Murder in the Brothel

The Maggie Monroe Series: Book Three

Helene Mitchell

Green Sweater Girl
Columbus, Montana

Praise for the *Maggie Monroe* series

"Helene Mitchell brings the 'extra panache' with her *Maggie Monroe* books. She weaves a PERFECT tapestry of unpredictable mystery plots with colorful, imperfect, and unconventional characters. After working four decades in law enforcement, I thought I had seen it all. Then along came Helene Mitchell...you will absolutely love these books!"

— **Mike Moser**
Ada County Sheriff's Office (Retired)

"Thirty years in law enforcement, I have seen all kinds of criminal behavior. Helene Mitchell's *Maggie Monroe* books spin those behaviors into quirky mysteries. Fun reads!"

— **Shaun Gough**
Gooding County Sheriff

"Settle into your easy chair and put on your detective hat, Helene Mitchell will give you clues throughout the story, *Murder in the Brothel*, so you can try to figure out who done it. Sheriff Maggie has to unravel a complicated family story. They came to Barrier, Nevada to escape the notoriety of the unsolved murder of their mother. And they don't want their secrets known so they are a bit deceitful. Meanwhile at home Maggie and Brick are uncovering mysterious things in their own yard. Are they connected? Read on, fellow detectives."

— **Dona Frey**

"Instantly draws you into the story! Unable to quit reading until you get to the end! Full of surprises and can't wait to read the next book in this series!"

—**Sharon**
Amazon Customer

This is a work of fiction. Names, characters, businesses, places, events, locales, and incidents are either the products of the author's imagination or used in a fictitious manner. Any resemblance to actual persons, living or dead, or actual events is purely coincidental.

Copyright © 2024 Green Sweater Girl Publishing, LLC

All rights reserved. No part of this book may be reproduced or used in any manner without written permission of the copyright owner except for the use of quotations in a book review.

Edited by AnnaMarie McHargue and Anita Stephens
Designed by Leslie Hertling and Eric Hendrickson

Library of Congress Control Number: 2024912941

ISBN (paperback): 979-8-9895968-3-6
ISBN (ebook): 979-8-9895968-4-3

www.gailcushman.com

Green Sweater Girl, Columbus, Montana

Dedication

*To those women who are serving
behind the badge.*

It's not what you look at,
but what you see.

–Henry David Thoreau

Acknowledgments

Murder in the Brothel took form when I learned of an unsolved murder near my home, a beloved woman who was brutally murdered and as of today, her perpetrator is still unfound. I could only imagine what her family has gone through. It is the kind of book that authors hope will result in reopening of the cold case with another hard look at the evidence.

I am indebted to many people who have encouraged my stories and given me the opportunity to write. I have been fortunate to have had two husbands who have supported and encouraged me to write, and have now penned eleven books, nine are published. Tom, RIP, believed in me and said I could do anything. He forgot about a few things I could never conquer, namely golf. And my new love, Robert, who is filling my life with new adventures, getting married in Paris, enjoying the Beartooth Mountains in Montana, and floating down the Erie Canal on our boat.

Murder in the Brothel was a bit of a challenge. I have done a lot of interesting things in my life, including serving as a Marine during Viet Nam and working within the prison walls, but I have never been in a brothel!

Thank you Anna Marie McHargue, Anita Stephens, and Eric Hendrickson for reading and rereading my work, making sure that everything is just right. And thank you to my blog readers for your support and kindness. You are my push-me-pull-me critters and you never disappoint.

I hope you enjoy knowing Maggie, Brick, and Brandi in *Murder in the Brothel*.

Chapter 1

Brandi, Candice, and Ginger
Five Years Ago

Candice Dumont's house lay smack in the center of a tight-knit, Reno subdivision where everybody knew everybody. Her small, aging, two-story colonial, while nothing special, boasted a well-kept yard, updated paint, and even a potted daisy or two that always made her neighbors feel welcome. Candice's community prided itself on being a team that watched out for one another, often checking in each afternoon to see that all was well. Candice never worried about locking up before her daily catnaps or as part of her nightly routine because her neighborhood had proven itself safe year after year. That night, she had drifted off into a deep slumber, so deep that she heard nothing, not even footsteps on her creaking hardwood. All fell silent to her dead-to-the-world ears. Her panicked eyes flashed open only as the first bullet ripped into her chest. She never knew of the other three bullets or the number of blows that had been inflicted on her torso—the cool serene morning destroyed by the person hell-bent on butchering her body.

Candice's older daughter, Brandi, lived in an apartment nearby, having moved from her mother's home a few weeks before. Throughout her years at university, she had bunked with her mom, but now, halfway through her second year-long teaching contract, she had earned enough money to rent a small place of her own. It wasn't that she hadn't loved being in her mom's home, after all she and her mom were more than mother and daughter. They had grown to become friends with similar interests, who not only enjoyed their time together but shared clothes and hairdressers, always laughing when someone remarked on their physical similarities. They were both tall and slender, with similar hair color, and they both wore it pulled back into a ponytail. Brandi's hair was brunette and Candice's was the same color, except that hers had recently become woven with gray. Brandi's nearby move was merely a next logical step in her well-planned life.

After the move, Brandi was sure to see her mom whenever she could, but always stopped by on Friday mornings for an early morning cup of coffee and toast before heading to school to teach her fifth graders. That morning, the door was unlocked and ajar, which was not unusual, but on that morning, Candice did not respond when Brandi called her name, which was unusual. She popped an English muffin into the toaster, poured her coffee, and called out, "Mom, where are you? Do you want an English muffin, too?" She was met by silence and shouted louder this time, before heading up the stairs to her mother's bedroom, coffee sloshing from the cup as she ascended the stairs. "Mom, are you okay?" Seconds later, Brandi dropped the coffee cup when she discovered her mother's battered and shredded body motionless in her bed.

The violent murder shocked the Reno citizens so fiercely that even the casino trade slowed down for a time, as the town came to grips with the murder. During the first days, the news media carried daily stories of law enforcement's progress on the case, which was nothing. The police roped off Candice's house with lime green tape and recommended that Brandi take extra safety precautions, explaining that perhaps the perpetrator meant to kill her instead of her mother. After all, they resembled each other so closely. Brandi, filled with trepidation, in shock over finding her mother's body, listened to their advice and holed up, never returning to her classroom.

Except for the police, she talked to no one and had no interaction with her friends, colleagues, or her sister, Ginger.

Chapter 2

Ginger and Ace
Five Years Prior

Ginger, Candice's younger daughter, briefly attended a community college in southern Texas where she met and married a homely man who hailed from a small town near the Texas-Mexico border. A small port wine mark stretched across his long face, giving him a perpetually sad looking face. Added to that were long drooping ears, a crooked nose, and vivid red hair that combined to create an odd-looking man. She had married him on the rebound, after having been jilted at the altar. He was called Ace and was a Texan's Texan, living, breathing, and bragging about his Texas roots and pride. As their marriage wore on, so did his tendency for mental and emotional abuse, and after four years and a few months in the local slammer for mistreating Ginger, he agreed to relocate to Reno where they could make a fresh start.

Ginger was short and plump with a pretty face and dimples that appeared when she smiled. She kept her blondish hair cropped short and wore bows clipped on either side of her head. It had been a fad at her college, and she liked how they looked, thinking that they brightened her face and eyes, and made her look younger, so she continued wearing them. Ginger and Brandi were as different as water and wine. Whereas Brandi resembled her mother and was outgoing and energetic, Ginger was more like her father and tended to be bitter and indolent, never finding a job that she liked enough to stay with it. She and her mother disagreed on nearly everything, and she despised Brandi's abilities and successes. When they decided to move to Reno, she entertained the idea of reconciling their differences, but Ace didn't trust Brandi or Candice. But then again, he didn't trust anybody.

A small casino hired Ace in security, and his job was to keep his eyes peeled for wayward activities. Ace eyed everyone who came into the casino as suspicious, and within a few weeks, the casino switched him to a less stressful job, cleaning slot machines and gaming tables on the graveyard shift. He didn't mind much because he had sleep issues, which meant that he could avoid talking to Ginger. She half-heartedly accepted a job as a waitress at the same casino, but after the two-week trial period, her boss suggested she look elsewhere, and she spent her days watching soap operas and reading romance novels. Ace worked at night and slept during the day, so they seldom saw or spoke to each other. Their fresh start grew staler by the day.

Brandi phoned the Reno police, followed by a call to Ginger. "Mom's dead," Brandi wailed into the phone after it had rung several times. "She's been shot and beaten. She's all mashed up. There's blood all over the place." She looked out the window and saw the police arrive. "You should come here now," she told her sister.

Ginger was half asleep and slow to answer the phone, "What do you want, Brandi, I'm not up yet. What do you want?"

"Mom, I'm talking about Mom. She's dead!" Brandi cried into the mouthpiece.

"What are you talking about? I talked to her yesterday and she was fine. Complaining about her arthritis, but fine."

"She was murdered. You need to come to her house now," Brandi insisted. "There's a lot of blood."

"Murdered? Why would anyone murder her? Did you call the police?" Ginger asked.

"Of course, I did. They just got here, six or eight cop cars, maybe more."

"Well, Ace just walked in from work. I'll fix him something to eat and head over in a while. I'm barely awake," Ginger yawned.

Chapter 3

Brandi and Candice
Seven Years Prior

"Mom, it's sunny and warm out, so why don't we do something to take your mind off Dad." Candice's husband, Jacque, had walked out on her recently, without telling anyone where he was going, and Candice had closed herself down, not going anywhere, even eliminating her favorite activity—golf. Although their marriage had been on the fritz for a long time, having him leave without notice had shaken her.

"What do you have in mind? We can't afford to shop or hang out at the mall. The current movies are a bust and I don't want to drive far because gas costs too much," Candice said.

"I don't know. We could go yard sale-ing, maybe we'll find something fun." Brandi picked up the local paper and saw an expanded list of garage and estate sales advertised in the area. "It says here that Mrs. Maxwell's estate sale starts today. You remember her. She's that rich lady who lived in that enormous colonial on Fort Street. Her husband died a year ago. Maybe we'll find something good."

The pair visited two estate sales and four garage sales that day. Candice bought a used soft jean jacket for four dollars, but the other garage sales reaped nothing. At the Maxwell's estate sale, Brandi spied a box in the corner filled with used dress-up clothes for children and a sign that said free.

Since Brandi was on the lookout for clothes for a Little House on the Prairie school production for her fifth graders, she thought it might be useful and rifled through the box. She pulled out a wide brim prairie woman's hat and a couple of checked dresses that might work for costumes, along with a small, locked jewelry box adorned with a western logo. She gathered the items in her arms and showed them to the estate sale manager, "Are all these free?" she confirmed with the manager. "If so, I'll take them all."

They were hungry and almost avoided the final estate sale, but it turned out to be the best of all of them. They picked up a couple baskets for a dollar and a brightly colored painting with a lot of circles for three dollars. Brandi had a double major in art and education and recognized it as a Kandinsky. Although she didn't know its actual value, she did know it was worth much more than the three-dollar price tag that was taped to the frame. She convinced the salesperson that two dollars was more than it was worth, and moments later walked away with her treasures.

"We spent eight dollars today and I had a ton of fun," Brandi said as she pulled on and modeled the jean jacket that Candice had purchased. "And this will fit both of us." She smoothed the jacket in the mirror and noticed a small bulge in the breast pocket. She opened the pocket, dipped her fingers in, and squealed, "Finders, keepers, look here." She pulled out a small wad of bills, two one-hundred-dollar bills, a fifty and a few ones. "We made money today, Mom. What a day! I've never had a hundred-dollar bill."

Candice lifted her head from what she was doing and smiled, "Shouldn't we return that money, I am sure they didn't mean to leave it in the pocket. Isn't it stealing?"

"No way. It's not stealing. It's finders, keepers, like I said," Brandi said.

Her mother frowned, followed by a quick smile, "Well, then, I paid for it, so shouldn't I earn half?"

Brandi handed her one of the hundreds, "Here you go, but this wad is peanuts compared to this Kandinsky because I know it's worth four hundred dollars, maybe more. I'm sure it's an original and we can sell it online for at least three hundred."

Candice opened her eyes wide and quipped, "What are you talking about? You mean that painting with all the squiggly circles? Kadin-who? Four hundred dollars? For wiggly lines that look like children's art? Maybe I should become a painter." Candice wasn't familiar with the art world and had never heard of Kandinsky. Her work experience was limited to answering phones and filing notes from parents at a local elementary school. She looked at the painting and shook her head in disbelief before turning her attention to the rest of their haul. "Hey, did you open the little jewelry box yet?"

Brandi retrieved a pocketknife to pry open the box that had been with the pioneer garments, and said, "Mom, Kandinsky is an incredibly sought-after artist," as she wedged the knife into the crack under the lid. "Wait a second, I've almost opened it." She pushed the knife in farther and said, "It's a children's jewelry box, but I can't get the lid off." She paused and looked down at her hand. "Dang, I chipped a nail, but I think I have the lid loose." She twisted the knife and the box finally opened, and her eyes fell on a pair of earrings and a ring. The small cubic zirconia earrings were probably valued at nothing, but the ring consisted of a small grape-sized emerald centered with a diamond on either side. "The earrings are worth nothing, but this ring could be worth a fortune, maybe several thousand dollars. The setting is a mess, all bent and tangled, probably unsalvageable, but the emerald alone is a good find. And the little diamonds could be cleaned and polished, maybe even mounted on posts for earrings."

"How do you tell the difference between a zirconia and a diamond? They look the same to me," Candice asked, knitting her brow.

"Don't worry about that, Mom, I know how to differentiate. I can teach you. Today was probably a once in a lifetime day, but we should try again. We have nearly five thousand dollars' worth of merchandise and paid eight lousy dollars for everything, including four bucks for the jean jacket. A steal, no matter how much return we receive on it. That's a lot of money, for danged sure, and tonight, we can celebrate by eating at the best restaurant in town."

Chapter 4

Candice and Brandi
Seven Years Prior

Candice and Brandi began frequenting various neighborhood sales every weekend and found a treasure trove of unbelievably valuable jewelry and gems selling at next to nothing. Since Brandi knew enough about quality jewelry, she could easily negotiate an even lower price with those who didn't know the trade. Two weeks after their first big find, Brandi, who had spent two years during high school working in a jewelry store, had learned how to differentiate good quality gems from inferior ones, discovered a full carat diamond that was being marketed as a cubic zirconia. She bargained the owner from five dollars to three, and the owner tossed in a mismatched set of earrings that unfortunately actually were cubic zirconia. Candice had never dealt with jewelry, beyond being on the receiving end of occasional gifts from her husband, Jacque. Brandi, on the other hand, had an artistic eye, skill and knowledge about gemstones, and with her creative mind was able to see beyond the dirty, scratched stones to imagine new pieces more beautiful and valuable than their original settings.

The third weekend they went out again, this time finding a single ruby earring that Brandi later turned into a dinner ring and a broken watch with an opal-studded watchband that became a necklace, turning her six-dollar expenditure into five hundred. Their newly found avocation quickly became a passion, and they cruised neighborhood sales every weekend looking for anything that sparkled or had the potential to sparkle. Brandi favored emeralds, but Candice looked out for diamonds. Unfortunately, she still could not tell the difference between a real diamond and a fake one, which caused a couple forgivable errors.

"You have an artistic brain, Brandi, which you got from your father, not me," Candice told her daughter. "I'm happy you have it, because I don't see these gems like you do. I'm more basic and mainly see dollar signs floating around these scratched gems. If we clean and polish them, they will be worth a lot more. Maybe we can contribute to my retirement account."

"I feel like Michelangelo," Brandi told Candice after she had redesigned a ruby and diamond ring into a stunning necklace. "When he carved statues, he talked about setting people free from the stones. I feel the same way, not setting people free, of course, but releasing the gem's splendor so that others can see it. I feel like I'm renewing the stone's spirit."

They became adept at renewing the gems, repairing settings or creating whole new pieces of jewelry, more modern and swankier than that of its original owner. They realized they could make something out of nothing, buying a pair of broken earrings for five dollars or one earring for a dollar, resetting the stones into a dinner ring or brooch, and selling it on the internet for much more. This gave them a clear path to marketing and selling the gems they had recovered, and Brandi soon developed an active list of clients and had no trouble turning a quick and healthy profit.

Brandi and Candice set paying off her student loans as a top priority, and every cent they earned for the first few months went toward the loan debt that, before long, disappeared. Brandi dreamed of a higher standard of living, and their jewelry business seemed to be the answer. She used the trite aphorism of a beer budget with champagne tastes and attempted to find a stockbroker who could help them invest the money. Neither of them knew anyone, which pleased Candice as she didn't want to give their money to someone they didn't know. Instead, she suggested that they stuff it in a lock box and hide it under her bed. Brandi argued against that approach, and they finally agreed to rent a safe deposit box until they found a stockbroker they could trust. They agreed to live on their current salaries, Brandi on her teacher's salary and Candice on her pension and social security. They would have plenty of time to figure out their investment strategy, but the safe deposit box would work for now.

During the week, Brandi's school duties kept her busy and, on the weekend, she spent her time working their jewelry project, going to estate sales, designing, and internet marketing. She was glad when Candice volunteered to become the caretaker of the money and jewelry, storing the cash and gems in their box. Candice began to allocate a small cash draw every month for each and the rest of the money sat untouched. When they finally found a stockbroker, they would be able to give him a sizable chunk of money to invest.

Brandi became the driving force of their business partnership. She assumed responsibility for designing new pieces and became an expert at bargaining with the estate sale personnel, while Candice handled the drudgery of cleaning and shining each gemstone, sometimes taking hours to polish them to Brandi's satisfaction. Candice knew nothing about the internet, so Brandi took over that end of the business as well as the selling end. She primarily used eBay, but there were a handful of other sites as well. Neither of them had a business background and didn't know how to set up a business, so they agreed that they would simply split whatever money came their way. Each week, Candice deposited their earnings and withdrew a little for herself and Brandi. Unbeknownst to Brandi, though, Candice rented a second safe deposit box, and when she split the money between the two, she put a little extra in the second box. She realized that she had retired too early, and the extra money would keep her solid as she aged.

Busy with school, Brandi didn't pay much attention to the amounts they earned and knew when she needed the money, it would be available. She trusted her mother and knew their business was profitable. Upon graduation, with her loans paid off, Brandi replaced her beat-up Toyota with a new BMW. It was a celebration gift to herself, she reasoned.

Their venture had been successful and so far, in one year, they had earned more money restoring jewelry than Brandi's first-year teaching position or Candice's social security. Besides the extra income, they had developed a real friendship. It was quality time, Candice laughed, quality time as well as quantity time. A quality mother-daughter friendship and a good quantity of money. They called their business Q2.

Chapter 5

Candice and Jacque
Five Years Prior

The solo administrative assistant at Liberty Bell Elementary, a small elementary school in Reno, Candice managed daily affronts offered by grade schoolers and their parents, handled the schedules and classroom aides, and left each day satisfied with her work. She loved the kids and teachers and having the summers and holidays to herself. Without an education, good paying jobs were scarce and this one fit her needs and wants perfectly. Her salary supplemented the family income, and she was able to support her golfing habit and provide a few extras for herself and husband, Jacque. She adored playing golf, while Jacque abhorred it, but she managed to play several times a week, mostly after school when the rates were lower. She settled for playing the nearby public course, a poorly maintained facility, because it was less expensive, but she made friends and golfed as often as possible. Despite lessons and practice, her handicap didn't improve, but she kept at it.

Jacque was never without work, sometimes holding down two or three jobs at once, but they were scattered and short-term with unpredictable and unreliable incomes. He was a jack-of-all-trades, had good carpentry skills, in much in demand as a handyman. He also memorized much of Mr. Boston's Bartender's Guide. Unfortunately, he had never developed scheduling skills and more than once forgot to finish or show up for a job. He had been the drummer in his high school band and had practiced enough so that when the local band advertised for a drummer, he stepped forward and did the best he could. He wasn't Ringo Starr but could keep up with the other members, who were also not Beatles quality, but still good enough to play gigs at local bars. Unfortunately for Candice, he developed an eye for the ladies, and his roving eye caused difficulty between them, ultimately leading to their separation and divorce. He was of French heritage, tall, dark skinned, and a step beyond flirtatious. His good sense of humor let him hold an audience and command their attention. Candice said she first loved him because he was a ray of sunshine in a dreary world.

Jacque's father had been a trained carpenter and taught him plenty of useful skills, but Jacque didn't think that carpentry paid well enough, so he joined the Army after high school and became a rifleman. He worked his way up to corporal, but with his snarky sense of humor, promotion to sergeant would not be in the cards, so he left the Army after three years, happy to be on his way. He used his GI Bill to attend real estate school at the local college and schemed to learn real estate with a get-rich-quick plan, but he didn't earn enough to keep him in the style to which he and Candice wanted to become accustomed.

Candice's salary was low, and the school district limited her to 30 hours a week, but since she liked her job and the school, she remained a dedicated Liberty Bell employee for more than a decade. She only left because the school district decided to close the school and transfer her to a larger one, several miles away. Learning she also would need to move to a 40-hour workweek, her only thought was her golf game. How could she fit that in each day with this new workload? Brandi encouraged her to move to the new school, but Candice was tired of working. She had reached the age of early retirement and decided to step down, even though it was four years early and would be at the lowest rate of retirement pay. Jacque earned enough money to support them, and they could live on his salary alone if they lived frugally. Candice had no financial worries until the fall when Jacque left without a word and she found herself alone and without enough income to support both herself and her golf habit. Brandi was nearly finished with college when her dad left, so she moved from her college apartment to her mother's house to help with expenses, but even together, they barely eked out enough for necessities so golf came to a screeching halt.

Within a few months of their jewelry venture, Q2 had taken off, affording her a new set of golf clubs, a golf cart, membership to a country club, albeit a medium quality club and more weekly golf days than she had ever enjoyed before.

Chapter 6

Brandi and Candice
Six Years Prior

It was the country club and golf cart that made Brandi wonder about how much money Q2 was making. She knew they were turning a profit and since her own teaching job kept her busy, she hadn't paid attention to the amount of money that went into the safe deposit box. She trusted her mother, of course, and Candice gave her a monthly draw, which Brandi considered mad money, enough to do something fun but not enough to make a life-style change, although that seemed to be exactly what she saw Candice doing. Golf was expensive, and her mother's pension and social security were barely enough to pay the rent and utilities. So how much money were they earning, and why wasn't she seeing it when she received her cut?

Brandi questioned the new top-of-the-line clubs, the golf club membership, and the cost for daily play. Her mother loved golf, but had never been extravagant, and lived within her budget. She knew the amount of her mother's income and expenditures, everything except her new hobbies, but golf was pricey. She wouldn't have thought anything about the cost if her mother had continued playing on the local public course, using the same clubs she had owned for years and walking the course, but this was new. She called the golf club and learned that the membership fee was more than her student debt had been, and the new golf cart cost more than her beat-up Toyota was worth.

"Mom, how can you afford to play golf? Did you come into an inheritance? Did one of your not-rich aunts die or something? Or did Q2 become more profitable than you let on? What's up?"

Candice looked away. She had known Brandi would ask questions, but she hadn't prepared herself and stammered, "No, no, it was your father. He finally came through. I don't know why, but he decided to front me the money for golf. I think he realized how much I loved it and missed it and felt guilty when he left us. He called me out of the blue and asked how much money I would need to play golf again. I told him and he sent me double what I asked for. End of story."

"Is he in town?" Brandi asked. "I haven't seen or heard from him in a few months and assumed he moved. Besides, he hated you playing golf, Mom, he complained it was a waste of time and money. What made him change his mind?"

"I don't know, but maybe he feels guilty about his new blonde friend," Candice said. She knew Jacque didn't feel guilty at all, but she couldn't let Brandi know about hiding the money.

"Is he planning to come back and see us?" Brandi asked, hesitantly. She thought it unlikely that he would return, but she also wondered about her mother's story because it sounded nothing like the dad she knew. He had earned the reputation of being a scoundrel and seldom gave anybody anything, and invariably found other uses for his money than giving to his family. Yet, Candice was her mother, and as far as she knew, Candice had never lied to her before.

Chapter 7

Candice and Ginger
Six Years Prior

Candice and Brandi were surprised, delighted, and apprehensive when Ginger suddenly moved to Reno. They saw it as her attempt to mend the family rifts, after all, they were adults now and should be able to put past animosities behind them. Candice invited Ginger to join them on their various excursions and help them with their Q2 jewelry project, although Brandi wasn't sold on her joining their business. "We will rename our business Q3," Candice offered to Ginger, but she declined, always with some excuse. She was too busy or she and Ace had plans or she didn't feel well. It was always something. Candice and Brandi knew the real reason she wouldn't officially join their business was because of Ace. After all, how could Ginger cater to Ace's every need if she had familial work obligations.

Ginger had learned through the years not to cross Ace and stayed home, kept the house clean, watched television, and cooked his favorites, some of his mother's southern cooking recipes, which she didn't care for, but he loved. Although she felt bored and trapped, she remained quiet and didn't complain. Ace didn't like it when she mentioned finding a job or even volunteering. One time she mentioned her mother's offer, but he laughed and told her she was being foolish. If she worked at a real job, she would be absent from the house, and her mother and sister's silly pastime was exactly that, a silly hobby that wouldn't profit her. He didn't fathom that they were earning a profit, but had he known, he might have pushed Ginger to join Q2. Brandi never mentioned their financial successes to either of them and let Ace and Ginger think it was an inane way of passing time. Candice was a little more charitable, but also held back because neither of them wanted Ace to know that their project was prosperous.

When Ginger's phone jangled, she picked it up to find her mother's smiling face on the screen. She sighed and pursed her lips. She and her mother had never gotten along well, especially when she was a teenager and now, whenever she talked to her mother, she felt like her mother was spying on her. The rancor and animosity bloomed like the first pansies of summer. She turned the television louder, knowing it would irritate Candice. "Hi, Mom," she mumbled, "what do ya want?"

"Just checking in. I haven't seen you in a couple weeks, and I'm wondering what's happening with you and Ace. Have you been able to find a job?" Candice asked.

"No, I quit looking because there's nothin' out there," Ginger said. "I told you that. Why do you keep asking me the same questions over and over? Can't you remember anything? You got Alzheimer's or something?" She had told her mother repeatedly that Ace didn't want her working, but Candice asked the same questions every time.

"Sorry, I forgot," Candice said. She hadn't forgotten, but Ginger's sullen attitude, which soured to surliness, concerned her. She thought Ginger would be happier if she had a job or a distraction other than watching soap operas all day waiting for Men-Ace to return. Candice's brain had nicknamed him, Men-Ace, which she thought fitting. In Candice's mind, keeping busy helped maintain good physical and mental health. She thought of the adage of idle hands being the devil's workshop with Ace playing the role of the devil.

"Would you like to go to lunch?" Candice asked her brightly. "We could go to the club because they have great salads, and I know you'd enjoy it. Or another restaurant downtown. It would be my treat."

That offer was met with silence, so Candice asked a different one. "How about a game of golf? Do you still have the clubs I gave you? I bought a golf cart recently, and we could play eighteen holes, or nine if you prefer. How about that?"

"No, I sold my clubs, so don't have them anymore and haven't played in a long time, so no, thank you," Ginger pursed her lips and thought, *Don't you understand, Mom? I'm not interested in being with you.*

Candice sighed, "How about this? Last weekend Brandi picked up a matching necklace, earrings, bracelet, and even an ankle bracelet. Rubies. I can show you how to remove the jewels from their settings, and I think we can make an attractive piece of jewelry—with the emphasis on pricey. They need sprucing up, you know, cleaning and polishing, but they are high end. It would be a good opportunity to visit because we haven't seen each other in a while, you know. Would you like to help me? We'll make a pretty penny on this find when we clean and polish these pieces, and we'd be happy to pay you." Candice knew that Ace had not advanced beyond entry level in his casino job and thought she might change Ginger's mind with the offer of money. Q2 was turning a good profit, and she and Brandi had talked about adding someone to help, but they didn't want someone they didn't know. Although they distrusted Ace, they thought Ginger might be helpful. Besides, she was family, while they considered Ace to be an add on.

"No, Mom, I won't enjoy working on the jewelry project like you and Brandi do. I'm fine at home, so don't worry about us. I'll call you next week." She pieced her words together to sound pleasant and polite. Her words weren't ill tempered, but her tone was. Both Ginger and her mother knew that was an idle promise, that she wouldn't call. Ginger hadn't and didn't disguise her feelings about her mother. The thought of actually phoning her mother simply wasn't in the cards.

The phone call never happened, and a few days later, Candice was dead. The police had no immediate suspects, but promptly questioned Ginger, Brandi, and, of course, Ace, who received special scrutinization because of his previous jail time. The murder had occurred pre-dawn, and Brandi and Ginger said they had been asleep, each in their own quarters. Ace had been at work, so his alibi was the most solid, but the police didn't believe anything that anybody said.

They asked about Candice's ex-husband, Jacque, but no one admitted to knowing where he was. Brandi knew that her mother said he gave her money for golf, but remained silent when questioned by the police. Her time with her mother over the years afforded her the luxury of learning her mother's unspoken cues. She wouldn't have been surprised to learn that her mother hadn't been forthcoming about Jacque or his whereabouts. The feeling nagged at her, but she kept her unconfirmed notions to herself. Ace, with his odd look, odd behavior, and sketchy background remained high on the police watch list, and although Brandi and Ginger seemed unlikely murderers, the detectives kept a close eye on them, always turning up out of nowhere. Brandi was outgoing and pleasant, and taught school, but Ginger was as timid as a mouse. Both women were distraught that their mother had been murdered, but Brandi, especially, grieved at the loss of her mother and business partner. The police had nobody in their line of sight, and Brandi feared it would stay that way for a while, if not forever.

Chapter 8

Five Years Prior
Brandi and Ginger

The police investigation recovered nothing, no clues, no hints of anything that would help them discover Candice's murderer. For weeks, they conducted interview after interview with anyone and everyone in Candice's community. Nothing ever came of those talks, so the authorities turned their eyes toward the homeless population and the local ne'er-do-wells, but they couldn't find anyone who had a motive. They even ran a search for Jacque, but he had disappeared with no trace of where he had gone or what he was doing. Apparently, Candice had no enemies, everyone loved her. By the time the police finished interviewing her friends and acquaintances, they concluded it was likely she could have been nominated for sainthood.

The police began a routine of persistent and extensive questioning, and the media flocked to Candice's residence to shove microphones in the faces of everyone who might have known her, especially Brandi, Ginger, and Ace. Brandi couldn't walk outside without reporters heckling her, and Ginger stayed inside with curtains drawn. Only occasionally did she peek out the windows, quickly vanishing if someone spied her. Ace snarled at the reporters when he went to work and answered no questions.

Reno Detectives Burns and Lawrence led the case and haunted the sisters, calling or showing up at their homes at all times of the day or night, asking questions and making insinuations. They would go back and forth, from one home to the other, returning for another conversation during the same day, probing, repeating the same questions time and again. Detective Burns, the more experienced of the two, played a grandfatherly type and offered the sisters every opportunity to share what they knew. Detective Lawrence acted as if he wanted to be their friend, but both resembled snooping beagles, nose down, whiffing their prey.

The first day Brandi and Ginger met the detectives, Burns wore a gray suit with a gray and white striped tie. With his ash-colored hair and pallid face, he took on the same characteristics of some statue in the center of a park. He was expressionless but gave a half-smile when he introduced himself. The younger detective, Lawrence, had blond curly hair drawn back into a manbun with short wisps of hair sticking out. He looked more like a bartender than a detective with his rolled-up sleeves and slightly crooked tie that hung loose at his collar. The two detectives were of similar height and weight and both looked fit although Lawrence, the younger, looked better. Brandi thought he was cute, but he was a cop, and she dismissed any idea of pursuing anything more than a quick conversation with him.

"My mom and I worked together," Brandi informed the detectives. "We ran a business and called it Q2. It wasn't really a formal business, not registered or anything, and we named it for no reason. We bought old jewelry, cleaned and polished it, and resold it on the internet. Maybe one of our buyers or other business associates is to blame for her death? It's all confusing and upsetting though, because I can't think of anyone who didn't like my mother. She worked as a school secretary, popular with students and staff. She retired not long ago."

"I see. Where's your dad?" Detective Burns inquired. He asked the questions, and Detective Lawrence wrote down the answers in his small notebook.

"I'm not exactly sure, maybe Los Angeles," Brandi told him. "He left a couple years ago and we haven't seen or heard from him since he left. Mom divorced him, but I'm not confident he signed the papers. Mom never discussed him with me, so I really am only guessing. His name is Jacque, Jacque Dumont, and he could be dead for all we know." She filled them in on their father's occupations while Lawrence jotted everything down. Brandi didn't tell them about Jacque's sudden generosity of golf equipment.

Brandi handed Lawrence a list of buyers and sellers and other interested parties, which he stuck in his shirt pocket for further reference. Burns shook his head and said, "I doubt that will reap anything, but we'll check it out." Burns was more interested in Ace and the sisters than the names that Brandi fed them. They admitted that Q2 might be an interesting angle, and they would investigate the list of names, but most buyers lived outside of Nevada, and the detectives felt that the perpetrator was local, maybe someone who knew she wasn't careful about locking her door.

The detectives searched for motives and anything that would lead them to the killer, while Brandi, Ginger, Ace, and Jacque continued to be at the top as persons of interest. As is often the case, the motive for this murder was either money or personal vendetta, fueled by anger or jealousy, but the detective didn't see any of those when they looked at Brandi, Ginger, and Ace. Jacque had apparently vanished, and no one admitted knowing anything about him, even alluded that he might have died, although no one said how or when. And while clearly none of them had much money, they didn't seem bitter or angry about it. Certainly not enough to toy with murder. Brandi, of course, told them about the Q2, but the detectives viewed it as a hobby, never realizing that real money was involved, and Brandi saw no need to fill that detail in for them. Ginger also seemed genuinely disinterested in learning about it. The detectives filed for warrants and searched their houses and examined their bank accounts but again came up empty. Brandi never mentioned the safe deposit box and was unsure whether the detectives had discovered it or not, so she happily thought they had missed it. Ginger knew nothing about it either and Brandi enjoyed keeping it her secret.

The detectives questioned Ginger multiple times, but she had solid answers, and they could not shake anything loose from her. Although the police named her as a possible suspect, her soft voice and meek and mild manner dropped her to the bottom of their list. They continued questioning both women, which yielded nothing, and they slowly began to look for other suspects.

Cocky and arrogant, Ace promptly gained the police's attention, but he claimed ignorance about his mother-in-law's murder. His attitude annoyed the detectives, and he stayed on their radar as a person of interest, but their interviews produced nothing new. Nada, nil, zero. The police felt as if they had crashed into a roadblock.

While law enforcement constructed several antennas for Jacque, they always came up empty. His cell phone number went to voice mail and they couldn't trace it. They left messages, but he never returned their calls. The divorce papers had never been returned to the attorney. It was almost like he had vanished, or simply hadn't wanted to be found.

Two weeks passed, and the police announced that they would release Candice's body for burial. However, because the cause of death continued to be under investigation, they left the security tape on the doorways to the house and denied Brandi and Ginger entrance.

Brandi was eager to access her mother's house. She didn't complain to the police or let them know she wanted to go inside, instead she patiently bided her time. The night the police finally released Candice's body for burial, Brandi sneaked into the house to look for a burial dress. While she was inside, she did a quick, but thorough, search for the gemstones that her mother had most recently been preparing for sale. She knew her mother's hiding places, after all she had hidden many things from her daughters and husband through the years. Brandi carefully opened the kitchen canisters, one by one, flour, sugar, coffee, and tea and found small plastic bags of loose gemstones, rubies, and emeralds. The fourth canister, the smallest, also held treasures, but Brandi did not find gems inside, rather she unveiled two safe deposit keys. Two keys, not one. She gathered up the keys, packets of gems, the burial dress, and hurried home. Brandi and Ginger laid Candice to rest within a few days while the investigation continued.

At the funeral, Brandi informed Ginger that she had found nothing except the title to her car, a two-year-old Ford, in excellent condition, which she had located at the bottom of a box of tissue, another hiding place that Brandi knew. She handed it to Ginger and said, "Take it, you and Ace need another car." Ace and Ginger owned a pickup, but no other vehicle, and she knew that they would put a second vehicle to use. She reasoned that if she gave Ginger the car, she wouldn't make a fuss about whatever else she might find. The less Ginger knew, the better.

Weeks passed before Brandi entered the bank to clear out her mother's safe deposit boxes. She carried an oversized purse hoping it was large enough to stow the contents of the box.

"No, Ma'am, I can't let you in," the bank manager told her. "The investigation has not been concluded. Law enforcement put a hold on Candice's banking activities, which included her safe deposit boxes, so you'll have to wait until the police clear them for opening. Unfortunately, I don't know when that will be." Brandi hadn't realized that the police knew about the safe deposit boxes and left the bank disappointed, wondering how she could access them. She knew they had accumulated a substantial amount of money, not to mention a good cache of gemstones and jewelry, but she didn't know why her mother had two different boxes. Candice had never shared that information with her.

Two days later she returned to the bank when the manager was at lunch and approached a different banker, a youthful college student, who clearly knew far less about the case than the manager. Brandi cleaned out both boxes, hoping that the bank would not fire the young banker. One box held money and jewels, and the other held cash, a substantial amount of cash, making her wonder why her mother had been keeping a secret stash. She dropped the contents into her oversized purse and left the bank.

After several more weeks passed without making progress on the case, newspaper coverage dwindled to a page three blurb, and the television people ceased calling. Drivers stopped rubbernecking as they drove by the house, although the lime green tape fluttered aimlessly in the wind.

Chapter 9

Brandi
Four Years Prior

It had been just under a year since Candice's death, and Brandi was still haunted by the memories of her mother's murder. She couldn't sleep, couldn't eat, couldn't concentrate. She abandoned her classroom and her students and spent her days holed up in her house with her curtains drawn, wondering why her mother had been murdered and worried that someone would do the same to her. She didn't answer her phone and kept her lights off, always lowering the sound of the television so that no one would detect she was home. She lost weight and interest in doing anything that had been normal a few weeks earlier. The police interviewed her time and again, asking the same questions for which she had no answers.

Before her mother's murder, Brandi had been a simple schoolteacher, teaching fifth graders the basics, preparing them for the big jump from elementary school to middle school. Knowing she liked teaching and because her tragic experience was extraordinary, the school district tolerated her absence for the rest of the school year, but after summer break, the superintendent's patience ran thin. He hired a substitute for the fall semester, but as the months passed with no answers, he told her he was reassigning her classroom to another teacher. The news hit her with a force she hadn't anticipated. One more thing that left her shaken. Her thoughts spiraled after months of being holed up inside her small home until she convinced herself that she needed to make a drastic change. She needed to find a new path, one that wasn't as frightening, and one that helped her feel safe.

With the first anniversary of her mother's death looming and no new information or clues, Brandi's frustration grew with the constant badgering by Burns and Lawrence. She, Ginger, and Ace were still their only suspects, as Jacque had fallen off their radar. She put in place a plan to do whatever she could to reestablish her life. She canceled her lease, stowed her household goods and her BMW in a storage unit, and with a huge backpack strapped to her body, carried an oversized purse to the largest truck stop in town where she convinced a truck driver to let her ride with him. She asked him where he was headed, not that it mattered. He pointed east, and she told him that was where she wanted to go, too. She had hoped for California, but east would be fine, whatever lay to the east of Reno is where she would lay her head. Didn't matter what kind of town or what kind of job, only that the police wouldn't be breathing down her neck. Her plan was to exit the eighteen-wheeler the first time it stopped. It wasn't a well-thought-out plan, but she didn't care.

Inside her backpack were the contents of her mother's safe deposit boxes as well as a few changes of clothes. Even those few things made the bag heavier than she anticipated, but the wads of cash her mom had squirreled away would provide her all she needed for at least a year, as long as she stayed careful. With an open mind, a variety of skills, and no attachments—except Ginger, who seemed disinterested in any type of sisterly relationship—Brandi felt confident that no matter where she landed, she could find work doing something she liked while also finally feeling safe, or at least a little safer than she had the last year. An adventure, she thought to herself. Brandi was open to whatever came her way. A couple years to lose herself and she would be able to disappear for good. She didn't tell anyone that she was leaving, not the police, her sister, or any of her teacher friends. She simply vanished.

Four hours later, the truck driver pulled his semi into the parking lot of the Chicken Dinner Ranch in Barrier, Nevada. She exited the cab of his truck, looking around. She had never been to Barrier, and it looked as desolate as most rural Nevada towns did. Maybe it was a mistake, but her plan was her plan, and she forked over a hundred bucks to the driver and told him to forget he had seen her. He grinned and said, "You betcha," as he grabbed the money and proceeded upstairs, saying he wanted a shower, while she sat in a booth at the bar and watched the comings and goings of the establishment, puzzled at what services the establishment provided.

After a time, Brandi, having finished her third glass of Chardonnay, ordered the house specialty, the chicken dinner with all the trimmings. Mashed potatoes, salad, and corn on the cob. She hadn't been to a restaurant since her mother had been killed, and the chicken dinner tasted good, good enough that she ordered a second green salad. Her year-long diet of hard-boiled eggs and peanut butter sandwiches had grown old, and a real dinner sat well with her.

"How do you like it?" a brawny man said as he paused at her table on the way through the bar. "Any complaints? We specialize in chicken dinners, so why else would we be named the Chicken Dinner Ranch?" He let out a loud chuckle and clapped his hands together. Heads turned and looked at him, and he gave them a big grin, but he returned his attention to Brandi.

"No complaints, none at all, it's yummy," Brandi answered.

The stranger said, "Do you mind if I sit for a minute?" and before she answered, he sat down on the opposite side of the booth and reached over to shake her hand, "I'm Jay Guzman, the owner of the Chicken Dinner Ranch. Welcome. We don't have many single women stop to see us. Mostly truck drivers and couples, but not many women alone." He exuded confidence and courtesy and carried a broad smile.

Brandi squinted her eyes and replied, "Why is that? You don't like single women?"

"On the contrary, we love single women. In fact, I was hoping you were here to apply for a job," he said, signaling the bartender to bring them each a drink. This would be her fourth in as many hours.

Brandi lifted an eyebrow, "Really, what job?" She was keen on finding a job, and here was a job offer, seated across the table.

"We have lots of jobs available. Some pay well, but others, not so much. It all depends on what skills you have," Jay said, smiling. He looked at her hands and saw two ruby rings, no diamonds, and no wedding band or finger indentation suggesting that she had worn one, at least not recently. He continued, "Are you married? Family?"

"I am looking for a job and no, I'm not married. I have a sister, Ginger, but I don't know where she lives, in another state I think, which works fine because we don't talk much." She wanted to kick herself for giving too much information. Jay was easy to talk to, but she didn't know anything about him.

"What's your name and where are you from?" Jay asked. The question was direct, but he grinned when he spoke to her, and his tone was pleasant and easy going.

She blurted out her first name, but paused, considering what to say. It had been a year since she had a conversation with anyone except Burns and Lawrence and a few phone conversations with her sister. Finding the words seemed difficult. He might have heard of her mother's death in Reno and connected it with her, so she lied, "I'm from California."

"California? What part of California, Brandi?" Jay continued.

"Southern California," Brandi said. He was asking a lot of questions, which made her uneasy, yet he was pleasant, had a great smile, and she liked him. She had heard of the Chicken Dinner Ranch but couldn't recall the context. Egg farm? Truck stop? It wasn't coming to her.

"What kind of jobs do you have available, Mr. Guzman?" she asked. "I don't really want to waitress or tend bar. I'm a teacher, but don't have a contract this year." This was a half-truth and half-lie because the superintendent had offered her a second-semester contract. She hadn't accepted it though, and now she was gone. She looked around the room. It wasn't a bad restaurant, so even if his offer was for waitressing or bartending, she could make that work, too, at least for a time. She could find a better job later, maybe in a more prosperous looking town.

"Jay, call me Jay. Haven't you heard of the Chicken Dinner Ranch?" Jay asked, unsure if she really knew what his main source of income was. "We're kinda notorious."

The word notorious flicked on Brandi's memory. A brothel. The Chicken Dinner Ranch was a brothel. Oh, my God, she thought. Her brain turned flipflops, and she gasped in a chunk of air, followed by a small coughing spasm. She was sitting with the owner of a Nevada brothel, and she didn't know how to respond. Jay seemed pleasant enough but working in a brothel had never entered her mind. Her mother would be giggling in her grave, and her teacher friends would cackle at the thought. She had trained as a teacher, and teachers didn't do that type of work. "Well, I know that the trucker I hitched a ride with was hell-bent to arrive at the Chicken Dinner Ranch. He went up the stairs two at a time, and hasn't come down the stairs yet. I doubt he's cleaning chicken eggs, is he?" She gave him a questioning smile and laughed aloud.

Jay laughed, "You've got a quick sense of humor. You've got that right, I doubt that he's cleaning eggs, and it's equally doubtful that he's eating chicken. At least right now," Jay said, his eyes sparkling with a tease.

Brandi shook her head, "No, I'm not interested in that kind of job. I'm a schoolteacher. I don't have anything against it, you understand, it's just that, well, simply put, it's not me. It would take a huge amount of money to get me on my back." She laughed, "What would my fifth graders think?" She blushed as the image of her being a working girl flew across her brain.

"Your fifth graders would probably never know," Jay responded quickly. He liked this woman. She was open and honest with a positive attitude and a good sense of humor, all excellent qualities for someone working in a brothel. She was obviously inexperienced, which was both a bad and good thing, but she was smart. She was easy on the eyes, tall, and fit, too, which was a plus because many of the working girls let themselves go physically and became saggy before their time. He was down one girl, and this one was a real looker. If his instincts were right, Brandi would quickly become a favorite, and drum up the business of two.

"Pity," Jay said, sighing, "I can dream, can't I? I do have another job available, though. Dishwashing. It pays minimum wage, but it's available because my last dishwasher landed himself in jail." He placed his business card on the table beside her and scribbled something on the back. "Here's my card, Brandi, check the other side if you change your mind. It's a legitimate job offer, and it was nice to meet you." He clasped her hand and gently kissed the back of it. He slid out of the booth and disappeared through the bar.

Brandi shook her head and looked after him, silently giggling at the thought of working in a brothel. She knew that brothels were legal in a few Nevada counties, but not all, and Washoe county where Reno was located was one of those counties in which brothels were illegal. Brothels were so far from the center of her brain that she had never bothered investigating how they operated. Why would she? She was a certified teacher with a job that she liked and paid well.

She had never given a single thought to working in a brothel and pushed away his card on the table, snorting to herself. The server came by and gave Brandi a look, "Jay must have liked you because he paid for your dinner and wine. He doesn't do that often. What else would you like?"

Brandi told her she was finished and then twisted her head to watch as Jay disappeared. She tiptoed her fingers across the table and picked up the card but slapped it down on the table and turned her head away. The card remained on the table, upside down, and she stared at it suspiciously, as if she expected it to evaporate or explode, but reconsidered and picked it up. She focused her eyes on the card, scolding herself for even considering his job offer. Yet, she couldn't help but wonder what was on its reverse, and after a few seconds, her curiosity won. She closed her eyes and flipped it over, opened them, and her eyes grew big. She had told him it would take a huge amount of money to get her on her back. Jay had written an amount that would be difficult to turn down, no matter what the job. It was a larger amount than she made teaching and repairing jewelry combined, that was for dang sure. Almost into six figures. At the bottom of the card, he had scrawled, *And maybe more,* and signed it, Jay.

Brandi's mind flashed back to her mother's horrific death and determined that being a working girl could not be much worse than what her mother had endured. She picked up her purse, backpack, and duffel bag and made her way to the direction she had seen Jay just a few minutes earlier. He smiled when he saw her and repeated, aloud this time: "And maybe more. Welcome, Brandi."

Chapter 10

Sheriff Maggie
Present Day

Maggie's eyes opened wide in a flash, and she swung her feet over the edge of the bed hitting the floor with a thud. She had heard something, a screech followed by a noise, not a pleasant sound, but a scraping sound, like a door scraping on rusty hinges or grating across the floor. Her mama bear instinct immediately kicked in. She glanced at the alarm clock by their bed. It read one minute past midnight, twelve minutes earlier than she had heard similar noises the night before. The screeches and scrapings had started a month ago, occurring nearly every night, each time between twelve and three. Tonight's was right on target, but the scraping sound was new. She reached over and shook her husband, "Brick, Brick, did you hear that?"

Brick stirred and rasped, "Hear what? I'm 'sleep." He jammed his pillow over his eyes and mumbled something that vaguely sounded like go away.

"No, no, Brick, wake up," she said, shaking him again. "I heard the noises again, and this time they were louder and longer. We should check," Maggie was frightened at the thought of an intruder but the thought of the unknown terrified her. She knew Brick had deadbolted the doors because he obsessed about locking their doors at night, although they remained wide open during the day, so during light hours anyone could walk in. As the elected county sheriff, she kept on the lookout for anyone who might hold a grudge against her or Brick, her school-principal husband. She also thought about the safety of her twin boys, asleep in their bedroom.

She blinked both eyes open, stretching her eyelids to help focus, but her brain wasn't totally functioning yet. She stood up, threw her robe over her shoulders, and grabbed Brick's arm with a more persuasive shake. "Wake up, Brick, Honey, we both should check because I did hear a screech again, followed by a creaking noise, like a door with rusty hinges opening. I've never heard this much noise before. None of our doors creak, so I don't know where it was coming from, but it was loud enough to wake me up. Maybe it came from the yard? We should look to see if anything or anyone is outside. You peek in on the boys, and I'll check the outside." She stopped babbling and pulled a pair of jeans over her nightgown. She turned and punched in the code for the lock on her bureau drawer and withdrew her stowed pistol. She jammed it deep into the pocket of her pants.

Brick O'Brien and Maggie Monroe had been married six years and were the parents of Jimmy and Sean, four-year old twins. They had recently built a new house, rather they had rebuilt the one they owned, adding two bedrooms and expanding the kitchen for additional space with new appliances and cupboards. Maggie insisted on two additional bathrooms because the one-bathroom concept from the early nineteen-hundreds caused stress and inevitable pleading when four people, soon to be five, needed to use the bathroom, often all at once. They had endured the ambiance of house and agreed that it was tired and needed updating. Houses in Barrier were hard to come by, at least brick and mortar houses.

Their house was a brick-and-mortar house, well, at least three-quarters of it was. Like many homes in rural Nevada, one side of the house was constructed with liquor bottles, an estimated twenty-five thousand emptied bottles, which was a good amount of whiskey. At the turn of the previous century, lumber in rural Nevada had been expensive and difficult to find, transporting it by rail or wagon had precluded many homes being built. However, empty liquor bottles were readily available, and residents began recycling bottles into whiskey walls. The original house had been acceptable for two people, but adding the twins, and now with another baby on its way, there was no doubt they needed more room, and fast. Maggie and Brick had upgraded the plumbing, electricity, and appliances, all of which had been left over from the seventies and were not compatible with the electronic devices their boys would eventually desire. The new additions did not create a dream house by any stretch, but they did improve the functionality for five people, or even six, if they had another surprise set of twins.

Brick sighed, "Are you sure? I didn't hear anything. We've heard things before and found nothing, but maybe teenagers are trying to scare us. It could also be the construction crew who told me they would arrive early today to dig the hole for our pool. Two weeks of shoveling and we can fill it up with water and jump in. The boys are counting the minutes." He yawned as he threw off the blankets, put his feet on the floor, and stretched his long body.

"You must have been dead asleep not to have heard the screeching and scraping. It is midnight, too late for kids to be out terrorizing the high school principal and too early for Terry and his crew to arrive. In my world early is five o'clock, not midnight, at least on my sleep schedule. I didn't hear any vehicles and doubt that Terry will arrive before nine," Maggie protested.

"Do you want me to check outside? I can," Brick answered, as he slipped into a pair of Levi's, leaving his feet bare.

"No, I'll go outside. I already have my boots on and you can check on the boys." Maggie grabbed a flashlight and cupped the pistol in her hand as she walked through the kitchen toward the back of the house.

Brick peeked into the boys' room and verified they were tucked tightly in their beds asleep. He moved to the doorway and watched as Maggie rounded the corner of their house, gun in one hand, flashlight in the other. He had been a Los Angeles cop before he had moved to Barrier to teach high school social studies and coach basketball. Later, he became the principal, and now he served from time to time as Maggie's one reserve deputy, keeping his pistol nearby, except when he was at school. His ten years in Los Angeles had given him good judgment, a level head, and self-discipline, which served him well in all three areas of his professional life, working in the Los Angeles Police Department, with the Barrier sheriff's office, and as school principal.

Brick's parents had named him Rockford, like the James Garner television show of years' past, but his taunting brothers labeled him Brickford because as a young boy, he could not shoot the basketball through the basketball hoop. They said he threw bricks. The moniker stuck and followed him into adulthood. Few people knew his real name.

"Did you see anything? Are you sure it wasn't a dream?" Brick asked Maggie after she came back in. She had circumnavigated their newly improved house twice but had seen nothing amiss.

Maggie shook her head, "No, we've both heard these sounds other times, so it's not a dream. But the scraping noises were different tonight. Something creaked, went silent, and started again, like someone opening a door, stopping, and then continuing after a few seconds. It sounded like a door hinge needing oil, but it quit and went quiet. Are the boys asleep?"

"Yes, the boys are down for the count," Brick answered. "Are you sure nothing was outside? Do you want me to check, too? I can put on my boots."

"No, nothing abnormal, but the inside lights were on at Bob Givens' house, as well as at our other neighbors', whatever their names are, so I'll check tomorrow to see if either family heard or saw anything. Neither house had their exterior lights on. It will wait until tomorrow," Maggie answered yawning.

"Maybe you imagined it," Brick said. "That's what prego ladies do, imagine all kinds of things. Let's go back to bed."

"Yes, bed sounds good, but I don't think I can sleep," she answered, "I'm wide awake, and the baby's kicking like mad. I don't think Sarah likes being awakened in the middle of the night, either."

"Sarah? Are we having a girl? Snuggle up to me, and I'll calm both of you," Brick offered. He pulled off his pants and nestled her close beside him. "Go to sleep, Mother of Sarah."

Chapter 11

Maggie and Brick
Present Day

Born and reared in Barrier, Nevada, Sheriff Maggie Monroe was in year three of her second term as the sheriff. After high school, she had escaped from the dreariness of Barrier to attend college and earn a degree at UNLV. She swore on a stack of badges that she would never return to her hometown. She considered it too small with nothing to do, but when her father developed dementia, she rethought her self-proclaimed oath and came back to help her mother. She had majored in criminal justice, and within a year of her returning to Barrier, fresh out of college, the town's former sheriff retired, and she ran for office and won. She was baptized by fire immediately with a high-profile case involving the murder of a beloved priest, who had served as the high school principal, as well as being the local Catholic priest. The unraveling of the murder led to a series of child pornography incidents, and the townspeople had forgiven her inexperience and fully embraced her law enforcement style. It had been Maggie's first big case, and she appreciated Brick's help. She was intuitively honest and direct, but Brick taught her to be thorough. She was precisely the sheriff the residents of Barrier wanted, and they had re-elected her easily.

Maggie was tall and fit and over seven months pregnant. She kept her long brown hair tied back in a ponytail, a beautiful woman by any definition, and Brick had been instantly entranced and smitten when he first met her. She was athletic, but their twins kept her busy and had slowed down her exercise routine. She had a quick smile and a good sense of humor, and Brick loved her dearly.

Brick had arrived in town the same night that the priest was murdered. He stepped up to help her but stepped cautiously, not wanting to tread on her toes. He had come to Barrier with the promise of a teaching and coaching position offered by the priest/high school principal, Father Fitzwater. When Fitzwater died, Brick became a novice teacher, and the staff worked to assimilate him into the school. He coached basketball, and winning a few games endeared him to the town. He picked up the few classes he needed to become the principal and married Maggie, which helped him integrate into the small town of Barrier.

After college, Brick had gone to work as a police officer, despite having received a teaching certificate, but enrolled in enough education classes to keep the certificate active through the years. "Just in case," he said, not thinking much about the classroom. After he had back-to-back close calls involving firearms while arresting people, he reconsidered. While he was recovering from an injury, he decided he needed to make a change in his life. He wasn't sure what he would do when, out of nowhere, Father Fitzwater called, asking him if he wanted to teach school and coach basketball. Fitzwater and Brick had met on one of his trips through rural Nevada. The timing was right, and he had no commitments, so it was an easy transfer, and yet, some moments felt more difficult than others. Had he actually decided to throw away ten years of dedicated law enforcement service? The moment he met the lovely, somewhat naïve, unmarried sheriff, with a type-A personality and the bonus of beauty and enchanting green eyes, he knew that his decision was right. Change was good, and this change was better than good.

Brick stood six-foot-three, bulging with muscle and not an ounce of fat. When he arrived in town more than six years earlier, his black hair had been peppered with gray but now, the gray hairs had nearly taken over the black.

He teased Maggie that it was married life that caused it, but he knew it was in his genes, and he would be totally white-haired soon.

Maggie's lone deputy, Kenneth Garrison, whom everyone called Cagey, knew his job well and had been instrumental in solving the murder case. Cagey struggled with personal issues carried over from his childhood that resulted in him being an odd duck, quiet and reclusive, but he respected Maggie and afforded her unquestionable loyalty. He reminded Maggie of a tall bulldog with a hardened face. His teeth, now yellowed from years of smoking, protruded a bit and somehow seemed to highlight the scar on his left cheek. He was a burly man with fleshy arms that stretched the sleeves of his short-sleeved shirt. He seemed taller than his six-foot-two-inches because of his erect stature, including an oversized chest and sturdy legs. His formerly black moustache and beard had grayed in recent years, and he concealed his thinning hair with a WCSO baseball cap. One sleeve of tattoos on his arm that ran from his wrist to his neck, mostly of random designs that he said held no meaning, only rounded out his rough appearance.

"What's on your agenda today?" Brick asked, as they rallied from their sleep when a stream of sunshine notified them that it was time to arise. "Are you planning to catch any crooks?" He loved to tease and asked her about catching crooks every day, although crook catching didn't happen often. Barrier was a small town and relatively crime-free. Most of her time was spent answering complaints about dogs and trespassing.

"Crooks? Maybe, it all depends on whether one shows up. If one shows up, I'll nab him," she laughed. "Or Cagey will. Either way, the Barrier sheriff's office aims to keep our fair city crook-free. But never mind the crooks, I am concerned about the creaking sounds I heard last night. I'll have another look around while you fix Sarah and me a bacon and egg sandwich. Sarah is starving. Since you are on your summer schedule and don't have much else to do, it seems fair that you cater to me and the boys, and this sweet one." She patted her belly, which had grown large in the past month with the baby who was due in seven weeks. Last night I dreamed that we named her Sarah. Do you like that name?"

"You mentioned that last night, but was that before or after the noise woke us up? What if it's a boy? We decided not to find out the gender, so while Sarah is a fine name for a little girl, I don't think it fits for a boy, do you think?" Brick smirked.

Maggie shrugged and said, "We'll see. I think she's a girl though, and I really like the name Sarah. So, unless you object, Sarah it is." Brick knew better than to argue with this particular pregnant woman and wisely agreed.

Maggie finished dressing and headed outside to look for what might have caused the noises she heard. She paced the property's outer perimeter once before she moved toward the house and made two more laps trying to see if anything was out of place. They had a large yard with a short picket fence that needed painting. It was an easy step-over, but she saw nothing unusual, nothing that might have generated the noise she heard. She walked across the open area where they had demolished the garage that had been present when they purchased the home but saw nothing. Her phone chimed. and she knew it was time to go to work. She ran back inside the house, grabbed her sandwich, gave a goodbye kiss to the three men in her life, and headed to work to verify the crook or no crook status in her town. She also planned to take another stab at locating wherever or whatever the nightly noises might be.

Chapter 12

Maggie and Cagey
Present Day

"Cagey, we had a visitor last night," Maggie said, "well, maybe." She quit speaking mid-sentence, as she had second thoughts. Cagey might think she was prego-crazy, too, since she hadn't found anything. Brick would double check, though, after he finished fixing breakfast for the boys. She had searched quickly at midnight, but it had been a moonless night that left it pitch black outside, and a flashlight could only reveal so much. A repeat, systematic search before coming to work in the light of day revealed nothing either. Everything around the perimeter and the house seemed intact. She didn't want to come across as paranoid, so she hoped Cagey hadn't been listening.

"A visitor? Who came by?" he asked.

She sighed, *Dang it. I should have kept my mouth shut. Now I'm going to have to tell him.* The nightly screeching had persisted off and on for a month, but she had not shared anything about it with Cagey. "I'm not sure, we, rather I, heard some noises, but we don't know where they came from. I checked the perimeter and saw nothing, but the Givens' interior lights came on, too, so perhaps we should give them a whirl and see if they heard or saw anything. I did a walkaround after it happened, about midnight, and combed through the property before I came to work this morning, but I saw nothing either time."

"What about your other neighbor? I know Bob and Joyce live across the way, but what about the other house on your cul-de-sac?" Cagey asked.

"Yeah, they've lived on our street for about a year, and I've barely seen them, except for when he is crawling out of his pickup. They have another car, but nobody drives it. It's parked in their garage, as far as I know. And they have a heavy-weight, long-toothed dog that scares the dickens out of me, but I don't know what kind it is. I just know that it has sharp teeth, and is big, ugly, and scary," Maggie told him.

"I'll visit both of them to see if they saw or heard anything. Bob Givens' wife doesn't miss much, so I'll check with her first. That woman is the seed of all gossip in Barrier. I'll also check with your other neighbor, but I will keep my pepper spray handy for that one, since I am not a fan of big scary dogs either. Tell me again what you heard," Cagey said.

Maggie repeated her story, "I heard a screech or a scratch, loud and long. It was loud enough to wake me up, but it didn't awaken Brick because he was totally out. After that, I heard a squeaky creak, like a rusted door being opened, hinges, or scraping on a floor. I'm not quite sure but then there was silence. It lasted a few seconds but, like I said, it was loud enough to gain my attention. I worried about an intruder, but Brick is diligent about locking the doors, as you know. All those years in Los Angeles taught him that doors should be locked at night. I looked at the clock and it was a minute past twelve. I woke Brick and checked outside and saw nothing out of place. Brick checked the boys, who were sound asleep and fine, and then went back to sleep. Maggie rubbed her belly and said, "Baby Sarah decided it was time to practice jumping, so I didn't rest much."

"No problem, I'll have a look and, like I said, pay a visit to Bob and Joyce and the other neighbor," Cagey said. He paused and added, "I don't know if these run together, but Jay called early this morning, about seven o'clock, and said one of his employees is missing. We'll need to do a missing person search. She was one of his long-timers, and he doesn't want to lose her."

Jay Guzman, the town's largest employer, owned the Chicken Dinner Ranch, which offered an extensive western bar, chicken dinners with all the fixings, and a solid menu of females working in the world's oldest profession. The CDR, as it was called by the local citizens, lay on Highway 50, nicknamed the Loneliest Highway in America, but with the expansive services of the CDR, including a bar, food, and women, it had gained an intriguing reputation among travelers.

Jay was a natural businessman with both chutzpah and charisma. Some called him a wheeler-dealer-banana peeler. He owned two other popular businesses, the Barrier B & B, a medieval-themed bed and breakfast that was popular year-round as a must-see-to-believe destination resort, as well as the Panorama, an ancient hotel with a colorful past that drew patrons for its meals and history. Its staff and menu were second to none, and guests enjoyed its ambiance and menu. Barrier, once a thriving city with an abundance of high-producing gold fields, now dwindled, with a few stores and more empty storefronts. Somehow, Jay's businesses thrived, and he had been Barrier's reigning business kingpin for over ten years. If anyone knew how to turn a dollar, he did. People liked him, but knew to hold him at arm's length.

He had smooth-talked himself into politics and had been elected mayor during the last election cycle. When he said he would do something, it got done, with no ifs, ands, or buts about it. He focused his eye on everything Barrier, and no one complained.

Jay and Cagey were brothers.

Chapter 13

Brick and Terry
Present Day

The backhoe, along with three workmen and Terry, the supervisor wearing a white hard hat, arrived early, nine o'clock, an hour after Maggie had left for her office. The sun was out offering the promise of a warm day. They positioned the backhoe within the bounds of the ribboned-off twenty-three by forty-three-foot area, the dimensions needed to install the six-foot deep, twenty-by-forty-foot pool. They had allowed a few extra inches of maneuvering room, for when they inserted the plastic liner. The extra space would be filled in when they finished. With no swimming pool construction company closer than Reno, which was two hundred miles away, Brick had ordered a kit, a do-it-yourself swimming pool. With school out of session, he wanted a practical project to keep him busy, and he thought that he and a few high school basketball players could spend the first couple weeks of their summer vacation building one. It was a matter of digging the hole to the proper depth, leveling the dirt, adding and leveling a layer of sand, and inserting the plastic liner, which he thought might take the whole basketball team, including substitutes.

After they finished, he would hire a concrete company to pour a sidewalk around the pool and to the house. Maggie insisted that they add an expansive patio for sunbathing and family picnics. They would also add a high locking fence around the area to secure the attractive nuisance, as the insurance company called it. The accompanying literature said it would take a week to build, but Brick had never undertaken a project like this and thought one week might be a push. He instead estimated two, maybe three weeks, in case they ran into inevitable snags. Their goal was to have a pool party on the Fourth of July, five weeks away, which was two weeks before the new baby arrived. Brick reasoned that buying pizza for the basketball team several times would be cheaper than hiring a construction team out of Reno.

Activities and jobs for kids were sparse in Barrier and other nearby small towns. And, with summer temperatures often hovering around one hundred degrees, surely his team would welcome the work knowing a dip in the swimming pool would be their summer reward. There was little moisture but plenty of wind for weeks on end. Brick and Maggie thought a swimming pool would be a wonderful addition to their house and fun for the boys. While building it would be a challenge, everyone would enjoy a pool during the summer months. Maggie was already planning the July barbecue/pool shindig, inviting everyone she knew. Maggie and Brick both enjoyed a nice swim at the local swimming hole, and although they lived in a desert, they wanted the boys to learn to swim. Everyone was anticipating their first splashes. The only kink they could foresee was that Maggie's baby would arrive about the same time. By the end of the summer, though, Maggie would be back in her bikini, a sight Brick eagerly anticipated.

The supervisor, Terry Stevens, positioned the backhoe and his team for the dig. They had checked for gas lines and electrical wires the previous day, and everything was a go. The backhoe began its work, but with its first dig, it crunched to a halt. The operator tried again, but the backhoe hit something that caused it to clank, come to a standstill, and refuse to move. The operator rolled the machine a few feet forward and tried again, but the scoop ground to a halt once again at a foot below the surface.

"What in the heck is under here?" Terry grumbled to the operator, "Back it up and try again." He picked up a hand spade and moved toward the spot where the backhoe had made its initial dig. He rammed the spade into the ground and scooped out a couple shovels of dirt, but, again, it hit something solid.

He knelt on the surface of whatever was stopping their progress and brushed away the dirt. "What the heck? It's a slab of concrete. Why in the world is it there?" Terry asked, mostly to himself, but ordered one of the workmen, "Go and find Brick, and tell him to come out here."

Chapter 14

Brick and Terry
Present Day

"What the heck's under here?" Terry demanded of Brick, as soon as he appeared, pointing down at the concrete slab he was standing on. Terry was all business, wanting his employees to start back to work. The twins, decked out in their swimming suits in anticipation of going swimming, trailed behind Brick to the site. They ran to keep up with their dad's long strides and jumped over the plastic tape marking the proposed pool boundary.

"Nothing, at least I don't know of anything," Brick answered, falling to his knees to view the concrete. He scrunched up his face in puzzlement, clearly annoyed at the glitch in his plans.

Terry slammed the spade into the ground, "It's somethin', Brick, not nothin'. It's a slab of concrete, and this damn backhoe ain't gonna dig through that concrete floor or ceiling or whatever it is. The cement hasn't bent the scoop blade yet, but it will if we keep at it. We're gonna have to dig some of this by hand to figure out what this slab is." Terry frowned as he surveyed the slab.

Brick's mind immediately flashed to the massive tunnel system that crisscrossed below the surface throughout Barrier. During the Barrier gold heyday, mining companies found extensive gold deposits and excavated the ore using miles of tunnels to access and extract it. The mining companies paid premium prices to raze many of the houses in Barrier, leaving the community with few places to live. Barrier now resembled a construction zone with trailers, sheds, campers, and container houses, with a few traditional homes made of wood, brick, stucco, or whiskey bottles. The tunnels snaked below the surface like spaghetti, and the mining companies used the tunnels to transport metals and workers easily from one site to another. When the mining industry in Barrier shut down, the tunnels remained, but now, one by one, the mining companies closed them off, either filling them in or blocking their entrances. It was a slow process as the mining companies didn't care about the vacant tunnels and placed blocking them low on their list of priorities.

Brick shrugged and pointed toward the back of his property, "There's a defunct tunnel by our old garage site that runs to the CDR from our house, but we sealed it off after we bought the house. Maggie thought it had bad juju and didn't want our kids to discover the tunnels and hurt themselves or find out it connected to the CDR." Brick had reluctantly bought this house, the site of the priest's murder. It had plenty of bad vibes on its own, and they didn't want more.

"This cul-de-sac sits on an incline, too small to be called a hill, and I thought the mining companies didn't tunnel anything except the main part of town. I didn't know they searched for gold in this area," Terry said.

Brick had lived in Barrier fewer years than Terry, but he had learned about the tunnels as he and Maggie solved the priest's murder, so he told him what he knew. "Most of the tunnels were in town and led to lucrative gold pockets that were excavated and later abandoned, but they dug at least one tunnel up here. I suspect that they searched for gold but didn't find enough trace elements to mine, so abandoned it. One of the previous owners of this house, before Fitzwater, thought a tunnel to the CDR might be lucrative, people going to and from the CDR without anyone knowing the obscure route to the brothel. Its construction is far better than the tunnels I've passed through in the town area and even had some electric lighting. You can walk through the whole thing, except for the last few yards near the CDR where the tunnel has a low ceiling. It is only a couple feet high so you've got to crawl through on your hands and knees. The Chicken Dinner Ranch was its own gold mine." He thought of his first trip through the tunnel because that's where he had asked Maggie on a date. He had been wearing running shorts as he had been out for his daily run, and when they finished passing through the tunnel, his bare knees were scratched and bloody.

"Yes, the Chicken Dinner Ranch is a gold mine, but I wouldn't want to be in that kind of business," Terry said, continuing. "Maybe this is a septic tank. Septic services used to be common, but I know you have city services now. Your house is old, and somebody might have dug a septic tank that they covered with concrete after the city kicked in with its services. People do odd things."

"I don't know. The title company included some history of the house, but I don't recall anything about a septic system, although Maggie might know more because she grew up here," Brick said. "She'll be home for lunch. We can ask her then."

"We can scrape down a foot to see how big this whole slab is, but it looks like it is fairly large, at least twelve or fifteen feet. I don't think your swimming pool is going to work here, Brick. Do you and Maggie have a Plan B?"

Brick moved the boys outside the lime green tape to watch the backhoe do its job. It scraped a foot of soil off the concrete revealing a patch of concrete that was about fifteen by fifteen with two pipes protruding from the slab, each about six inches above the concrete's surface, both with removable caps. "What do you think those are?" Brick asked Terry, "Chimneys? What the heck?" The last scrape with the backhoe revealed a two-doored hatch, green with rusted metal and a padlock.

Terry huffed, "Brick, my friend, you have a bomb shelter, and those pipes are air holes, I believe. A bomb shelter right here in Barrier." He shook his head in disbelief. "They were popular during the Cold War scare, but I've never seen one here. If people wanted to dig around here, they dug for gold, not for a bomb shelter. This one looks like it's been closed up for a while. Somebody must have covered it with dirt years ago."

"Damn," Brick said, "what will I do about my swimming pool?"

Chapter 15

Brick and Terry
Present Day

"I don't have a bolt cutter, but Maggie does. I'll ask her to bring it when she comes home for lunch," Brick said as he hit speed dial on his cell phone. "I'd better call Maggie's mom, too. The boys don't need to see whatever this might be."

A few minutes later Maggie's mother appeared and took the boys in tow, bribing them with visions of making cookies.

"You'll have to come and get it yourself," Maggie told him when he called and asked for the bolt cutters, "because we are busy catching crooks." She wasn't really catching crooks, but rather looking into a missing brothel worker, but Brick didn't need to know everything.

Brick made the short trip to Maggie's office and returned home a few minutes later. "I brought Super Sadie," Brick said snipping the air with the tool. "She'll slice and dice anything. Let's cut."

Super Sadie had a two-foot-long handle, and five-inch jaws. Brick snipped the lock off in one short stroke. "She's a wonder woman," Brick noted. "A mighty fine clip artist."

The bomb shelter hatch swung open with a loud creak and a groan reminding Brick of Maggie's claim of hearing a grating creak in the middle of the night. The hatch cover had been buried and the dirt undisturbed, so he dismissed it as a source of the noise.

Terry and Brick started toward the door and peered down the stairs, but with no lights, they saw nothing but black. Terry pulled a flashlight from his toolkit, and Brick flipped on his cell phone flashlight. They lit the way, eyeing the steps, a handrail, and some dark-colored growth on the walls. They descended the steps, eighteen by actual count, trailing their lights from floor to ceiling trying to see what it looked like. The steps were moss-covered, steep, and narrow. When Brick reached for the handrail, it crashed to the floor as soon as he placed his hand on it. Another loud clank.

"This place stinks," Brick sputtered, trying not to breathe. "It smells like rotten eggs or a wet dog or even a dead animal. I've been in a lot of basements before, and they usually smell musty, but this one is foul."

"It could be this moss with some mold or mildew," Terry answered, "or it could be a dead animal, like a mouse or a gopher or something, some animal that digs or crawls through dirt. I don't think anyone has been down here for a long time, so who knows? This is downright creepy," Terry said. "Give me a backhoe any day. I don't know how you law enforcement types do this."

"We don't do this type of thing every day, that's for sure. Is that a water tank?" Brick asked aloud, quite sure it was. It was a gray metal tank lying prone, balanced on two concrete blocks, up to his shoulders high with a four-foot girth. "What do you think? I have no idea how much water it would hold." He passed his flashlight over the entire surface and focused it near a tap but saw nothing helpful. "I wonder if it's full." He knocked on the metal tank with his fist, and it echoed back a thud. "It sounds like it's full, but if it is, I can't help but wonder how long the water has been in the tank. Since the 50's?"

The entire shelter was indeed about fifteen feet by fifteen feet, one room with a half-wall separating it into two areas, eating and sleeping. A curtained-off lavatory, not much larger than a linen closet, sat in the corner, holding a toilet, sink, and shower. The shower had been installed over the sink to save space with two sets of faucets, presumably one set for the sink and one for the shower. The rust-stained toilet was devoid of water, and the tank lid was cracked. A wooden toilet seat was broken, making it a half seat, and half of it lay on the floor. Terry twisted one of the faucets, and it turned, but no water sputtered out. "Nothing here," he said.

Sitting in the kitchen area was a large table covered by an oversized faded plastic red-and-white checked tablecloth. The table was hinged to the wall, and the legs moved up and down so it could either lie flat against the wall or sit like a table. Four folding chairs leaned against the wall. A painted shelf contained a three-inch pile of paper plates, a couple coffee cups, and a roll of duct tape.

On the other side of the room rested six narrow bunkbeds, three high with black and white striped mattress pads, all attached to the wall. The top two beds had hinges and lay flush to the walls, but the lowest ones would serve as a place to sit. "These beds remind me of pictures I've seen of submarines," Brick said. "I wonder if they put a second door in here anywhere, you know, an escape route." They both moved around the room, looking for a second door but came up dry.

"Well," Terry said, "I don't think you want to build your new pool on top of a bomb shelter, and you probably don't want to remove it, so what's next?"

Brick's expression dulled as he held his breath for a second, "I don't know. I guess we have no choice but to find a different place to build our pool."

Chapter 16

Maggie and Jay
Present Day

Maggie called Jay on his cell phone and asked, "Cagey told me you lost someone, so who's the missing girl? Have you heard anything from her yet?"

"Hi, Maggie, no, we've heard nothing. She left behind her purse, but nothing seems to be disturbed. She's just gone. It's Brandi. She's been here for four years. I'm worried because no one saw her after lunch, and she didn't work last night. She sometimes goes on long early morning walks, but she's usually back before breakfast. She's nowhere to be seen. It's unlike her."

"Where does she walk? In town? Or does she venture out on the highway?" Maggie asked, thinking the town was safe enough, but walking on the highway might lead to something dangerous for a woman walking alone in the dark.

"She stays in town, as far as I know. I hear she likes to walk past the old buildings on her way to the Panorama for breakfast. They open early, so she often spent a bit of time talking to the young women she met there," Jay said. The Panorama employees were legal immigrants coming to America to start new lives, mostly from Asia or the Pacific Islands, but a few were from Europe and Africa. Jay collaborated with a team of casino owners and arranged their travel. They spent a year or more learning American culture and language before Jay helped them negotiate with Las Vegas or Reno casinos for permanent jobs and living quarters. With their training and language skills, they urged international gamblers to lighten their own pockets and increase the casino coffers. His mother had been a Panorama worker years before, and he prided himself in helping these young women gain fresh starts. He often said this was his contribution to harmony in the world.

"Tell me about Brandi," Maggie persisted, "anything you remember."

Jay began to talk, "There's not much to tell, she didn't talk much about her past. She said she was from California, but most of the women who work here list California as their place of residency, so I'm not sure it's true. I asked her a couple times, but she fired back, 'Why do you ask?' She said she was a teacher, but that is hard to believe, because why would a teacher come to work here? She didn't like to talk about herself, and I never got clear answers. Most times she answered a question with a question. She was about twenty-five when she first arrived and has been here four years, so she's not quite thirty now. I think her birthday is in January. She has stayed with me all four years, which is a record. Most women work a year or two or even less, become restless, and move on, either to another brothel, another work choice, or off with some guy who promises them the world but gives them nothing. Now and then, someone goes back to school. Brandi never connected with anyone special, although she was popular and had a steady line of return clients. She was always very careful, practicing safe-sex as far as I knew, although we never talked about it, which is probably why she never contracted any diseases. The state's doctors regularly inspect our workers, and they said she really took care of herself, eating right, exercising, and did not have evidence of drug use and was in good physical shape. She was pleasant and enjoyed people, and people liked her. As I said, she seldom talked about herself, but she could con others into telling their life's stories. She did mention having a sister, but I don't know if that was true or where the sister is, if it were true."

"Is Brandi her real name or a name she adapted for your business? And what's her last name?" Maggie asked.

"As far as I know, it's her real name, at least she had a Social Security card listing it as her name. If it's not her real name, she must have had it legally changed. Her last name is Dumont. Brandi Dumont," Jay answered. "If you drop by, I'll give you a photo. We photograph our employees when they first come to work for us, then again every six months. Sometimes, though, they leave without a word, like Brandi did. In this business, people age faster than usual, and the women change their hair, make-up, and skin tones every few weeks. I'll make you a copy of her last two photos. I hope you can find her and that she is ok."

"I'd like to talk to some of the others at the CDR to see if they know where she might have gone. They might have heard her say something or seen someone with her. Does she have a vehicle or access to a vehicle?" Maggie asked.

Jay shook his head, not remembering that he was on the phone with Maggie, and she couldn't see him, "No, she doesn't have a car. She said cars were too expensive, and she was saving her money for bigger and better things. She never indicated what those bigger or better things were, though. When she did go out, she walked. She said it was good exercise and gave her time to clear her head. She usually walked in the morning because business picks up after lunch, but she had the whole day off yesterday and didn't work the night before either. I don't know when she left, so she could have been gone for thirty-six hours."

"Okay, I'll come by in a little while. I'll need to talk to all your employees," Maggie continued.

Chapter 17

Cagey
Present Day

Brick and Maggie's cul-de-sac contained three houses. The trio were spread out—close enough to be called neighbors but far enough to stay out of each other's business. Cagey knew Brick and Maggie, of course, and the residents of one of the other houses, Bob and Joyce Givens, but not the third house, which the Givens' owned, but rented out. The tenants there usually didn't stay long. Bob was the counter man and manager of the local pizza shop, and Joyce kept her eye on the rental and the comings and goings of the neighborhood. She was the neighborhood yenta, a busybody. She meant no harm but seemed to know everything about everybody and was willing to tell.

Bob Givens answered the door on Cagey's first knock, and Cagey greeted him by jumping right in, "I'm wondering, Bob, did you or Joyce hear anything last night? Someone reported a prowler in this area."

"Maybe. Joyce woke up about one thirty or a little before and looked outside. She said she thought she heard somebody on our steps because they creak when someone walks on them, but she didn't see anything. I ought to replace these steps, but it's a lot of work."

"Did you hear anything earlier, like at midnight?" Cagey continued.

"No, I didn't hear anything at midnight," Joyce said, as she approached the door where Bob and Cagey stood. "But at one-thirty, I heard a creak, a loud creak, and I figured it was the neighbors. Not Maggie and Brick, of course, but the tenants renting our other property, Ace and Ginger. They are a strange pair."

"What do you mean, strange? Strange how?" Cagey continued.

"Well, I really shouldn't say. It's gossip, you see, but he locked her out of the house one evening two months back. Ginger rattled the door, but it must have been locked because she stayed outside for a long time. It was spring, and we were having warm days, but it cooled right down at night. And...she was naked, naked as a chicken. It was like he had thrown her out of the house while she was taking a shower. I saw her grab a bath towel off the clothesline and wrap it around herself as best she could. Then she sat on the front steps. It was a small towel and barely covered the necessities. She must have been sitting outside for an hour or more, like it was the most normal thing in the world. I watched from the front window deciding if I should help, I don't like to interfere, you know. After a while, Ace opened the door and let her in. That was followed by a lot of yelling and swearing, but they quieted down after a few minutes. I thought about calling you or Maggie, but I didn't because it stopped. It wasn't that late, maybe eight or nine, I mean not in the middle of the night or anything, but anybody could have seen her."

"Did you say anything to Maggie? Or mention it to Ginger?" Cagey asked.

"No, I didn't say anything to Maggie. She's so busy with those cute little boys, and I don't like to bother her. It never happened again, so I think it was a one-time event," Joyce said. "But that's not all. Sometime after dark the same night, I saw someone running down the hill. I don't know if it was a man or woman," Joyce continued. "The person obviously wasn't from our house or from Brick's, so they must have come from Ginger's house."

"How long have they lived here?" Cagey asked.

"They moved in about a year ago, but I've never talked to her, other than at the mailbox. We swap hellos occasionally, but she's not much of a talker. She told me her name was Ginger, but nothing more. Bob dealt with all the rental paperwork when they moved in because I wasn't feeling well that day. Bob sees Ace at the Pizza Shoppe now and again, but not her. He works at the Barrier B & B as a groundskeeper, mowing and clipping and stuff like that. He wears one of their logoed shirts, you know the dark green with BBB printed across the front. I don't think she works, at least I've never seen her leave the house except to go to the mailbox. As far as I know, they own one vehicle—that big, white, hot-rod pickup, but she doesn't go anywhere unless she walks, and I've never seen her walking to town or exercising. Maybe she's one of those people who works from home via the internet."

"They only have one car?"

"I believe so, but if they do have another one, it could be in the garage. Maybe she doesn't drive."

Chapter 18

Maggie and Brick
Present Day

Maggie stopped at the CDR for the photos of Brandi Dumont and once again talked with Jay. Both photos were good quality head shots, likely taken with a cell phone. Maggie didn't recall ever having seen her. Brandi was an attractive woman, as Jay had said. In one photo, her hair was short with blond highlights, but in the other, she had red hair that fell to her shoulders. She wore turtlenecked shirts in both pictures.

"Is she wearing a wig in either of these pictures?" Maggie asked. "What's her natural color?"

"No, both photos show her real hair. Some of the women wear wigs, but I don't allow wigs for their biannual photos. Brandi's natural hair is dark brown, but she highlights and colors it periodically," Jay said.

"What color was her hair the last time you saw her?" Maggie asked.

"I'm not sure, she changes it often, but short and red, I think. Shorter than in this photo," Jay said, pointing at the photo with the blonde hair. "I think she changes it so often because it masks who she really is. She's a good employee, and makes a lot of money, that is to say that she makes me a lot of money," he admitted with a little smirk. "I pay her well, too, but I knew this wasn't what she wanted to do with her life. Something else is going on with her, but I don't know what. I've asked, but like I said, she clams up about herself."

"Do you have any guesses as to what her issues might be?" Maggie asked.

"I don't know. I've thought about it, but she's never indicated anything. She showed up one day with a truck driver, and I thought she was pretty and offered her a job. She is classier than most who work here. I didn't really think she'd take it, but she thought about it for maybe fifteen minutes, said okay, and went to work. That was about four years ago. She never said anything about why she came or what she wanted. She likes the money and makes a good amount, but as far as knowing much about her, I don't. Most of my employees have some sort of tale you can latch onto, you know, they've got something in their past that leaks out and you know why they came to Barrier, but not Brandi. I know she has a sister. That's it," Jay said.

Maggie looked at the photos again and noted that Brandi had regular features, but her eyes seemed to sparkle in both pictures, like she had a secret. Maggie was curious about why she was working at the CDR. If she were a certified teacher, she had other employment options. Of course, she may have been motivated by money, as she knew Jay paid and treated "his girls" well. But why did she need that much?

By brothel standards it was early, and most of the employees had not yet arrived to work, so Maggie backtracked to her house to check on the progress of their swimming pool project.

The whole work crew was standing around, looking like they had nothing to do. "What's going on?" Her eyes grew wide as she noticed the open hatch. "What's down those steps, and what did you do with the boys?" She looked at the idle backhoe, then at Brick. She squinted her eyes down the dark staircase, and asked, "What's this?"

Brick answered, "Everything's good, well, I don't really know. Grandma is baking cookies with the boys, but we have a bomb shelter instead of a swimming pool. It's throwing a wrench in our plans. We have to make a choice, either we're going to cancel the pool, fill the bomb shelter with water and swim in it, or find another place to install it." Brick scanned their yard, wondering where they could make it fit. A twenty-by-forty-foot pool would fit in several areas of their yard, but other considerations, such as privacy, trees, convenience, and the required fencing made the decision more difficult. The area they had chosen had been perfect, and now they had to refigure their options. Since the backhoe team was ready to rumble, Brick was annoyed at the inconvenience of a bomb shelter in their yard.

Terry interjected, "Yes, Sir, it's a problem, but I think it's solvable. Why don't you two take a couple hours to figure it out while we go for an early lunch. We can talk about it when we return. The backhoe's not going any place. We'll have to check for gas and electric lines, but that won't take long. If you can decide today, we can mark it off and fire up the backhoe first thing tomorrow. This is just an unforeseen snag, but it's solvable, that's for sure, and we'll get 'er done. No problem."

Maggie nodded, "Okay, that'll work. We'll figure it out. We might have to cut back a tree or two, but we'll figure it out. I'm in the middle of something right now, so I'll leave it to Brick. Hopefully, I can get back here in an hour or two, but before I go, though, I want to take a gander at the bomb shelter. My dad talked about bomb shelters being built in the forties and fifties when people worried about the Cold War, but I never saw one here in Barrier. I don't recall him ever mentioning a bomb shelter here, either. It's not like Barrier is a hot bed for the communists. Let's look."

Terry headed toward his truck, and Brick and Maggie switched on their phone flashlights and proceeded down the stairs. The moss or mold growing on the narrow steps made them a little damp, and Brick was concerned about Maggie slipping, so he took her arm, "Careful, Maggie, we don't want Sarah tumbling down the staircase. Also, it's stinky. I'm not sure you two should breathe in this foul air, so we better make this a quick trip."

They aimed their flashlights around the room, noting the same things that Terry and Brick had seen until Maggie bent down and peered under the table. "What do you suppose is in these?" she said, pushing the hinged table toward the wall and snapping its hook to the wall. Two boxes, sealed with gray duct tape, frayed and old, and unlabeled, sat next to each other. The larger one was cardboard, a small banker's box with the lid attached, and the smaller one was wooden about the size of a cigar box. A third container, a cloth bag sat on top of the others.

"I don't know, Sheriff, but we didn't see them earlier," Brick said, dragging the largest box toward him. Maggie jammed a pair of gloves into his hands, and he stopped what he was doing. "Roger, Sheriff, I forgot protocol. I guess I'm out of practice because I don't have to glove up when I'm at school." He stretched the gloves onto his fingers and began to strip off the tape.

"It's probably some sort of food, you know, the kind people buy when they worry about the end of the world. Food staples, like pasta and flour, stuff that either never goes bad, or takes a long time to rot," Maggie said, adding, "like Twinkies. Maybe our end-of-the-world under-grounders were addicted to all things Hostess, and these boxes will be loaded with them. I used to love Twinkies but haven't had one in eons. Do they still even make Twinkies?"

"Yes, I'm pretty sure grocery stores still have them, but we're not buying them for the boys," Brick said. "With their love of sweets, they would probably become addicted. If these boxes hold Twinkies, we're tossing them."

"We can toss them after Sarah and I have our fill, not before," Maggie answered quickly. "I'd like a Twinkie right now."

"That's my prego girl talking," Brick said as he peeled the tape off, finding that the top was also sealed with glue. "Somebody didn't want these Twinkies to be found," Brick said, straining his fingers to pry off the top, ripping the cardboard. "Oh, my God, what is this?"

Chapter 19

Ace and Ginger
One Year Prior

"It's been a horrible day. I can't deal with this anymore. The police showed up again today," Ginger sobbed to Ace when he returned from work. She had been crying, and her eyes were bloodshot with mascara running down her cheeks. "More questions about Mom. It's been three years since she was murdered. Aren't they ever going to leave us alone?" Her body drooped, and she looked older than her years.

"Not only the police, but a few minutes ago, I received a call from Dad, who wanted to come by tonight. I don't want to see him, so I told him that we weren't going to be home. He asked me a bunch of questions about Brandi, like where she was and how he could reach her. I think he's looking for her, but I don't know why."

"What did the police want now?" Ace growled. "I'm sick of them bothering us. Maybe we ought to move back to Texas." He leaned over and hugged her. Despite his domineering and sometimes aggressive behavior, he loved her and didn't like seeing her weepy side.

"No, we can't move back to Texas because of everything that happened there. The cops asked me the usual question, Where is Brandi?" Ginger choked on her sobs and sputtered, "I've told them that we don't know, but they don't believe me. They'll be back next week, for sure. Can't we make them stop?"

Ace went to the refrigerator and pulled out two beers, "Yes, it's been three years since your mom died, and the fools haven't a clue about who killed her. The police are convinced that Brandi murdered her, based on the fact that she disappeared, which is a sign of guilt as far as they are concerned. Maybe her disappearance is their lone piece of evidence. I thought they would stop after a couple years, but these idiots haven't. It's a cold case, but they keep trying to reheat it. Their constant harassment has got to end. You'd think they'd work harder to find Brandi if they think she killed your mom. Even those inept cops should be able to see that we don't know where she is."

Ginger looked at Ace while she nibbled on her bottom lip, "Maybe you're right, Ace, we should move, not to Texas though, maybe someplace else, like one of the small towns near here. We could just disappear, like Brandi did. Become invisible and lose ourselves. Does it really make any difference who killed her after all this time? Brandi worried that she would be a target of the murderer, but I'm guessing she's safe now, and nobody's harassing her. If we move to a small town, maybe like Barrier, the cops won't know where we live and won't hound us every week. I doubt they would be able to find us if we moved to some dinky town in the middle of nowhere. I wouldn't mind moving because we have nothing keeping us here. Mom's dead, and Brandi's gone. Nothing."

"Barrier? Barrier where? Is it in Nevada? I've never even heard of it," Ace said, taking a swig from his beer bottle.

"Yes, Barrier, Nevada. It might be a good place to live. It's a gold mining town a couple hundred miles east of here. I looked it up on the internet," Ginger answered.

Ace listened, not believing what he was hearing, "What are you talking about? Barrier? Where the heck is that? I have a job, and small towns often don't have much work. And what if Brandi returns, and she can't find us," Ace continued, looking at Ginger as if she had lost her mind.

"Well, if we moved, we wouldn't have to worry about Dad finding us, because he's not smart enough to look in a town like Barrier. We know that Brandi didn't kill her, and the cops should know that, too, but they think she's the logical suspect because she disappeared. Brandi's probably hiding someplace safe, and I don't think they'll ever find her. I hated Mom and Brandi because they were so tight, but we both know that Brandi didn't kill her," Ginger said. "She's been hiding out a long time, and the police have no idea where she is, but I know she's safe."

Ace looked at Ginger as if he had never seen her before. His forehead vein turned purple, and his face flushed, "Do you know where Brandi is?" Ace asked with disbelief. "Have you heard from her?"

"Sort of. She sent me a couple postcards, nothing was written on them but my name and address, but I know her handwriting. She wrote these, I'm sure of it. This is the second card I've received in two months." She pulled them from under the seat cushion and handed Ace the two postcards, one with a photo of the Barrier B & B and the other from a bar and restaurant called the Chicken Dinner Ranch, Barrier, Nevada, both black and white cards.

Ace looked at the postcards skeptically and turned them over a couple times. "Did you show these to the police? I've heard of the Chicken Dinner Ranch, it's a ..., but where's Barrier again?" Ace asked suspiciously, leaving out the word brothel.

Ginger bit her lip, "No, the police don't know about the postcards, and I'm not telling them. Like I said, I looked up Barrier and learned it's a former gold mining town a couple hundred miles from here. I don't know what she's doing, maybe digging for gold because you know how she and Mom liked finding gems and jewelry."

"Yeah, I forgot about their business—the Q2 or whatever they called it. Did they make much money from it? It seemed like a lot of busy work, going to the sales to buy old jewelry and clean it up. It seemed a silly thing to do," Ace commented.

"Well, besides buying it, they repaired it and resold it on the internet, and they made good money. Brandi told me they would sometimes pay five bucks for a pair of earrings, clean them up, and then sell them for several hundred or even thousands of dollars. I'm not sure how much they made, but a long time ago, Brandi told me that she repaid her college loans and bought herself a new car. She also told me that Mom squirreled away a bunch of gems, and she could sell them anytime on the internet. It might have been a lot of money, but I don't know what their income was before Mom died," Ginger told him. "Mom offered me a job helping her, but I knew you didn't like me working, so I said no."

"I didn't know they actually sold that jewelry. I thought they kept it for themselves. You should have helped them, maybe we'd be better fixed now," Ace said, now interested in knowing about the money side of Q2.

Ginger smiled, knowing that Ace was hooked, "To me, Barrier is the perfect place to hide because it's tiny but close enough to Reno, right under the noses of the police. I've never wanted to live near Brandi, but she loved jewelry, and I'll bet she's still selling gems. Maybe we could cash in on that, too? Why don't we take a road trip and see what it's like? It's only a couple hundred miles, maybe three or four hours."

Chapter 20

Ace and Ginger
One Year Prior

Twenty minutes later, Ace decided to aim their car toward Barrier to have a look and attempt to locate Brandi if she were in Barrier. When Ginger told him that Candice and Brandi were selling gems on the internet, he interpreted her comments as loaded with dough, and since Candice was dead, it was reasonable to deduct that now Brandi was the one who was loaded with dough. He figured that she had been hiding and selling jewelry all these years.

Brandi didn't answer her phone, so maybe she had a new one, and they had no way of notifying her that they were coming. They arrived in Barrier late afternoon and pulled into the parking lot of the Chicken Dinner Ranch. Brandi had mailed a Chicken Dinner Ranch postcard, and they had seen billboards along the highway advertising its classic chicken dinners for only five dollars. Ace knew a bargain when he saw one. Ace's casino coworkers had told him about the Chicken Dinner Ranch, famous for lots of things, not limited to just chicken dinners. They also reminded him that the CDR was a brothel, but he kept that jewel of information a secret from Ginger. He knew Brandi well and figured that she might send a card from the CDR as a joke. Brandi had earned a college degree and become a respected teacher and right now she probably was sitting in a room full of fifth graders, teaching them how to multiply or divide or something similar. She had loved teaching and was considered a straight arrow among her friends. She didn't smoke and barely drank more than a glass of beer or wine. She had been with a couple men in her first year of teaching, but nothing serious, and she hadn't lived with either of them. Ace knew that Brandi had gone off the deep end when her mother died, but obviously not enough to work in a brothel, for God's sake.

They entered the bar and Ace ordered a craft beer. Ginger ordered a glass of the house Chardonnay while they waited for their meal. A long movie set-type bar, like those seen in John Wayne movies, complete with full mirror and mahogany trim filled one end of the room. Matching mahogany chairs and tables were scattered throughout the center of the room and red Naugahyde booths lined the exterior walls. People had taped and stapled dollar bills covering the walls and ceiling like wallpaper. Some were signed, some dated, some without anything. "Damn," Ace said, "look at all those dollar bills, we could be sitting pretty if we peeled all these off. Do you think anyone would notice?"

No other customers were in the bar, and when Ginger commented about the lack of patrons, the server smiled and said, "Hold on for a little while! It'll be filled before you're done. If you don't eat too fast."

Their meal arrived, and they dug into the fried chicken, mashed potatoes and gravy, corn on the cob, and slaw. Since they had skipped lunch, both were hungry, and they concentrated on their meals. A few people entered and headed directly to the bar, followed by a few more, and as the server predicted, the room began to fill.

They were nearly finished when Ace suddenly nudged Ginger, "There's Brandi. I see her, that's Brandi," he rasped, not too quietly. He gestured and pointed. "Isn't that her? Is she a hooker? She looks like a hooker with that blonde hair and makeup."

They had not seen Brandi in three years, the last time being at their mother's funeral. She looked different, yet the same, except for her bleached hair, saggy clothes, and overdone makeup. Ginger squinted and said, "I don't know, Ace, maybe, maybe not." Ginger knew it was Brandi, no doubt about it, but she looked so different. Her sallow skin and sunken eyes gave her a scarecrow appearance, and her usual smile was absent.

"Brandi? Brandi? Is that you?" Ace called to her. "I didn't think we would find you so quickly."

Brandi turned around and stared at Ace and her sister. Her eyes grew large and darted from one to the other. She had been at the CDR for three years without telling anyone of past attachments or family, and now her stupid sister shows up with her ne'er-do-well husband. She should never have mailed those postcards. Stupid, stupid, stupid.

"You must be mistaken, I'm Brandi, but I don't know you," she scowled, gazing at Ginger without blinking. She half-turned to gaze at Ace. "I'm late, I need to be somewhere." She turned on her heel and headed toward the back of the room.

Ginger grabbed her sleeve, "Of course, you remember me, I'm Ginger, your sister, your lone sister. We grew up together in Reno. Do you have amnesia or dementia or something?"

Brandi ignored her and slapped her hand away. She continued walking toward the rear of the bar, but Ginger didn't give up, "Come on, Brandi, you know us. Don't pretend that you don't. What's with you?"

Brandi was adamant and answered Ginger as she once more brushed her hand from her arm and snapped, "Stop it," at the same moment, Jay walked by. Ace stood and moved toward Brandi, "It's me, Brandi, I'm Ace your favorite brother-in-law."

Jay faced Ace and stepped among the trio putting Brandi behind him, "What's wrong, Honey, is he bothering you? Do you know these people?"

Brandi stepped back and looked away, muttering, "No, I don't. I've never seen them before in my life."

Jay grabbed ahold of Ace's arm and squeezed it a little tighter than he needed and said, "Okay, Cowboy, you need to leave now," and began steering him toward the exit. Jay, a large person with a monumental persona, caused heads to turn as the few guests watched the standoff. Ace was also a large man, but his largeness was more located in his stomach. He did not have the presence that Jay had. "I can call the police, or you can exit now, but leave this young lady alone."

Ginger watched as Jay escorted Ace from the building, but she didn't say anything. Puzzled, she sat down again in the booth, not knowing what to do. Brandi was ignoring her, claiming she had never seen her before, and she didn't understand why. They had maintained a rocky relationship through the years, but this was not what she expected. And who was this other guy? Her husband?

While Ginger picked at the rest of her dinner, Jay accompanied Ace to the parking lot. Ace complained the whole way, unsuccessfully twisting to remove himself from Jay's grip. Brandi picked up the rest of Ace's dinner and winked at Ginger, giving a little nod of her head, one that said, Follow me. Ginger waited a couple minutes and asked the server about a restroom and moved toward the rear of the building. Brandi stood outside the bathroom and scooted her sister in, closing and locking the door behind them.

The two sisters hugged each other, and Brandi whispered, "You shouldn't have come, but it's good to see you, Sis. No one here knows about Mom's death or you or Ace. I'm kind of shocked that you are still married to him, actually. I told people that I had a sister but I'm pretty sure I didn't tell anyone your name. Jay might have figured it out, though. I don't want any connection to Mom and Reno, and I don't want Jay to know that you are my sister."

Ginger whispered back, "What? Why not? We're moving here, Brandi, at least I think we are. Ace agreed to move, but he might change his mind since that man hustled him out of the bar. Who was the guy anyway? Your husband?"

Brandi's jaw tightened, "That's Jay, the owner. This is a brothel, and he runs a clean house and doesn't like scandals. I don't want him or anyone else to know about Mom being murdered because people might figure things out. I don't want the police to find me. Jay has been good to me. I've been here for four years, and I have earned a ton of money. Now you and I can go somewhere, you and I—without Ace—and become invisible. We can go away from the police and accusations and this, all the men." She raised her arm and passed it between them, gesturing toward the building. "It's about losing ourselves." She paused for a moment and looked at her sister. Until this moment, she had not realized how much she missed her and said, "I'm glad to see you, Sis."

Ginger wrinkled her brow and bombarded Brandi with questions, "Become invisible and lose ourselves, and go off somewhere? Are you kidding? Without Ace? What's this about? Do you work here? Are you... you know...are you a...?"

Brandi squeezed Ginger's arm and nodded, "Yes, it's all about Mom. And Dad. I've figured it out, and I'll explain it some time," she said before she unlocked the door and ran out of the room and up the stairs.

Chapter 21

Ace and Ginger
One Year Prior

Ginger returned to their car and joined Ace who was sitting behind the wheel. His face was blotched red, and he gripped the steering wheel so tightly that his knuckles had turned white. His voice quivered as he growled, "I don't know what that guy was so mad about. It was like he had something against me, and he'd never even met me. It was like he was protecting Brandi, what's up with her anyway? Are they married or together? I'm hungry, did you bring my dinner? We paid for it, but I didn't finish it or drink the whole beer."

Ginger was quiet for a minute, trying to sort out what had happened and how much she wanted to tell Ace. "I talked to Brandi. That guy was the owner, Jay, and doesn't like people interfering with his business, and Brandi is his business, apparently. The server removed your dinner before I could ask her to put it in a doggy bag. I'm sorry, but we can find another place to eat."

Ace responded, "I gotta say, I'm not that thrilled about this place, for obvious reasons, but since we are here, let's at least look around." The possibility of Brandi having earned a fortune with the gemstones recently dawned on him, and he added in that her earnings as a working girl might increase his calculations. "We need a little more information, like housing and jobs. This town is smaller than I thought, so I'm even less sure that this is the place for us. I actually haven't seen many houses. A couple of trailers and a few more container houses, but that's it. And why did Brandi treat us like that. She clearly wasn't that happy to see us. She acted like she had never laid eyes on you before, and that big guy shoved me out of the bar. What else did Brandi say to you?"

"I talked briefly to Brandi, finished my dinner and wine, and boogied. I don't know what's up with her, but when I told her we were thinking of moving here, she didn't seem to be bothered by it, but she also didn't want anyone to know we were related. Can you believe that? She said it was all about Mom and Dad and that she had figured something out. I don't know what that meant, but that's what she said. Maybe Mom's death, I mean her murder. And Dad? He called recently, but he's been gone a long time. Do you think she knows who murdered Mom?"

Ace was thinking hard and remembering the times he had been a guest at a local jail in his hometown in Texas. He had done many things that could have put him back there, but he and Ginger had left Texas before the police figured it out. Nothing was so serious as to be extradited back to Texas, but he figured it was only a matter of time before the Reno police started asking questions about the Texas issues. Barrier might prove to be a good hiding place with the bonus of having a backwoods police department. If he behaved himself, no one would ever find him.

Ginger thought for a minute, "Do you have any idea what she's talking about? When Brandi said that she didn't want Jay to know we were related, it made me think again about whether Brandi was involved in our mother's death. Maybe she was."

This was the quandary Ace and Ginger had mulled over many times, especially with Reno law enforcement asking the same questions more times than they could recall. Could they not stay away from Candice's murder issues? It was bad enough that she had been murdered, the newspapers used the term slaughtered, but the constant haranguing needed to end.

Ginger was tired of it all, the constant questioning by the police each week, reaffirming what the police already knew. She wanted to hide. Mom was dead and that wouldn't change, but couldn't they all be safe together in Barrier, even if Brandi were involved? What could they do to make it go away?

They busied themselves with the task of house hunting and found the situation bleak. The rentals were run down and small. They first looked for an apartment complex, but didn't find one. Ginger drew a deep, dark line in the sand on container houses, although some had been fixed up enough that they looked tolerable. A few single-wide trailers were available, but they were small and hadn't seen care of any kind for decades. Ginger said no to them also. She said she was done with alternative-type housing because once they had lived in a houseboat for few months. They had docked it on a slow-moving river in Texas with a floating flower garden behind it. Torrential winter rains began one night and sent it downstream while they were asleep, and they had awakened in a different town, and their flower garden was gone. She had said no more alternative houses and meant it, and now, she insisted on having a regular house, wood, brick, or stucco on solid ground. A regular house.

They registered for a room at the Panorama Hotel and walked across the street to the Pizza Shoppe to order a pizza and beer. Ace was hungry and cranky, having missed his lunch and being frustrated and disappointed with the housing situation.

Several tables were full, mostly with teenagers, and the room was noisy, which made him even crankier. The man behind the counter moved toward them and said, "What can I do you for?"

Ace looked around for a menu, and seeing none said, "I'm starving. I'll take an extra-large pizza with the works and a Coors, and she'll have a small pineapple and Canadian bacon pizza and a Pepsi."

The man behind the counter twisted his mouth and sighed, "You must be new in town. We have one kind of pizza, pepperoni, and one size, large.

And Oly, no Coors. Coke, no Pepsi. Do you want one pizza or two? Pizza is pizza, beer is beer, and cola is cola, meaning we stock one kind of each. This is Barrier, not Vegas."

Ace gazed at the chubby man, "You got that right. Nothing but Oly? Okay, Oly. It'll have to do. And she'll have a Coke. We'll take two pizzas. She doesn't like pepperoni, so she can peel the slices off if that's all you've got."

"You got it. I'll be right back with your drinks," the man said.

Ace faked a smile, "He's right, this is Barrier, not Vegas. Hell, it's not even Pahrump. Are we sure we want to move here? So far, no houses, no Coors, no Pepsi, and only one measly kind of pizza. I don't have a job and as of now, nothing to live in. Maybe we should rethink our moving here."

The man behind the counter brought their drinks, "I heard you say something about no houses. Do you want to move here?"

"We've been thinking about it, but it's up in the air as of now because we have two issues. I need a job, and we can't move if we don't have a place to live. She's nixed trailers and container houses, and I haven't seen many houses that are built with sticks or stones," Ace said. "Do you know of anything?"

"I might be able to fix you up. I have a rental house that will be available in a few days. Nobody's in it right now but the toilet leaked, and I have to replace the flooring. I can show it to you tomorrow if you want. My wife usually takes care of it, but she's under the weather, so I'll open it up for you to see. As for a job, try the Barrier B & B, on the other side of town. They hire workers constantly, and since it's summer, some groundskeeping jobs could be available if you can handle a rake and lawnmower."

Ginger looked skeptical, "Is your house a trailer or a container house, or is it a real house?"

The man behind the counter chuckled, "That's a common question for people moving here, but it's a real house, made of wood and whiskey bottles, like a lot of Barrier houses. Do you have kids or dogs?"

Ginger answered, puzzled at what he said, "Whiskey bottles? I don't know what you are talking about. How can a house be made of bottles?"

Bob gave a little smile, "Whiskey bottles are strong structurally, and the miners drank a lot of whiskey. Hell, they still drink a lot of whiskey, but we don't have as many miners these days. It was easy to build a wall with the bottles, and they didn't cost anything. People gathered them up and plastered them together. It didn't take long to accumulate a few thousand bottles, and they could cement them together as one of the walls in a house. The bottles filter the light making the inside twinkly, which is rather quaint and a little romantic. Structurally, they'll last forever."

Ginger shook her head, "Something new, I guess, and I could say I lived in a glass house. No, we don't have any kids, but we've been wanting to adopt a dog, you know a watchdog, something that will keep me safe while he's at work. We live in an apartment in Reno, and dogs aren't allowed."

"Sure, most people in Barrier have dogs, except us because Joyce, that's my wife, is allergic. By the way, I'm Bob Givens. Do you know anyone here, you know family or friends? What are your names?" He reached over to shake Ace's hand.

"I'm Ace Wray, and..."

Ginger interrupted, "I'm Ginger, Ginger Wray, and we don't know anyone here."

Chapter 22

Brandi and Ginger
One Year Prior—A Few Weeks Later

Two days after Ginger and Ace moved to Barrier, Ginger called the CDR and asked to speak to Brandi. Brandi had not offered her cell phone number, and Ginger was reluctant to go into the brothel. Brothels were a foreign concept to her, and the idea of Brandi being a working girl made her feel awkward and uncomfortable. Ginger was no prude, but she had her standards, and brothels were way down the list. Ace would be shocked at the idea of her even walking into a brothel.

In the four years that Brandi had worked at the CDR, she had never taken a phone call and hesitated to answer when told she had one. All of her regular gentlemen friends made appointments through the receptionist, so she couldn't imagine who would be calling. Not wanting to be discovered, she had let her cell phone contract lapse long ago.

When Brandi finally answered, Ginger said, "We've gotta talk, why don't you come over tonight? We rented a house from the pizza place owner. It's been a long time since we've had a real chat, and I think it's time to get reacquainted. I feel like we don't even know each other any longer. Ace got a job at the B & B and is working late tonight, so we can chat alone. I'll fix dinner for us, baked ham and deviled eggs, your favorite, or at least they used to be. It'll be fun, and Ace can have the leftovers when he comes home from work."

Brandi answered quickly, "Yes, we have a lot to talk about. Sounds like a good idea, but I'm working tonight."

While Ginger was disappointed by the rejection, she jumped in with a new idea. "I can take time tomorrow at lunch if you can manage to pull yourself away from your...clients."

"I can do that. Let's go to the Panorama. Their menu is incredible. It's anybody's guess what they'll have, but I promise it'll be wonderful. They have a couple private rooms, and I'll call the manager to reserve one and remind her of my eating habits. I want to keep my weight down."

"Ace is anxious to talk with you, too, but I don't want him to join us, at least for our first visit since you left Reno. He obsesses when I'm gone, but he is scheduled to work, so I'll come alone. If his work schedule has changed for some reason, I won't come. Do you have a cell phone?"

"No, I don't have a cell phone. I'd rather not have Ace come tomorrow, too, because he might not like what I'm going to say. We have a lot to talk about, so how about noon tomorrow? You can ask me whatever you want. I have an appointment at two, but he won't mind if I'm a few minutes late. When you arrive at the Panorama, give the manager your name, and she'll point you in the right direction."

Chapter 23

Ginger and Brandi
One Year Prior

Ginger changed her clothes four times that morning, trying to look chic and sophisticated. She wanted to look nice for her sister, to give the impression that she and Ace were successful and doing well, even though things were often scant and rocky. They seldom splurged or went out so her wardrobe was dated and tired, having been laundered too many times. Meeting her sister who worked in a brothel presented a dilemma, as she didn't want to look too sisterly and certainly not sexy, or people might get the wrong idea. She finally settled on black slacks with a white turtleneck sweater that she had purchased at a thrift store several years before, but had never worn. It had a nearly invisible spot on the waist, but today she covered it up with a coral scarf that had been in her mother's closet when they emptied her house. She had avoided wearing makeup since the murder but dug out her old cosmetic kit and carefully applied foundation, eye shadow, and lipstick. Her mascara was dry. She stared at herself in the mirror, surprised that she looked younger and relatively put together. And she felt good. Maybe she would apply her makeup more often and added mascara to her grocery list.

The manager of the Panorama opened one of the private rooms for Ginger and Brandi, and the two women sat across the table, gazing at each other but saying nothing for the first couple minutes. It was an awkward silence, neither knowing how to begin. Finally, Ginger broke the silence, "You look good, Brandi, but you are terribly thin."

Brandi laughed, "Do you remember how Mom said that you couldn't be too thin or too rich? I've been working on both."

"And I've been working on neither," Ginger answered, opening her eyes wide and giving out an uncomfortable giggle. "Since Ace doesn't want me to work, I cook and like to eat and have the belly rolls to prove it." She pinched her abdomen and shrugged. "Ace doesn't care, so I don't either."

"I don't care how you look, I am just happy to see you. I hope it's ok that I pre-ordered our lunches. They should be here in a few minutes. Today is French day, and I asked for salads, a cheese plate, and deviled eggs. They will bring baguettes and some spread that the chef creates, which is different every day and always amazingly delicious. I also ordered a bottle of white wine. I hope you like white," Brandi commented, smiling, and continued talking about the Panorama's history. She was as uncomfortable as Ginger and didn't know where the conversation would go, "The Panorama is a strange business in a rural town like Barrier. Most restaurants serve up hamburgers, hot dogs, fries, and slaw, with weekly specials of grilled cheese and a soup-of-the-day, but the Panorama offers an upscale international menu that changes constantly. I'm always surprised by the unique assortment of cuisine. Jay, you've met Jay, owns the restaurant as well as the CDR, and he has insisted on preserving its unique ambiance, which has remained the same since it was built many years ago. It was a part of the railway system carrying weary travelers from St. Louis to San Francisco. The menu might be Russian one day and Swedish the next, followed by French or Polynesian. Except for American hamburgers and hotdogs, anything might be available sometime during the year. The menu is unpredictable, but unforgettable." Brandi was talking non-stop and barely stopped to take a breath.

"No American food?" Ginger interrupted, thinking she'd never convince Ace to eat here, although it wouldn't matter because he didn't like to go out for meals. They couldn't afford to eat out anyway.

"Jay says that if people want run-of-the-mill meals, they can opt for pizza or a hamburger elsewhere. The international flavor here is a selling point, one that he likely won't change," Brandi continued. "The servers come from other countries, so it adds to the international flair. I don't eat here often, but sometimes stop in for breakfast because they brew tea that is to die for, and they have incredible breakfast pastries."

Ginger was half-listening to what Brandi was saying, as she had a lot of questions she wanted to ask. Brandi finally paused when the waitress dropped off their food order, which gave Ginger the opportunity to jump in. "I've been wanting to ask you since I first saw you at the CDR, why do you work in a brothel, Brandi? You have a college degree, enjoyed teaching, and certainly neither Mom nor I could imagine you would end up as a working girl, so why? Doesn't the school have positions?"

Brandi began to nibble on a deviled egg, "I've never looked for a job at the school, and I don't know why I went to work for Jay. I didn't really think about it, and Jay made it easy to stay. I had never been in a brothel before, and it was the farthest thing from my mind when I arrived, but the money is good, I mean really good, and Jay pays for everything—food, clothing, rent, medical—so I've been able to save a lot of money. Not only that, but I earn a lot of tips that nobody knows about, including Jay and the IRS. I have all that cash stashed in a safe place. When I decide to quit, I'll have plenty of money, more than I could ever have made teaching."

"Are you planning to quit, Brandi?" Ginger ventured, "It sounds like the money's good, but you were a good teacher, and you could start again. This job will make you old before your time."

Brandi laughed aloud, "I don't think I could pass the background check, at least not in Nevada. Who's gonna hire a former call girl to teach fifth graders? Besides, as I said, I don't need the money."

"Why did you leave Reno anyway? You didn't say a word to me or your friends. Nobody knew where you were until you sent those postcards a few weeks ago, and even then, I wasn't sure. Since both postcards had pictures of businesses in Barrier, I convinced Ace to come here on a lark, thinking you were a teacher here or something like that," Ginger continued as she poured more dressing on her salad. "We didn't know where to look for you and only stopped at the CDR because of the billboards that advertised cheap chicken dinners. You know how Ace likes to save a buck."

Brandi tipped her head to one side and said, "It was a mistake to send those cards to you, because I didn't really want you to find me. I left Reno because I hated it after Mom was murdered. The police hounded us, day after day, and I felt like I had to quit my job and couldn't even go to the grocery store without someone approaching me. I stopped eating and lost a lot of weight. Mom was dead, which brought our Q2 project to a standstill, and I had put my whole being into that venture. I couldn't manage the jewelry business alone, and you weren't interested. I knew that you wanted to remain in hiding because Ace killed Mom, and you wouldn't want him to go to jail and that you would never turn him in and..."

Ginger looked up and snapped, "What are you talking about, Brandi? Ace didn't kill Mom. We thought you did. Ace disliked her, but he didn't kill her."

A slight flush crept up Brandi's neck, "I know that I didn't kill her, and you didn't kill her, so that leaves Ace. Plus, he hated her. I heard him say that he wished she were dead more than once. I never heard him say anything nice about Mom," Brandi continued. "He had a lot of guns and a motive and opportunity. He could have left work at the casino during a break, popped in, and killed her, and no one would have missed him."

Ginger interrupted, "Dad had a lot of guns, too, so having guns doesn't automatically make you a suspect in a murder. He was the one who taught me how to shoot."

"That's true, but it would have been easy for Ace. He might have told you that he didn't kill her, but he's lying. I'm surprised that the police haven't figured it out."

Ginger was growing angry, and her face reddened. "No, it wasn't him! Quit saying that! The police already looked at him, but it wasn't him. When he said that he wished she were dead, it was Ace being Ace, nothing more," Ginger said. "He would never really hurt anyone."

"Not true, he's hurt you. I've seen the bruises, so don't stick up for him by saying he would never hurt anyone," After a moment, Brandi continued, "So, if you don't think it was him, who do you think it was?"

Chapter 24

Cagey and Ginger
Present Day

"Thanks, Joyce, Bob, you've been helpful," Cagey said as he began to walk down the steps, bouncing on the creaky one a couple times to see how loud it would be. "I don't think this is the creak that Maggie heard. It's not nearly as loud as she said it was."

"Okay, Cagey, keep us in the loop," Bob requested. "If you hear of a prowler, we want to know about it. We'll keep an eye out and let you know if we see anything, too. Joyce specializes in looking out for the neighborhood." He looked down at the creaky steps under Cagey's feet and said, "Maybe I shouldn't replace these steps because they kinda work like a security system and are much cheaper to boot. Plus, I don't have to do the work," he joked as Cagey walked away.

Cagey texted Maggie to let her know his next move and drove his rig closer to the Givens' rental. A light shined inside the house, so he knocked on the door, but no one answered. He heard a series of impressive barks from inside the house and noticed a shadow and motion behind the front window curtains, but no one came. He had forgotten to ask Bob what Ginger and Ace's surname was, and called out "Ginger?" as he tried the door again, pounding harder this time. "Ginger? It's Deputy Garrison from the sheriff's office. Could I talk to you for a minute?" He heard nothing except a few more loud barks, followed by silence.

He banged a third time, and the door cracked open. A woman in shorts and a doesn't-leave-much-to-the-imagination tank-top peeked out, along with the prominent nose of a large brown dog with a white ear, red eyes, and a mouthful of white teeth. The woman's stringy hair hung over her left eye, and her cheek had a red mark on it. "Ma'am, Ginger, I'm Deputy Cagey Garrison with the sheriff's office. I need to ask you a few questions. May I come in for a few minutes?" Cagey's voice was firm, yet kind.

Ginger shook her head and rasped, "What do you want?"

"We've been alerted about noises in your neighborhood last night. The sounds were like screeches and creaks. I'm looking for information about a potential prowler. Did you see or hear anything?" Cagey asked, trying not to look at her bare shoulder, which contained a rather large dark blue and gray-green bruise.

"No, I didn't see nothin'. Nothin' at all. Didn't hear nothin' either," she whispered and began to close the door. The dog yelped when the door caught its nose. She inched the door open again and pulled the dog back, but in doing so, she revealed more bare skin with several bruises from the waist up. She adjusted her shirt and pushed her hair from her eye, disclosing the mark on her cheek and newly blackened eye. She released the dog, and he nosed the door open and joined Cagey on the step, paws on his shoulders, and teeth bared. She grabbed the dog again, but she couldn't budge him from Cagey's shoulders.

Cagey pushed the dog off him, stepped back, and said, "Whoa, puppy, take it easy. I'm not going to hurt you," but the dog snarled and stepped toward Cagey again.

Ginger came forward and grabbed the dog's collar, "Come on, Peaches, come back in the house," she ordered, as she yanked him through the door. Cagey thought the dog was probably stronger than she and eyed the two retreating into the house.

"Ma'am, Ginger, where did all of your bruises come from? You're covered in them," Cagey inquired as she began to close the door.

"I fell in the shower last week. They're nothing," Ginger said, "I'm clumsy, that's all. Ace didn't hurt me if that's what you're wanting to know. He would never hurt me."

"Ace? That's your husband? I didn't say he hurt you, but now that you mention it, did he? How did you get those bruises?" Cagey asked again, clearly not buying that she fell in the shower.

A large white pickup interrupted him as it thundered up the hill and screeched to a halt in front of the house. Dust and debris flew into the air as a beefy man jumped out. Peaches escaped Ginger's grasp, bounded toward the man, and jumped on him, front paws landing on his shoulders. "Settle down, Peaches, be a good boy," the man said before aiming his remarks at Cagey. "Who are you, and what do you want? Ginger, for hell's sake, go back inside the house and put more clothes on. Take Peaches with you. And fix me some lunch, I'm hungry." Ginger vanished behind the door without a word.

Cagey reintroduced himself and started to explain why he had come, but Ace would have none of it. "You're standing here, talking to my damn wife. We don't know nothin' about no prowler, and we didn't hear any noises last night, so you can get the hell off my property. Now would not be too soon."

Cagey raised both hands in concession and began backing away. He remembered Joyce Givens' comment about them being a strange pair. The word strange was too mild, they were downright bizarre and rude. He and Maggie would need to take another look at Maggie's next-door neighbors though. And soon, before Ginger was hurt again.

Chapter 25

Maggie and Brick
Present Day

Maggie unfolded two chairs and placed them by the stash they had found. "Holy cow," she exclaimed as she looked at the contents of the first box. "How much do you think this is?" It was filled half-way with stacked paper money, and the top layer, at least, was all ten-dollar bills, nothing else. More money lay loose in the box, not banded. Brick fingered down a couple inches and found a variety of other denominations, ones, fives, and twenties, and a few fifties, also loose in the box.

"Is this a finders-keepers situation?" Brick asked. "The money is in our bomb shelter, after all. Maybe it's ours." He simultaneously twisted toward Maggie, giving her a big grin. "Wouldn't that be something?"

"It might be, but don't get your hopes up. Not that I wouldn't like to have it. It would sure help out with college for three kids." Maggie was realistic enough to know that finders-keepers might not be the answer, but she didn't rule it out either.

"I have no idea how much is in this box, but it's a lot of money," Brick replied.

"Do you think these hold money, too?" Maggie asked as she cocked her head toward the other box and the olive-green banker's bag.

"I don't know, but let's check. Let's open the bag first." It wasn't large, the size of a lunch bag, but it was heavy. It appeared to be half filled and was tightly bound. The opening was knotted with string.

Maggie slid it toward Brick. "I don't think this is money unless it's coins, but I can't be sure. It's heavy," she said, as she pulled out her multi-bladed knife, sliced off the string, and pulled it open. "Well, well, well, a pirate's booty." The bag was nearly filled with small plastic bags of gemstones, some stones were loose, others were a part of a piece of jewelry, rings, necklaces, bracelets, earrings, cufflinks. It did look like a pirate's treasure trove. "Holy cow, this could be fun," she said, picking up a necklace of red stones with two stones missing. She dove her fingers into another bag and pulled out a broken string of pearls. "Aye, aye, Matey."

"Whoa, where did this come from? I can't wait to see what the third one contains," Brick said as he seated himself and pulled the third box toward him. It was small and heavy considering its size. The box was a wooden cigar box that was labeled Cigars. At some point it had been screwed shut, but the screws had been broken off. It was heavier than it looked. "I don't know if our knives will work to pry this open," he said aloud to himself as much as to Maggie.

"Use my knife. It's bigger than yours, cuz I'm the sheriff," Maggie said as she handed him her multiblade knife, which had all the usual tools, including a prying device. He grasped it tightly and pried the nails from the box. After a few minutes, he lifted the lid. "You gave that knife to me for our first anniversary, mister romantic devil," she said, laughing. "I never thought I'd use it, but what do you know, it did come in handy."

At the sight of the wooden box's contents, Brick jumped up, "Oh, my God! Gold! Gold nuggets, at least I think it's gold. Holy cow, we've struck gold. Maggie, if this is finders-keepers, we can retire forever." The box held a dozen or more pebbles, smaller than marbles but larger than peas and two plastic bags that were filled with something granular. "This is gold dust,"

Brick said with awe. Maggie and Brick were not experts on minerals but had no doubt that they had discovered a lucrative jackpot.

"This morning, we didn't know this bomb shelter existed," Maggie noted, "and now, we have boxes of treasures, but we don't know who they belong to. They might be ours, but they might also be a whole lot of trouble."

Chapter 26

Maggie and Brick
Present Day

Before the onset of Nevada's casino industry in the middle part of the twentieth century, mining, mainly gold and silver, was the king of rural prosperity. People made and lost fortunes as they searched for the elusive minerals, similar to seeking fortunes in the casinos, taking chances, sometimes going from poverty to wealth on the same day. The other side of get-rich-quick schemes was get-poor-even-quicker, and many passed through that maze without knowing what they were doing. People pursued gold and silver fortunes believing that the nuggets lay on the ground waiting to be found, but in truth, gold mining proved to be hard work, with the minerals coming in the form of small stones, grain-like sand, or even dust, which had to be extracted from the soil and processed with no guarantee that it was even gold or silver. The minerals were present, available for the taking, but gold and silver mining was not an easy life.

Maggie and Brick were both stunned by their find, and they sat in silence for a long time, mulling, wondering, thinking, and dreaming, in no special order. The air reeked, and it was cold, but neither seemed to notice. They were wordless, totally perplexed, lost in their own thoughts about what the treasure could mean. Brick centered on finders-keepers, while Maggie focused on her legal responsibilities, when a voice called down the steps,

"Hey, Brick, it's Terry. Are you guys down there? If so, I'm coming down. I wanna talk about the pool. I have an idea."

Brick and Maggie raised their eyes to look at each other, and both shook their heads. Brick called out, "No, Terry, I'm coming up and Maggie, too. It reeks, and we aren't sure this smell is good for Maggie. She needs to get into the fresh air asap. Hold tight, we'll be right up."

Maggie quickly folded the table back in place, and they shoved the treasures under the table where they had been discovered. She pulled down the table, tossing the red-checked plastic tablecloth over it, yanked it down, and started toward the staircase. Maggie tugged on Brick's sleeve and whispered, "Nobody has access, so these treasures will be safe right here, but can you put a new padlock on the metal hatch again? Buy a good one. We don't want anyone finding this trove. I'll bring the handcart to carry them up the stairs when I come home from work tonight, and we can sneak them into the house until we figure out what to do. Neither of us should be breathing this foul-smelling air. Especially Sarah."

Brick nodded, "Good idea."

Terry was halfway down the stairs, but they turned him around, and the three of them headed back into the brightness of the afternoon sun. "I wish we had the pool today, it would be a lot of fun, even though it is a little cool. What's your idea, Terry?" Brick was usually upbeat, but now he sounded exceptionally chipper. He had prioritized the pool building into a much lower position since they had found the treasures, but he couldn't let Terry know that.

Terry shared his thoughts about a new site and suggested digging the pool on the opposite side of the house from the prior selected site. It would overlap where the garage had been, but they would have to remove a couple of mesquite trees, so leaves wouldn't blow into the water. They could add a doorway to the outside through their bedroom, which would be a convenient route to pass from the house to the pool with an added feature of a nearby bathroom. "Little boys love to pee in the pool," he laughed. The only negative Terry could see was that the new site offered less privacy than the previous site because it backed up toward the neighbor's house. In the year since their neighbors had moved in, Brick and Maggie had not seen them outside except when they retrieved Peaches, their vicious-looking dog. They had no idea of the neighbors' names.

Maggie was not thinking about either the swimming pool, their nearly invisible neighbors, the screeches, or Brandi, the missing woman. Her brain instead was wrapped around the findings that sat on the floor of the bomb shelter. She was clueless about what to do. In the past, she had asked for help from other law enforcement agencies when she ran into a snag, but this time she didn't want to seek help. She couldn't call the police chief or sheriff from Reno or any other nearby city. The county attorney wouldn't be any help either, because under the finders-keepers law, the boxes and bag belonged to Brick and her, yet she couldn't help thinking that some crazy crime had been committed. Why else would they be stored in the bottom of a bomb shelter?

"Maggie, what do you think?" Brick asked, nudging her. He was having an equally difficult time concentrating but wanted to lose Terry and buy a padlock to lock the bomb shelter down.

Maggie looked at him and smiled, "You decide. I've got other things on my mind right now. We'll make it work, whatever you come up with. I'm going back to my office." She winked at Brick, kissed him good-bye, and headed toward her rig.

Chapter 27

Cagey
Present Day

Cagey met Maggie at the sheriff's office and together made a dent in a pot of coffee while swapping information. Cagey apprised her of his visit to the Givens' house, and his distressing conversation and encounter with Ace and Ginger. Maggie reported what she knew about Brandi, but since her trip had been cut short by the discovery of gems, money, and gold, her information had a lot of holes. She didn't mention the bomb shelter because she was sure Cagey would want to see it, and she opposed revealing anything about the treasure trove until she and Brick knew what direction they would go. She and Brick had a lot of thinking to do, but that would need to come later.

Maggie said, "I know Jay will call us if Brandi contacts him or returns, but it never hurts to ask. I haven't talked to the rest of the staff yet, because it was too early in the morning. The bar, restaurant, and access to female companionship don't open until nearly noon, so nobody was available, but we need to ask. Someone there knows something."

"I'll head over to the CDR to see what I can find out. Do you want to speak with Ginger yourself? It might be a good idea for you to approach her, you know, the woman-to-woman thing. Ace has probably already returned to the B & B for work, but watch out for that dog, he's aggressive. His name is Peaches, which must be some sort of joke. He's big and a brute," Cagey warned.

"Yes, I've met Peaches," Maggie answered. "He barks a lot and isn't someone I want to tangle with. What is their last name? We can send out a request to the NCIC to see if either of them has done anything criminal. They've lived here for a while, and we haven't had any run-ins with them, in fact, neither Brick nor I have even met them. We've met their dog, Peaches, but not them. They apparently moved here for no reason. I've always thought that Barrier would be a good place to disappear if you needed to hide from somebody."

Cagey filled her in with what he knew, "They rent from Bob and Joyce Givens, so they'll know their last names. I forgot to ask when Ace showed up and rudely invited me to leave, but I'll give Bob a call. I don't know if he does a background check on his tenants, I doubt it, but Ace seems like a bully, and with Ginger's bruises, I suspect he's a wife beater. She said she fell in the shower, but the bruises look like handprints to me. He might have a criminal record, but Ginger is timid as a mouse. I'm willing to bet she's never even had a parking ticket."

Cagey dialed the phone and two minutes later, he hung up with Bob Givens, "Wray. His last name is Wray. Ace and Ginger Wray. W-R-A-Y." He spelled it out.

Maggie wrote it down, "Thanks, Ace isn't a common name, most likely a nickname, so there can't be too many of them. Will you please take care of the NCIC request? I'll be interested to see what pops up. I'm curious if they heard anything last night, and I'll ask about her bruises when I pay her a visit. I've never seen visitors at their house so she should be alone, except for Peaches, if Ace is working. I'll see what she has to say, and then we can meet back up and go to the B & B together and ask him a few questions. He'll be less objectionable if he's at work, unless he's involved in a crime. If he has been, who knows what can happen?"

"You're not going to want to meet Peaches without pepper spray," Cagey reminded her.

"Got it," Maggie said, patting one of her pockets.

Cagey systematically visited with every CDR employee, hoping to gain information about Brandi and where she might have gone, but he gained little information. Every employee liked her, thought she was a straight-up person, but offered him nothing about her past, except that she had a sister. No one knew where she came from, California being the standard answer, but he couldn't even narrow it down to northern or southern California, so it didn't help much.

Cagey asked Jay's permission to view her room to see if it divulged any kind of clue but found the room tidy and sparsely furnished with two small white dressers, a bed with a pink coverlet, a white chaise longue, and matching armchair. The pastel wallpaper created a bright and cheerful atmosphere. The closet held a few clothes on hangers, and a footlocker sat in the bottom of the closet. The lock on the box dangled loose from its hinge. A half dozen books rested on a shelf, along with her teaching certificate and pictures of her mother and father, but there were no pictures, no letters, no mementos about her previous life. Cagey opened the lid and looked in but didn't see anything unusual. He unzipped her purse and located a single credit card and a small notebook with a few notes, but mostly it was blank. He had hoped for addresses or phone numbers but found none. Next, he discovered a cell phone in a drawer, but it was turned off and drained of energy. He placed the phone in his pocket and kept the purse with him for safekeeping, intending to lock them up in the sheriff's vault until she was found.

"I don't see a bank card or checkbook or anything else. How is she paid?" Cagey asked Jay before he left. "You do pay her, don't you?" Cagey had never asked Jay about how his brothel employees were paid. Cash or check? Brothels were legal in Nevada, so Cagey assumed that social security was taken out of their pay and he paid his employees by check, but he wasn't sure.

"Of course, I pay her. I pay most of the female workers in cash because they like the fluidity of cash. Some of them have sketchy pasts and don't want a paper trail. They often owe a lot of money or have kids someplace and must pay child support. Some have legal histories with lawyer bills or fines to pay. She's the only one here without a car. She rode in a semi with some guy when she came and hasn't left Barrier since. I've never figured her out, she's been here a long time and doesn't spend much money. I suspect she has a tidy sum sitting somewhere because she's a popular woman. She never buys anything new for herself, except for an occasional meal and new lingerie, which is a tool of the trade," Jay said defensively. "And she doesn't drink or smoke, either. She's not a spender."

Chapter 28

Maggie and Ginger
Present Day

While Cagey visited the Chicken Dinner Ranch to learn more about Brandi, Maggie looked in on Ginger. The original purpose of Cagey's visit to Ginger was to learn if they had heard the middle-of-the-night noises, whatever they might have been, but he had refocused his concerns to the bruises on Ginger's face and torso and learned nothing about the nightly sounds. Maybe Ginger had screamed while being beaten by Ace. Was it a recent one-time event or a night-after-night happening? The sounds had occurred for about a month, and now Maggie feared that they had not searched deeply enough. Maggie, who was not shy about knocking on doors, rapped loudly on Ginger's door and called out, "Ginger Wray? It's Sheriff Monroe, the Barrier sheriff. I need to talk to you for a minute." She waited for a few seconds and re-knocked on her door, louder this time, and restated her message. She saw the front window curtain move and heard a menacing growl. Peaches, she thought as she dug in her pocket for her pepper spray.

"Mrs. Wray, could you open the door so we can talk?" Maggie called out. "It won't take long."

"No, I can't," came a call through the door. "Ace told me not to open the door for anyone, especially the police," her frail and rickety voice answered through the door. "You have to go away."

"Is Ace here?" Maggie shouted back, although more gently. "He doesn't have to know we talked. Please open the door. It will only take a couple minutes, and then I'll be gone."

"What's it about?" the skimpy voice asked. "The deputy was already here, and I told him I didn't know anything."

Maggie sighed, *This is the worst kind—battered woman afraid of her battering husband. Time to change my approach.*

"I live next door, and I'm nervous about an intruder that might be lurking around," Maggie said. *Appeal to the woman's own fears*, she thought, adding aloud, "I've got little children and am afraid for them."

The door inched open, and an eye and an ear appeared, along with facial bruises and straggly hair, maybe blonde, maybe blondish gray. She wore a long-sleeved shirt and jeans that covered her body from head to toe. She was thin, emaciated or anorexic perhaps. The skin on her face was sunken, as if she had lost a lot of weight, and her raspy voice squeaked when she spoke, "I didn't hear anything, like I told the deputy."

"Are you Mrs. Wray? I'm Maggie, your neighbor."

"Yes, I'm Ginger Wray. I've seen those cute little boys playing in the yard. Are they twins? We don't have any children. Ace didn't want any," Ginger answered.

"When did you move to Barrier?" Maggie asked. "I live next door, right over there, but I've never seen you." She pointed to her house where the workmen were busy. *Maybe if she kept talking, Ginger would venture outside or admit her to the house, and she could take a better look at the bruises.*

"My sissy lives here, and I wanted to be closer to family. Ace got a good job here, and we have this nice house, and I see my sissy nearly every day," Ginger added. "She comes most days, but I haven't seen her much this week."

"May I come in?" Maggie asked. "I'd like to meet your dog. Since we live next door, I don't want him to be afraid of me." *Okay, Maggie, you're putting yourself out on a limb. You'd rather stick your hand in a hornet's nest than* meet Peaches. All in the line of duty. She kept one hand on the pepper spray and the other near her Glock.

Ginger cracked the door a little more and scanned the cul-de-sac, perhaps on the lookout for Ace, and said, "Yes, I'll put Peaches on the back porch, and you can come in. He can be a scary dog. I'm not that crazy about him myself." Maggie waited while Peaches retreated, unwillingly, but Ginger held him by his collar, and he complied. Drool ran down the side of his head, and he licked at it. He moved his head to peer at Maggie, but Ginger finally moved him to the porch.

Ginger returned quickly, and widened the crack to allow Maggie entrance, "What did you say your name is?"

"Maggie. Maggie Monroe. I think neighbors should meet each other, don't you?"

Ginger nodded, "Well, yes, that's good. I don't know anyone in Barrier except my sissy. People probably think I'm a recluse. I'm not really, but, well, Ace thinks it's best if I stay home."

"Oh, my, you have bruises on your face and neck?" Maggie asked, as if she just noticed them. "How did you get them?"

"Silly me, they are nothing. I stood on a ladder and mis-stepped and fell. They're almost healed. I'll be fine. I'm clumsy and fall a lot," Ginger told her. Maggie squinted, recalling that Cagey's version was that Ginger had fallen in the shower.

"I can take you to the clinic if you want. The bruise on your eye is badly discolored. Maybe the doctor should have a look just to be sure. You don't want to lose your sight," Maggie advised her.

"No, Ace wouldn't like that. It'll heal, it always has before." Ginger touched her eye and grimaced but didn't say any more.

"Why doesn't Ace like you going to the doctor? I'd go in a heartbeat for that bruise, regardless of what my husband said," Maggie encouraged. "Especially for my eye. It looks serious, Ginger. Let me drive you. I'll stay with you and bring you home after you see the doctor. The clinic is seldom busy, so we can be back before Ace comes home. He wouldn't need to know."

"You ask a lot of questions. My husband doesn't like me going out," Ginger protested, "and I don't want to go to the doctor anyway."

"Why is that?" Maggie asked. "The people at the clinic will treat you right and won't tell anyone about your visit."

"No, somebody might...," she paused before continuing, "well, circumstances, you know, people might talk." She gazed at Maggie as if noticing the sheriff's uniform for the first time and said, "You should go now. I don't want to get in trouble."

Chapter 29

Maggie and Brick
Present Day

"Let's revisit the bomb shelter," Maggie suggested after they had put the twins to bed. "I've been thinking about it all day. Do you think it's connected to something criminal?"

Brick answered, "The cash could be stolen or saved, but the gems and jewelry and gold might be a whole different matter. We could claim the money, through the finders-keepers' laws, but it might create a stir, more than we want to deal with. But it's a lot of money, and it might be worth the bother. I can already read the Vegas headlines, Barrier Sheriff Absconds with Loot. We could try to keep it a secret, but if it got out, it would be hell to pay. If we leave it in the house, it could be stolen. Depositing it in a safe deposit box might also cause a stir, and we can't leave it in the sheriff's office vault. We need to be straightforward and try to figure it out."

"With the possibility of a prowler, we shouldn't leave the boys in the house alone, so I'll stay with them while you take the handcart and bring everything up, hopefully in one trip." Maggie smacked her head with her hand and moaned, "Duh, I forgot the handcart. I left it at the office. I don't know how I forgot it because I've been thinking about it all day. Another headline: Prego-girl Loses Memory. I'll go back and bring it home."

"That's okay, we can do it tomorrow. I padlocked the hatch tight, and I'm tired, so we can deal with it all tomorrow. It's been a heck of a day, and I'm ready for a glass of something amber, and I don't mean iced tea," Brick said.

"Go for it. Have a second glass for me, if you would," Maggie said laughing. "By the way, I met Ginger, our neighbor, today. I stopped to see if they had heard the screeching and scratching last night. Cagey had already talked to her, but Ace blackballed him from their property. I went back and met Ginger, battered wife of Ace Wray."

"She's battered? That's horrible. No wonder we haven't seen her out. Had they heard anything?" Brick asked.

"No, and Bob Givens hadn't either, although Joyce might have heard something, but she wasn't sure about it. When Cagey talked to him, Bob said it might have been his creaky steps."

"What's the story on the Wrays?" Brick asked. "They've lived in that house about a year, give or take, and this is the first time either of us has met them. Where did they come from? Do they have kids? I've seen their dog, and he's definitely not a friendly critter. I hope they secure their yard and fence because the pool will be close to their fence, and I'm sure that dog will be curious. For our peace of mind, I better double check that fence for gaps or loose posts."

"I talked to Ginger for a few minutes. She's mousy and acts like she's afraid of her own shadow. She seems terrified of Ace. She has some nasty bruises on her face, but when I tried to convince her to go to the clinic, she said that Ace didn't like her to leave the house, not even to go to the doctor. Cagey also noticed some bruising on her shoulder and midriff when he was talking to her. She's abused for sure, but she didn't want any help. We'll keep an eye on her," Maggie commented.

"How about that other girl from the CDR? Brandi? Any word on her?"

Maggie shook her head, "Nope, it was a strike-out day. Except for finding a bunch of cash, jewels, and a pound or two of gold. I guess that's something."

Brick laughed aloud, "Yeah, I guess that's something."

Chapter 30

Maggie and Cagey
Present Day

The night passed uneventfully, no noises or creaks, and the sun promised a bright day. No wind or clouds yet, and with luck, it would stay that way. Brick and Maggie arose at dawn, and Brick went for his morning run. Maggie had dispensed with jogging until the new baby came, but she went outside to drink a cup of coffee and do some yoga stretches. She did a few sun salutations as she awaited Brick's return and breakfast. She and Sarah were starving, as usual. The boys were asleep, and she appreciated the peacefulness of the cool, calm morning.

On the final stretch of her yoga routine, she heard a bark, followed by several more, and walked to the fence to see what was irritating so many dogs. Citizens of Barrier could own several dogs, but all had to be licensed and fenced or leashed. No free-running dogs allowed. The dog ordinance was one of the most violated laws in Barrier, and she dreaded the confrontations with pet owners who believed that all dog laws were for others and never their own pet.

She looked to her left and saw Peaches staring at her through the chain-link fence. His eyes were burned red, and he curled his lip in anticipation of introducing himself to her.

"Not today, Peaches," she said aloud. "I'm not interested in being your friend, and remember, you homely critter, I have a bullet with your name stenciled on it, if you ever go after my babies."

"I noticed you were talking to someone, are you and Peaches becoming best friends this morning?" Brick asked as he came up behind her.

"Oh, sure, I was explaining to him how my Glock works, especially if he messes with my babies, including you, but I doubt he listened," Maggie responded. "Let's eat breakfast before the twins wake up. Terry and his crew should be here shortly."

Their pancakes weren't on the griddle before Cagey phoned, "Good morning, Sheriff, we have a lead on Brandi Dumont."

"Really, how'd you do that?" Maggie was constantly amazed at Cagey and thankful for his initiative in working on their cases. His work was his life.

Cagey filled her in, "When I submitted the inquiry to NCIC about Ace Wray, I also submitted one about Brandi. I just had a hunch. Most of the working girls have histories, and I thought she probably did, too, and hoped something would pop up. Sure enough, we got info on two Brandi Dumonts. One is from Tulsa, and she's safely in prison on drug trafficking charges, but the other is from Reno. Her mother was murdered about five years ago, and she became a person of interest when she vanished shortly afterward. The case remains open. Mom had two daughters, and both have now disappeared from the Reno area and guess what. The sister's name was Ginger. I called the Reno police department wondering if they had information, but they said their investigation had stopped cold."

Maggie thought for a second, "Somebody at the CDR told me that she had a sister living here. Do we know of a Ginger Dumont who lives here?"

"Not Ginger Dumont, Ginger Wray. Brandi's sister's name is Ginger Wray," Cagey said.

Chapter 31

Maggie and Brick
Present Day

Maggie deposited the handcart on the patio as she trekked out to join Brick who was viewing the swimming pool progress. Terry and his staff had already left for the day, but they had taped off the dig area and positioned the backhoe, ready to start digging early the next morning. "This is a good place," she approved, "I like it. We'll definitely have to add an outside door by our bedroom, but that'll be an easy fix. I'd rather add a door than swim in a toilet, which will happen if we don't have easy access to a bathroom. It is less private than the other site, but we'll make it work." She looked over at the Ginger and Ace's house, "And, we'll have to deal with the dog."

Brick agreed, "Yeah, the dog." After a moment, he turned back to the pool area and said, "Terry said they'd start the dig tomorrow morning, early, they said, which probably is later than my idea of early. I like the other site better, but I guess we are beyond that now. I'll bribe my basketball team to pull out a couple mesquite trees, but we can do that after the pool is in. They can pull out those puny scrubs and will be happy if I buy them a pizza, so we won't have to hire anyone to do it."

"Even better. I left the handcart on the patio so after dark, you can bring everything to the house, and we can have a better look at them. We could leave them in the bomb shelter, and they'd be safe enough, except for the smell. I don't want to leave the boys alone while we document the contents, and I don't want to tell my mom too much about what's going on. I'm ok if she knows about the shelter, but not the money and gems."

After dark when the boys were asleep, Brick unlocked the hatch to the bomb shelter and bumped the handcart down the stairs. His phone gave enough light, but he carried Maggie's heavy grade flashlight as well. Maggie shifted the contents of their new walk-in closet to make room for the treasure trove. Thank heavens they had added it in the remodel. The treasure would remain hidden until they decided what to do, which would be soon.

Brick entered the kitchen area and trailed his light across the walls and floor, reviewing what they had seen during their previous visit. He stepped to the table and tossed the tablecloth on the floor and relatched the table to the wall. He gasped, "What the?" The floor was empty, no boxes, no bag. Everything was gone. He hit Maggie's number on speed dial, panicked, "They are gone. Everything is gone."

"What's gone?"

"The boxes, they disappeared, nothing is here."

"No, that can't be. Look around," she insisted. "Are you sure you locked the hatch?"

He flashed the big light around the room, and repeated, "Of course, I locked it. I even double checked it this morning. Nothing, no boxes, no bag of gems." He snapped a photo of the empty space and texted it to her.

"That's impossible. The bomb shelter only has one door," Maggie said when she looked at the photo he had sent. "Did you see any marks on the floor, you know like they had been dragged out or used a handcart or wagon? The containers would have been awkward to carry, and toting all three at once would be close to impossible. They didn't evaporate. Look under the cots and in the bathroom and in that tiny shower."

Brick had grown a little irritated with her questions. The bomb shelter was empty, "I'm telling you, Maggie. Nothing is here. Everything is gone."

They had not photographed the bomb shelter previously but now Brick began snapping shots of everything, the cots, the shelf, the bathroom. Even with the flashlight, the quality of the photos was poor, but they would have to do for now. Who knew about the bomb shelter? Terry and the crew, but no one else, except for Maggie's mother, but she didn't know what they had found. Had Maggie told anyone else? As far as he knew, she hadn't even told Cagey. And he knew that she wouldn't have mentioned them to Ginger. Or Bob or Joyce? No, that would be unlike Maggie.

Chapter 32

Maggie and Brick
Present Day

A town like Barrier, barren and bleak, lying miles from other communities that might offer a livelier existence is bound to attract diverse people, lifestyles, and events. Barrier fit that standard because it was a small town with a few thousand residents. Its population varied from year to year, sometimes month to month as people arrived and departed, with one thing on their mind, finding a better place, somewhere to dump their problems and allow them a more prosperous existence. The successful ones stayed, the unsuccessful ones moved on to another town, once again taking their problems with them.

Housing had been an issue from the time the area became populated, and residents grappled with the realities of finding shelter. Building materials in the desert had been at a premium, forcing residents to be innovative, hence the whiskey bottle construction, usually with one wall assembled from the bottles. Small houses needed twenty-five thousand bottles and the larger ones, many more. The miners laughed about contributing to the housing construction market as they finished one bottle and opened another.

Maggie had lived most of her life in Barrier and knew most of the residents, especially now that she wore the badge of sheriff. Two types of people were attracted to Barrier: law-abiding citizens who wanted nothing more than to live their lives out in a quiet town with outdoor activities to keep them busy, like hunting, fishing, and camping. They worked hard and played hard and enjoyed the lives they led. Maggie knew that finding work there was difficult, so she always felt pride when she saw the townspeople find creative ways to make enough money to be content. Sometimes they lived off the land, hunting and fishing and farming for food. They weren't rich in dollars but had the joy of living with nature. They watched the stars in the sky and looked for wild animals. They voted, went to church, and were good neighbors. They wanted little else and were happy to have Maggie as their sheriff, a local girl whom they knew and liked. She was solid and honest, and they knew they could go to her for help if they needed it. When she married Brick, their admiration for her increased.

The second type of resident was nearly the opposite because Barrier was an ideal place to lose yourself, to hide where no one would find you. These residents didn't want to be bothered with anything in Barrier. They often had no jobs and counted on others to provide for them, whether government or charity. They resented the laws, and if they never saw a policeman or other public official, they were happy as they could be. They didn't vote but complained about what others voted for, like the dog ordinances and curfews. Maggie viewed this group as transient, coming and going, often returning after long periods of absence. Were they looking for or running from something? When one of these people left, another would arrive to take his place, a constant circle. Everybody had a different story, and she wondered what made these folks tick. Did they have something to hide? She was sure that most of the women at the Chicken Dinner Ranch did, thus Brandi was probably hiding something, too, and now, Brick and Maggie's neighbors, Ace and Ginger, tumbled into this group as well.

Chapter 33

Maggie
Present Day

Brick scrutinized the interior of the bomb shelter once more by washing his flashlight over the entire walls, floor, and even the ceiling. He checked the steps for signs that anyone else had passed down them and inspected the clasp on the rusted latch. He exited the bomb shelter and relocked the door, shaking the padlock to verify that it was tight. Terry and crew had not replaced the dirt they had removed, and Brick tramped around in the dark, searching for signs of a second entrance or exit, but found none. He was sure at least one other access had been constructed, but where was it? It wasn't obvious. The exterior lights to the Givens house flipped on, and Brick doused his flashlight. Joyce Givens, he knew, might ask a lot of questions, and he wasn't ready to answer them.

Maggie and Brick talked well into night about the bomb shelter and the boxes and bag, making wild guesses as to how they disappeared. They talked about the other rather disturbing things that seemed to be attached to their house, and how its creepy persona had increased. They had spent all five years of their marriage in the whiskey bottle house and largely ignored its saggy atmosphere and sometimes bizarre aura. Even with newly painted walls, the fatigue hung over the cottage like a thick, faded drapery. The recent remodeling had brightened it up, but the creepy, gloomy aura never left.

Five years earlier, the house had witnessed the murder of a priest who had been watching a Saturday afternoon movie on television before reciting mass. The beloved, yet devious, possibly sociopathic priest had been murdered in this house. Since then, the house had seemed restless. Brick and Maggie both felt the unquiet but tried to ignore the vibes that emanated between those walls.

Brick, newly arrived in Barrier at the time of the priest's murder, needed a place to live and had searched the town for something livable for days, but with Barrier's housing shortage, he had been forced to choose between a container house with no windows and this murder house. He decided the murder house was the lesser of two evils. Now, though, he wasn't so sure. He purchased it, and when he and Maggie married, it became theirs.

The house creaked and groaned, and the newly married couple first attributed the noises to their south-facing whiskey bottle wall, which felt especially loud when the wind picked up. The erratic sounds were sometimes soft, sometimes shrill, sometimes loud. Long or short, occasional whistling noises. While ninety percent of the wall's bottles faced inward, meaning the business end of the bottle toward the inside of the house, the rest faced outside, and the wind whistled through them, singing eerie songs with no tunes. Although most of the whiskey bottle houses had been destroyed by the mining companies, several houses remained intact, but other homeowners reported no noises other than wind singing the blues. Brick and Maggie wondered if they could be sitting on a fault with minor earthquakes causing the house to belch and sigh, but they found no evidence of Barrier sitting on a fault. After their first year in the house, which had been filled with mysterious noises, they decided to pay no heed to the sounds and blamed them on the age of the house. Maggie reasoned that old people had aches and pains, so possibly their house did, too. They ignored the sounds and lived as they wanted, but the erratic noises didn't stop. Maggie and Brick convinced each other that they didn't believe in ghosts, rather the house had lived a grueling life and had tales to tell. Maybe they needed to rethink that.

Remodeling the house surely would scare away the house goblins, they reasoned, but the opposite had proven true. The goblins worked overtime. Maggie was the first to hear the unidentifiable sounds, screeching and scraping that no one else heard, but as summer approached, Brick started hearing them, too. Sounds were everywhere, except, of course, for the hidden bomb shelter, which one moment held an immense treasure and the next moment did not. Why didn't Maggie and Brick hear someone removing it?

Maggie and Sarah had slept fitfully, but Brick was once again out like a snuffed candle. She heard no screeches, but the creaks and groans started at midnight and continued for an hour or more, much longer than usual. They weren't coming from the house, yet they were.

It was nearly five when she swapped her bed clothes for a pair of sweats. Brick's jeans lay across the end of the bed, and she rifled through them for the padlock key. She grabbed her phone, the oversized flashlight, and her pistol, and murmured to herself, "Come on, Sarah, let's go to the bomb shelter and see what else is happening. Don't be scared, little one, I have my pistol."

The stench was overpowering, but she descended the stairs and swiped the flashlight beams across the walls searching for hidden doors or windows. Inch by inch. She pulled out the shelves and the ancient microwave to see if they hid an egress. She looked below the cots and double checked under the table. Nothing. She was getting nowhere. She surveyed the room, looking for something, anything, even eyeing the floor to see if the bomb shelter had a basement.

She was frustrated, and they both were hungry. She placed her hand on her abdomen, "A few more minutes, Sweetie, and we'll leave this yucky room and find something to eat. I know a door is here someplace. These items did not magically vanish into this stinky air." She plopped down on the cot and splayed the light across the walls when the beam homed in on a light switch hidden behind the water tank. She had not seen it before and doubted Brick had either. She would have missed it if she were standing.

"This is progress, Sarah, I see a light switch," she said aloud, "I wonder if it's connected. I doubt it, but I'll give it a go." She leaned over and flipped it on and nothing happened for a second, but she heard another creak, this one longer than the various creaks she had heard before. She aimed both the flashlight and pistol at the noise and backed up on the cot. After a few seconds, a dim ceiling light pulled her out of total darkness, and the wall next to the curtained bathroom began to move and slowly scraped open, followed by a groan. Sarah jumped in her womb, and Maggie gave out a little yelp, "Come on, Sarah, this is no place for us to be alone, let's boogie out of here."

Chapter 34

Maggie and Brick
Present Day

Maggie left the light on and the wall open and fled up the stairs and into the house. Her hands were shaking, but she managed to lock the padlock and ran toward the safety of their home. She shook Brick, "Brick, wake up, I found it. I found the door. Sarah and I visited the bomb shelter, and we found it."

Brick, half asleep, blinked his eyes open and twisted his face. He stretched and yawned and squeaked out some groans, "Wait, you found another door to the bomb shelter? Why are you up so early? You should have waited for me," he growled.

"I'm not sure it's an actual egress. It could be another room, but it's something, and I didn't want to check it out alone," Maggie told him. She spewed out her words, a little breathless. If she hadn't been pregnant, she would have pursued the finding without Brick, but with Sarah tagging along, she wanted support.

"We were both awake and curious, so we decided to visit the shelter and look again. I didn't really expect to see anything. I figured it would be a wasted trip, and we would find nothing, like you did. It was Sarah's fault," she told him, "you know what a rascal she's going to be." Maggie was giddy with pleasure, and her eyes sparkled. "I found a light switch and flipped it on. First, an overhead light flickered, and then a few seconds later, the wall opened up with this weird sound, a combination of scraping and groaning and screeching. It wasn't loud, but it was long. The light bulb is dim, barely giving out any light, but better than nothing. Come on, Deputy Brick, let's look at what's on the other side of the wall. Or would you prefer that I call Cagey?"

Brick swung his feet out of the bed and pulled on his pants, "Light switch? What light switch? I didn't see anything. I noticed the lightbulb in the ceiling but assumed the bulb was burnt out, but nothing more. I should have assumed differently. I have lost my sharp-as-a-tack detective skills."

"Silly boy, that's why you serve as the deputy, and I'm the elected sharp-as-a-tack sheriff," she chided. "Come on, hurry up."

"Can't it wait until I'm awake," he complained, "or at least have some coffee?"

"You're a whiner this morning, but okay. We'll fix coffee and some toast, but that's all I'm fixing you until after we return to the bomb shelter. Get going!" She turned toward the kitchen to plug in the coffee pot and make a couple slices of toast.

He called after her, "What about the boys? We can't leave them alone. Especially if the prowler is lurking around. Let's ask your mom to watch them."

"It's still dark, too early to call her. She'd think it's an emergency, but you're right, they can't be alone. She won't be awake and alert for at least an hour, so let's plan to call her then. The sun will be up, and we'll be able to see better. I'm gonna call Cagey, too, because we don't know what we might find, and my running days are on hold until Sarah is born. It could be nothing, but it could be our prowler. Better safe than sorry. I'll call him now. He's up with the chickens and has probably already had his coffee, but he can join us for another cup of joe. We need to explain the whole thing, gold and all. If we find the lost stuff, we'll need to move it."

"Good idea. I left the cart in the bomb shelter. Ask Cagey to bring donuts," Brick said, wiggling his eyebrows.

Chapter 35

Cagey
Present Day

The NCIC report filled with information about Ace Wray sat on the fax machine when Cagey arrived at work before dawn. The sheriff of a small Texas county he had never heard of had faxed it in the middle of night. He scanned it twice quickly saying, "Holy shit," reading it to himself a third time, taking more time.

He called the number in Texas, and the Post County sheriff answered. Cagey verified a few things and had just hung up when he saw Maggie's name on his phone's screen. He greeted her, and she responded, "Cagey, good morning. Brick and I need your help for a few minutes. Could you come to our house if you aren't swamped?"

"Sure thing, Boss," he agreed, adding, "I've got something for you, too." Maggie hadn't indicated what was going on from her end, but she sounded excited, and he wanted to tell her about the news from Texas. "I'll bring donuts."

He dashed into the bakery and picked up a dozen. He could eat three or four, but he knew the twins and Brick would gobble the rest. He wasn't sure about Maggie, sometimes she watched her weight, other times not. Since she had become pregnant, she was unpredictable, and he was never sure what she would do, so he brought plenty for everyone.

Cagey had never married and had no children of his own, but had adopted the twins, sort of, like a friendly uncle. He enjoyed teasing them, and they teased back but had become leery of him since the time they clambered onto his back while he was talking to their mother about a case. He could be all play or all business, and that particular day, he had been all business. Annoyed at two three-year-old boys bouncing on his back while he was talking about a case, he snapped handcuffs on their ankles, tethering them together, leaving them wide eyed, unsure whether to laugh or cry. They did a little of both, and now were cautious around him.

Cagey grabbed a donut from the box and handed Brick the remainder. He began talking to Maggie immediately, "This is like something out of the twilight zone. We got a report back on Ace, a total shocker. As it turns out, the name Ace Wray is a common name, at least common in Post County, Texas, which is about as rural a community as there is. A whole family, eight of them, plus a few cousins have the same name. They also all have a whole bunch of the devil in them, some worse than others. I called the county sheriff, and he gave me the run down on the Wrays. Granny, her first name was Ann, is dead now, but was married to Ace, who was murdered, but I'll tell you about that story in a minute.

"The sheriff said the name Ace was short for Dennis, but I'm not sure how that worked. Anyway, it seems that Granny Wray had a bunch of babies, maybe fourteen or fifteen, but she couldn't read, write, or spell, so she named all the baby girls Ann, because it was the only name she knew how to spell. She called the girls by different names, like Anne Marie or Annie Mae or Annie Jo, but their birth certificates were identical, Ann Wray. They were all born at home without a doctor or nurse, and she had to fill out the birth certificates herself. Her husband was a scoundrel who often left her alone without any help. She named the boys, Ace, A-C-E, after their father because she also knew how to spell his name. Three of the Aces currently reside as guests at various Texas prisons but the others, five more boys, all eight named Ace Wray, have scattered. Some may be dead."

"You must be kidding," Maggie laughed, "she named all her sons and daughters the same? That would have been confusing for the kids, and what about the school?"

"I asked that question of the Post County sheriff, and he said the Wray family found it convenient. They were rascals, constantly in trouble, and they covered for each other, such as one brother being blamed for misdeeds of a different one. There were many times the police were unable to sort out the crimes, especially without the level of technology that we have today. Maybe it was a perfect solution for a crime family overloaded with criminals or ne'er-do-wells," Cagey replied as he shook his head in disbelief, before continuing.

"But wait, there's more. As I said, Ace Wray, Granny's husband, was killed, by, get this, Ace Wray, but they don't know which one. At least they think one of the Aces killed him. They cleared all of the Ace Wrays except one because they didn't know where he was. But recently, they discovered that a man named Ace Wray was wanted in Reno for the murder of Candice Dumont. As luck would have it, he disappeared, and the Reno police don't know where he is either, although they have been searching for over a year. That must be our Ace, one and the same, but we have to make sure we have the right one."

"So, a person named Ace Wray is wanted for murder in Texas, and Ace Wray, maybe the same one, is wanted for murder in Reno. Is that what you're saying?" Maggie asked.

Cagey blinked his eyes a couple times and smiled, "Yes. Confusing, but that's what I'm saying."

Maggie paused for a minute and wrinkled her brow. "Murders? Two Ace Wrays are wanted for murder, or one Ace Wray is wanted for two murders. Our Ace, I mean our next-door neighbor with the vicious dog Peaches, he's rude and an abuser, but murder? They've lived in Barrier for a year. Does the timing even work? Are you certain?"

"No, of course not," Cagey said, frowning, "but everything points that way. And you've often pointed out that Barrier is a perfect hiding place. It seems highly unlikely that two Ace Wrays live in Reno. Since we have an Ace Wray here, we need to find out if he is the same one who is wanted for murder in Post County, Texas and/or Reno, Nevada. What are the odds that they are different people than your neighbor?"

"Maybe, maybe not," Brick said. "It also seems highly unlikely that several Ace Wrays, brothers and cousins, would be anywhere, but it fits. You said the Wrays, our neighbors, were a strange pair."

"Cripes," Maggie said, "murder. Maybe a double."

Cagey looked from one to the other, "The sheriff said he would send me more details this morning, and they might have arrived already. You said you had something you needed help with? What is it?"

Maggie started to say something, but Brick interrupted her, "Nothing, really, it can wait. It can wait until we figure out how to untangle the Ace Wray phenomenon."

Chapter 36

Maggie and Cagey
Present Day

Maggie and Cagey arrived at the sheriff's office within minutes of each other, Cagey first. By the time Maggie had arrived, the fax machine had printed and ejected the information from Post County's sheriff's office. They sent a copy of a death certificate for Dennis Ace Wray and nothing more, and Cagey had already read it three times and memorized its sketchy details before Maggie arrived. It opened their eyes to a murder case in Texas that they didn't know about yesterday.

Maggie dialed the Reno police and talked to the chief. Within minutes, the fax machine had spewed out a near-parcel of documents that she bundled up to read. The death certificate listed basic information, such as Candice Dumont's name and address, parents' names, spouse's name, date and time of death, and, of course, cause of death, gunshot wounds and a severe battering with a blunt instrument.

"This is the Candice Dumont case, Maggie. I'm sure you remember it. You had recently been elected, and it was all over the news," Cagey said, excitedly.

Maggie knew the name sounded familiar and immediately remembered the case. "Yes, Candice Dumont in Reno. I recall this case well because it was both interesting and frightening. She was murdered about the same time that we were dealing with Fitzwater's case, so I probably missed some of the coverage, but the news media highlighted her case on TV and Reno newspaper, and as far as I know it has never been solved. I don't recall the details, but it was all over the news because of the violence displayed against her. Whoever did it shot Candice in the chest a bunch of times and bludgeoned her in a crime filled with rage for whatever reason. I recall the newspaper said it was as if the killer wanted to take no chances of leaving her alive. They speculated a golf club, but never found it. I am sure that it's been on the Reno police's agenda all these years, but they never discovered who did it. It's a cold case."

"I haven't thought about it in a long time," Cagey muttered. "We didn't know anything about Brandi and her sister until this week. And Ace and his escapades."

"Fast forward to today when we learn that our neighbor, Ace, is wanted for not only one but quite possibly two murders. If that's true, Brick and I live next door to a violent murderer. Brandi lives in Barrier, too. Or lived here, which might explain why she had been so secretive about her past. This can't be a coincidence," Maggie said. "The Reno police now believe that Ace killed Candice, and now Brandi has disappeared. The Post County sheriff says that Ace killed his father, but again, we don't know if it is the same Ace. This isn't a mere coincidence, but proving it is something else. I bet Ginger knows more than she's saying and Jay, too. Do you think he knows more about Brandi than he's telling?"

Cagey responded, "I don't know. Jay said she kept her past a secret. He is my brother and has always been honest with us, but we're missing something. We don't know where Brandi is, and we don't know much about any of the three of them for that matter. Brandi has been missing for a couple days, maybe three, but it is very possible that she simply left Barrier. She doesn't have a car so would be hitch-hiking or bumming a ride with somebody. The theory that son-in-law, Ace, kills mother-in-law, Candice, might have some holes in it."

Maggie set her mouth in a hard line and suggested, "Let's get an arrest warrant for Ace and let him unravel his story. Maybe he knows where Brandi is, too, which would be a bonus. Solving two murders and a missing person in one morning, a new record."

Cagey shook his head, and his shoulders drooped, "This started out with you hearing noises in the middle of the night. Now we're chasing a murderer or maybe a two-time murderer. Something tells me this isn't going to be easy."

Chapter 37

Brick, Maggie, and Cagey
Present Day

It was finally light outside when Maggie called her mother and once again asked her to babysit the twins. She enjoyed being with the boys and was eager to help. She was as proud of her daughter as her husband had been. He was now deceased two years, but he was her biggest fan and teased Maggie by calling her the high, by-God, county sheriff. He had suffered from dementia, but it didn't stop him from bragging about his only daughter at the local coffee shop.

Grandma arrived quickly with a list of errands that she and the twins had to do, starting with making pancakes before a trip to the grocery store, buying stamps at the post office, visiting the hardware store for a tape measure, and enjoying an ice cream sundae at the local ice cream shop. Her errands often had to do with food, but nobody, especially the twins, complained. Today they would also stop by the cemetery to leave a bouquet of flowers on her husband's grave. It would be a busy day.

Brick went on his morning run and stopped at the sheriff's office on his way home, curious about how Maggie and Cagey planned to handle the business with Ace. He had watched Ace roar out of the cul-de-sac earlier on his way to work and had tossed him a little wave, but Ace ignored him as the dust billowed behind his pickup. Arresting someone at work had different dynamics than arresting someone at home. If they were to arrest someone at home, they only had to worry about other family members and probable access to a weapon. Most Barrier residents had rifles and pistols stored someplace in their homes.

At a work site, other employees, often more than one, were curious, making it a little more difficult to put someone in cuffs. Arresting someone anywhere was fraught with hazards but weapons at work were more likely to remain hidden. In rural Nevada, concealed weapon permits, along with concealed weapons, caused law enforcement to have watchful eyes, maybe even stronger than watchful eyes, binoculars with X-ray vision being a better description. Both Maggie and Cagey were experienced law enforcement officers, but Brick worried about them anyway, especially Maggie and her pregnancy. With only two officers in the town, things could get out of hand quickly.

Brick looked at Maggie and shared his concerns, "I know you two are capable law enforcement officers, the best, but if this guy is as violent as we think he is, I'd prefer that Baby Sarah not be involved, so how about you delay for ten minutes while I jog home and collect my gear and change clothes? I'll be back in a few minutes."

Maggie looked down at her expanded belly and nodded, "Good idea, but I'll drive you. We'll be back after Brick suits up. Cagey, could you pick up the warrant from the judge and call the Reno police to tell them what we have learned and what we plan to do about Ace? They might want to know. Ask for Burns or Lawrence."

Terry and his workers were digging and scraping with the backhoe when they arrived and Maggie stopped to greet them, while she peered into the partially dug hole, "It looks like you're gonna dig the hole this time," she said.

"That's right, nothing is stopping us now. We're full speed ahead, but that vicious yapping dog is about to drive us crazy." He nodded toward Ace and Ginger's house where Peaches was balanced on his two hind legs, nose and front paws against the fence growling and barking. Maggie frowned, thinking of her vow to shoot Peaches if he attacked their family. Maybe she should include Terry and crew in her promise.

Maggie agreed, "Yeah, I'm not happy about that one. If we bring the boys outside to swim, I prefer not to have him around. He's a menace in my mind. I don't know if Ace will keep him inside or not." Her mind flew to Ace, and she was comforted to know that he would soon be in handcuffs.

Maggie saw Brick heading toward her rig. "Gotta go, Terry, duty calls."

Chapter 38

Maggie, Brick, and Ace
Present Day

Maggie and Brick texted Cagey that they were on their way to the Barrier B & B. Cagey had acquired the warrant, and the three of them were hyped about making an arrest. Barrier was a small town with little crime, so arrests were few and far between. The relatively stable population had few issues that needed the attention of law enforcement, other than Saturday night drunks and the never-ending dog complaints. Maggie and Cagey kept their eyes peeled for trouble but luckily, most days little trouble and few troublemakers were found.

The Barrier B & B was a real-life castle that a Swiss financier had built on Barrier's outskirts in the early twentieth century. The four-level authentic European structure held a battlement and a twenty-foot spire with windows situated three hundred and sixty degrees, offering a spectacular view of the surrounding landscapes, especially the valleys and mountains to the west. It was his winter home, and he had lived in it a few years before allowing the castle to fall into disrepair. The town council had no choice but to become castle owners once the home had been abandoned.

When the population boomed with the discovery of gold, the town council who hadn't yet realized the value in the estate, had fenced it off, fearful that someone would fall or jump from the battlement, and the council would be subjected to a lawsuit. The chain-link fence worked for a while, but the local teenagers discovered that a few quick snips by wire cutters would open it up, and it became a convenient teenage hangout. Many youths smoked their first joints in the castle, and young ladies routinely lost their innocence in the tower. Sometimes vagrants used it as a mid-route refuge and stayed a few nights if local law enforcement didn't roust them out. The city council repaired the fence many times, but finally gave up, acknowledging that it was beneficial to know where the teenagers congregated for their weekend parties.

Rumors among the local citizens, including teenagers, ran rampant about the strange and unexplained noises that some people heard late at night, after midnight. The possibility of a haunted castle both enticed and frightened visitors. Many townspeople claimed to have seen lights in the empty castle, while teenagers, who were fascinated at the idea of a haunted castle, dared each other to spend the night watching for ghosts. Law enforcement officers investigated many times but failed to verify that it was inhabited by either ghosts or a live person. One transient person begged to spend the night in jail after a night in the castle, swearing that he saw something that looked like a curtain flapping in the breeze and heard banging on the doors followed by laughter. Another talked about smelling roses in the tower and feeling chills in the air, but after investigating, law enforcement couldn't find anything and wrote the claims off as itinerants using drugs. But the unexplained noises, lights, and behaviors continued.

Jay Guzman first saw the castle as a young boy and grew fascinated by the structure and its mystique. He vowed to own it someday, although he had no idea what he would do with it. A creative entrepreneur, he turned it into a destination bed and breakfast with a medieval theme, and visitors from far and near added Barrier to their travels to stay in the refurbished, possibly haunted castle. Jay hired his former bookkeeper, Mary Grace Brownly, to oversee the daily workings, but quickly discovered her forte was creative management. The B & B became his most successful business, except for, of course, the Chicken Dinner Ranch.

Mary Grace tuned in to the possibility that the B & B was haunted and built related events, offering ghost watches and special tours of the tower, along with fictional ghost stories, about what might or might not have happened within the walls of the castle. Jay constantly rewarded her efforts, especially when she added spooky t-shirts and other memorabilia to the property offerings. "It seems to work, Jay," Mary Grace shared with her boss, "but I am sure you know that the hauntings are likely myths. Never has a ghost, or poltergeist, or alien ever crossed my path."

Maggie, Brick, and Cagey arrived in two police vehicles and parked toward the end of the driveway where they could not be easily seen. Ace sat on the steps of the B & B with two men, perhaps other maintenance staff, and the manager, Mary Grace, an easily recognizable woman who had likely missed few meals throughout the years. The three men were smoking and talking, and the three law enforcement officers could hear them laughing. Although it was mid-morning, the cool air chilled them. Dew had kissed the grass and flowers making the entire yard glisten in the morning sun. Maggie, Brick, and Cagey exited their vehicles and began walking up the sidewalk. They walked slowly, but before they got to the steps, Ace and the other two men saw them coming and bolted, moving quickly toward the rear of the house. Cagey and Brick increased their pace to catch up with them, while Maggie stepped to the porch to talk with Mary Grace.

"That was fast," Mary Grace laughed. "If I had shot off rockets, they couldn't have disappeared faster. What's going on?" She looked down at Maggie's expanded belly and said, "Oh! Baby time must be close."

Maggie ignored her question and said, "Good to see you, Mary Grace, her name is Sarah. Just a couple more months. I'm pretty sure she'll be a big baby," Maggie ran her hand over her swollen belly and smiled.

"It's wonderful that you can find out the sex of a baby before it's born. It wasn't that way when I was pregnant with Reese. I sure loved the surprise element, though, with the nurse exclaiming, 'It's a girl' with everyone surprised. When Reese was pregnant, she didn't want to know, and the prison wouldn't pay for the ultrasound anyway." Mary Grace's daughter Reese had been in prison when she gave birth to Mary Grace's grandson, so rearing responsibilities fell to Mary Grace until Reese's release. Reese, now off probation, lived with her son in Las Vegas.

Maggie stretched and twisted her neck toward the backyard, straining to see if there were any vehicles parked in the rear of the B & B. She saw two pickups, one black and the other white, in addition to a food delivery truck. Her eyes followed the route of the three men plus her two deputies. She said, "We're here to talk to Ace. We have a warrant for his arrest. It looks like he's not interested in talking to us, though."

"Arrest Ace? What for? He's such a nice young man, well, not that young, but he's more reliable than most. He likes to talk, though."

As Mary Grace spoke, the big, white pickup roared out of the driveway, leaving a trail of dirt, dust, and debris.

"That's Ace!" Maggie shouted. "He's leaving." She started to run toward her rig, but Brick ran past her, jumped in the SUV, and in a flash, he was gone with Cagey not far behind. "It looks like Sarah and I will stay behind," Maggie said, sitting down on the steps of the B & B.

Chapter 39

Maggie and Mary Grace
Present Day

Maggie hoped she could gain a little more information about Ace and asked, "How long has Ace been working for you? Is he a good employee?"

Mary Grace wrinkled her brow and paused for a minute while considering, "He's been here about a year, and he's not bad. My definition of a great employee is one who shows up, shows up on time, and does what is asked, and he's all that, so I guess he's a good employee. He's never come to work drunk, and as far as I know, he doesn't use drugs. But my personal opinion is that he is a jerk, and I don't know how his wife stands him."

"What do you know about him?" Maggie asked, wondering if she would learn anything sinister, hoping she would and wouldn't at the same time.

"I don't know much. I know he's married and from Reno. He and his wife used to live in Texas, and he's got a little drawl, which I think is cute. Doesn't he live next door to you and Brick?" Mary Grace asked.

Maggie nodded, "They do, he and his wife, but I never see them. I met her yesterday for the first time, and like you said, they've been here about a year. Have you met his wife?"

"No, never. He says she's shy and likes to stay home. Barrier doesn't have many activities, but most people introduce themselves to their neighbors or make friends in town, even if they are reclusive. Ace and Ginger don't have kids, so it seems like she might like to meet some people or something," Mary Grace added. "She doesn't work, so her day-to-day existence has to be boring. I am not sure I could do that."

Maggie thought of her own recent conversation with Ginger who said, "People probably think I'm a recluse. I'm not really, but Ace thinks it's best if I stay home." She also thought of the bruises on her face and shoulder.

"This is the weirdest thing," Mary Grace offered, "one of our employee perks is that Jay offers a free dinner for the staff every few months, usually when we aren't full. We've had two dinners since Ace came to work here, but they didn't come to either. It's too bad because Jay, as you know, offers wonderful meals, and they could meet other people in town, and best of all, it's free. Who doesn't like to go out to dinner when it's free? Jay only invites his own employees and their significant others, and it is fun, so I think it is odd."

"That does seem odd. I wouldn't mind taking their place," Maggie chuckled. "The food here is excellent, and with the twins, we don't go out much." Maggie's mind moved to Brandi, and she pulled from her pocket the two photos that Jay had given her. "By the way, Mary Grace, do you know this woman? We're trying to locate her."

Mary Grace took the two pictures and stared at one after the other and handed them back to Maggie. She didn't answer Maggie's question and at first said nothing, but finally asked, "Are they the same woman? The hair is different. Is she wearing a wig?"

"No, she colors it. I think she is bleached blonde right now, cut short and spikey, but I'm not sure. Do you know her?" Maggie asked again. Mary Grace had not answered her original question, and Maggie wondered why.

Suddenly, Mary Grace stood up, "I've got work to do. I'll see you later, Maggie. If you want anything, all you have to do is ask. That baby is probably hungry." She reached over and rubbed her hand across the baby bump.

Maggie sat alone on the steps for a while longer until her SUV rolled in. Brick was smiling, "Hey, prego-girl, do you want a lift into town?"

"Did you arrest Ace?" she asked. "Are he and Cagey okay?"

"Yes, to both questions, but let's skedaddle. Terry called with a couple questions about the pool, another issue, I think, so let's go home," Brick replied.

Chapter 40

Maggie and Brick
Present Day

By the time Brick and Maggie returned to their home, Terry's workers had halted their excavation and were sitting on a pile of dirt smoking cigarettes. "What's up?" Brick asked Terry. "Did you run into another bomb shelter? What's the hold up this time?" Brick was thinking, *This is my summer vacation, and so far, we've arrested a murderer and found and lost three containers of money, jewels, and gold. It's gonna be quite a summer, but can we please dig the damn hole?*

Terry mock-saluted Brick and Maggie and drawled, "It's probably nothin', but when we scraped around those trees to clear out the debris before we started to dig, we found that old gun safe that's sitting over by the tree. It's rusted shut, but we thought you would want to know about it, because who knows what's in it? It might be treasure, you know, pirate booty. Does Nevada have a finders-keepers law? If it does, you could be sitting on a gold mine."

Maggie and Brick forced a laugh and glanced at each other with knowing looks. This treasure was not a small gun safe, and if it were filled with weapons, rifles, or something else, it could be valuable, but it might also be part of a crime scene—just like the last treasure they found. Terry didn't know about the stash, and Brick and Maggie planned to keep it that way, at least for now.

Brick said, "Buried treasure in a gun safe, that would be something. It looks like our backyard is filled with surprises."

"We will take it to my office because maybe it has a history either about who owns it or its relation to criminal activity. It belongs or used to belong to someone, and I need someplace secure to open it. I wonder why someone would dump a gun safe into a yard," Maggie mused aloud.

Terry said, "It was half-covered with debris, like ashes and rotted stuff from an old burn barrel, the type everyone used to have in Barrier before the city council banned them. It's been here for a while." He pointed to an area of their yard and said, "It was wedged between that heap of dirt and the fence, covered by weeds and some rotted limbs from the mesquite trees. It must weigh over three-hundred pounds. I think it's going to need a scrubbing before you put it in your office. It's big, over four feet tall and two feet wide and deep. We could wash it down with a hose if you'd like."

"No, I'll wipe the gunk off at the office. Something might be under the sludge and slime that will tell us who it belongs to," Maggie said.

Terry continued, "At first, we thought it was an old electricity box, although it was a lot larger than most, but when we moved it, we had to use the backhoe because it was stuck and too heavy to move by hand. After we brushed some of the gunk off, we realized it was a gun safe and moved it from the pool area. It's heavy and rusted, but the combo isn't rusted through. You'll likely need a locksmith. It's going to be a bear to move."

Brick answered, "Yeah, gun safes weigh a lot on their own, and if it's filled with guns, that's another fifty or more pounds. I'll move my SUV closer so that we don't have to carry it so far." Four of them hoisted it and carried it like a casket, sliding it into the back of Brick's vehicle.

Terry offered, "I can go with you to the sheriff's office and help you unload it. Even with Cagey's help it's going to take more than muscles. In the sheriff's condition, she won't be much help. I am pretty curious about what's in it."

Brick shook his head, "Thanks, but we have a dolly at the office, so Cagey and I can handle it. We'll push it out onto the handcart and move it. I doubt we'll find a locksmith today. We'll probably have to pull somebody out of Reno anyway. I never thought I'd say this, but what we need is a safe-cracking felon who can open it for us, but we don't have anybody. Pity," Brick chuckled.

Maggie had been distracted, thinking about Ace, but now switched her brain to the gun safe. "I'll call the Reno sheriff. He's closer than my Vegas contact, and he's helped me before. Thanks for putting it in the rig, though."

Chapter 41

Maggie and Brick
Present Day

Maggie and Brick retreated to their kitchen, "What a week!" Brick said. He pulled out two bottles of water from the refrigerator and set them on the table. "And it's only Tuesday."

Maggie was silent, trying to come to grips with all of her projects, which now included a gun safe found in their backyard. Her thoughts were disjointed, but finally, she said, "We're going to need to find someone who can open that combination lock. Cagey might know someone, but if not, I will call the Reno sheriff. I know that moving the safe out of your vehicle into the station isn't going to be easy, but we will figure that out. You probably already guessed that I don't want to involve Terry. He seems like a nice enough guy and knows his digging trade, but we don't know much about him. I wonder how long the safe has been abandoned and if Bob and Joyce Givens know anything about it. Joyce watches everything."

Brick answered quickly, "That makes sense. Once Cagey and I get it out, we can store it in your office until we can find a locksmith to open it. It has wheels on the bottom, so once we get it through the office door, we should be able to roll it into your office where it'll be safe." He paused before continuing, "Like I said, it sure would be helpful if we had a lock-cracking felon nearby," he laughed. "Seriously though, where did it come from? Stealing a gun safe would require a lot of muscle."

Maggie said, "I need to deal with Ace right now, so I'm headed back to the office. This morning, all I was thinking about was digging the pool and figuring out where the noises were coming from, but look at us now." She held up her hand and ticked off five tasks, "The pool, the noises, the missing Brandi, and two murders, neither of which is in Barrier. She switched hands and restarted her count, "Suspected murderer Ace, abused Ginger, a bomb shelter, and we now added a mysterious gun safe. It never rains, but it pours, and it's pouring puzzles right now. I'll ask Mom to keep the boys at her house tonight, and we can visit the bomb shelter and figure out the moving wall. Maybe that will solve a puzzle or two. Maggie kissed Brick good-bye and drove her vehicle to the sheriff's office. Brick followed in his SUV.

When they arrived, Cagey's rig was gone. "Where is he?" she said to no one in particular. "We never leave prisoners alone in the jail. At least we never have." She hit the Cagey speed-dial button, and he answered on the first ring. "Where did you go? You should have called me," she barked. "You know we don't leave prisoners alone."

Cagey snapped back and panted his words, "You're right, Sheriff, but I had no time. I'm at the B & B. Mary Grace called, hysterical. The missing girl from the CDR, Brandi Dumont, is dead. Somebody murdered her."

Brick entered the sheriff's office, in search of the handcart. He was talking to himself, but Maggie waved him silent and continued her conversation with Cagey. "Okay, Cagey, I'll be right there. I'll ask Brick to tend to our prisoner. He can do the initial interview."

Maggie gave Brick a quick synopsis of what had happened, and said, "One thing is for sure, Ace is no longer a suspect in Brandi's murder."

Brick shook his head, "Maybe, maybe not, it all depends on when she was killed."

Chapter 42

Brick and Ace
Present Day

The words that Maggie had said a few days earlier, Crooks? If one shows up, I'll nab him, echoed through Brick's mind. Maggie had her hands full, and now that Brandi's disappearance had switched to a death, probably a murder, she would be even more swamped. Prisoners were time and energy intensive, too, and Ace might be locked up for a while. Brick also had other things on his mind. His summer priorities had been supervising his sons and the swimming pool construction, and he had looked forward to both, but now the pool had fallen toward the bottom of his list, and he regretted not spending more time with his twin sons.

An experienced police officer, Brick had interviewed many prisoners before. He didn't mind interviewing Ace but also didn't like infringing on Maggie's territory. Afterall, she was the elected sheriff, and the citizens had entrusted her with keeping them safe. At the same time, he knew that Brandi's death would take an inordinate amount of time and energy. Maggie was pregnant, and although healthy, she needed to take care of herself and their baby. He sighed and began to write out a few questions.

His mind darted back to the first time he had seen Maggie, when she was investigating the priest's murder in the house where they now lived. She intermingled among the crowd that had gathered. She knew most of the people shuffling around and greeted them easily with authority and confidence, although on the inside she was scared spitless. Fresh out of college, having little experience and a lone deputy, she was tasked to deal with a murder, and it had not been a run-of-the-mill murder. It was a high profile murder of a popular priest, and it opened all kinds of wormholes to explore. In his view, Cagey was the crown jewel of deputies, and she was fortunate to have him. He was honest and hardworking, and despite their age and experience differences, he respected her. He was the deputy, not the sheriff, and he deferred to her.

The night of the priest's murder, Brick had observed her working the crime scene as if she knew what she was doing. Collecting evidence. Interviewing witnesses and suspects. Following the clues. Sorting information to determine what was false or true. It hadn't been easy, yet she had handled it with professionalism, self-confidence, and ease and had ultimately unscrambled the clues to discover the murderer. He was sure that she had spent plenty of time on the phone with fellow law enforcement officers in other towns, but she had good instincts, a quick thought process, and she never faltered. That's my girl, he thought. That's just one reason I love her.

He looked at the questions he had written and escorted Ace to the interview room. Ace was antsy and grumbled about moving from his cell to the interview room although he had previously grumbled about being confined. Ace shifted in his chair and stared at the backs of his braceleted hands.

Brick: Okay, Ace, let's start. First things first, we're turning on the recorder. The sheriff has other things on her mind right now, so I am going to interview you and record our conversation to make sure the sheriff hears everything you say, without you having to repeat it to her later. Easier for you, that way.

Brick read Ace his rights and after a couple promptings, Ace acknowledged that he understood them.

Brick: Let's verify that you are who you say. What's your name?

Ace: Ace Wray. You already know that.

Brick: Is Ace your given name or a nickname? Do you have another more formal name?

Ace: No, Ace, just Ace. I was named after my daddy.

Brick: So, he was Ace, too?

Ace: As far as I know. My mama never called him anything else.

Brick: We have a murder warrant for you from Reno. What's that about?

Ace: Ah, that's about Ginger's mama, my mother-in-law. Somebody kilt her a few years ago and the stupid cops in Reno can't figure out who did it and keep harassing me and my wife. But I think Brandi did it and I've told them that. They acted like Ginger or I kilt her, but I was working when she got shot. They've talked to us many times, but I didn't know they planned to arrest me. I don't know why, cuz I didn't do it and they've got nothing on me.

Brick: What was your mother-in-law's name?

Ace: Candice Dumont.

Brick: What about your father-in-law? Was he in Reno, too?

Ace: I don't know exactly where he was. His name's Jacque Dumont. Jacque and Candice split a few years ago and I don't know where he went.

Brick: Why'd they split?

Ace: I don't know why he left. She liked to play golf and he didn't, but I don't think that was the reason he left. She liked to spend money on golfing, and they didn't have any money, so money might have been an issue. You should ask Brandi, but Ginger told me that he was a musician and liked to look at the ladies.

Brick: And what was your wife's sister's name? Your sister-in-law.

Ace: Brandi. Brandi Dumont. She's a teacher, except now she's a hooker at the Chicken Dinner Ranch. Ain't that a hoot? The schoolteacher is a working girl. She stuck her nose high in the air about going to college and she ends up a hooker.

He let out a chortle, which came out a snort.

Brick: Have you seen Brandi since you moved here?

Ace: Sure, we saw her the first day we drove in. She was in the CDR big as life, but she acted really snooty and wouldn't talk to us. She said she didn't know who we were, but after I left the CDR, my wife finally got her to talk, and since we've lived here, she comes to the house now and then. I'm not usually there, though.

Brick: When did you see her last?

Ace: A while back, I don't know when exactly. She and my wife don't get along well, and they started yelling and screaming at each other and I told her to leave and not come back, and she hasn't been back. I hope she never does. She upsets my wife.

Brick: What's your wife's name?

Ace looked squarely at Brick: Ginger Wray. He said it slowly, as if to chide Brick.

Brick: What do you know about your mother-in-law's death, murder?

Ace: I don't know nothing about it. The Reno cops thought one of us kilt her, but we didn't. It was somebody else. They pressured us a lot and that was one of the reasons Ginger wanted to move to Barrier. So, we wouldn't be hounded, but here we go again. Harassment never ends.

Brick: I see. How do you know that Brandi didn't kill her? Or Ginger?

Ace: Candice and Brandi got along well, but Brandi and Ginger are as different as peanuts and pork. Brandi is a selfish bitch and wanted to monopolize her mother and everything she had. She didn't want anything to do with Ginger. People think that Brandi is kind, but she's not, not at all. She is mean and vindictive, and it wouldn't surprise me that she killed her mother.

Brick: What about Ginger? How do you know she didn't kill her mother? You said you were working when Candice was killed, so how do you know that Ginger didn't sneak out of the house and shoot her.

Ace: What? No, of course she didn't. Candice treated my wife badly and favored Brandi over Ginger, but Ginger didn't kill her. And neither did I. I disliked Candice, but I didn't kill her either. Brandi is selfish and has a nasty disposition and I wouldn't put it past her to kill her mother. Look at her, she's a working girl now. Other than Brandi, I don't know who would have murdered Candice. Candice was no angel, but she didn't do bad things either and people mostly liked her.

Brick: Who do you think killed Candice?

Ace: Like I said, if you want Candice's murderer, check out Brandi. She did it, went into hiding in Reno after the murder. I mean, she hid in her apartment and didn't go out. She never called Ginger and didn't talk to anyone, but she split, completely disappeared when the cops were close. They couldn't find her, never dreamed she had become a working girl in a brothel, but if you ask me, she's the one who did it.

Brick: How can you be so sure? Did she tell you about it? Do you know if she had a gun?

Ace: No, sir, I was working. I worked at the casino. Ginger was home alone, asleep, and I didn't come home until after Candice died. I wasn't anywhere near, of course, but the police said she died at about three in the morning and I got home when the sun was coming up, maybe five or six. As for a gun, she never said, but it wouldn't surprise me. That's all I know. I've told this to the Reno police time and again. You can check if you want, you'll see, it's the same story I've told over and over.

Chapter 43

Maggie and Mary Grace
Present Day

When Maggie arrived at the Barrier B & B, Mary Grace was sitting in the sun on the front patio of the castle, and Cagey was standing in the moat with water up to his waist. His shoes, weapon, and radio had been abandoned and lay on the patio in a heap. The water sat mostly motionless as the flow spigots had been turned off. Only a small ripple trickled down the middle of the moat indicating that at least one of the spigots continued to flow. Cagey had asked that they drain the moat, but the depth had not diminished much since that request. The water was nearly four feet deep and not quite a hundred yards long, so he expected that it would take a while. Cagey was holding tight to something, and Maggie knew it was Brandi.

Maggie sat down beside Mary Grace, whose face was splotchy and red with tear streaks of mascara. She was dressed the same as she had been a few hours earlier, but looked far more rumpled, exhausted, and scared—mostly scared. Her knuckles grew white as she twisted her hands together. Her chest rose and fell with each breath.

Maggie noticed Mary Grace's breathlessness. "Are you okay, Mary Grace? Would you like a glass of water?"

"She's over there," Mary Grace sputtered, pointing, "in the moat. Cagey's holding her, she's dead." She fanned her face with her left hand.

When Jay renovated the castle into a bed and breakfast, he had cemented the dirt moat and filled it with a clear water. He added fountains and mini obstacle courses where visitors, especially children, could cool off from the Nevada heat, walking, splashing, and playing in the gently flowing water. It was one of the most popular features of the B & B, but right now the feature was void of guests. Two people, most likely other guests, stood at the door staring at Cagey in the stream.

Maggie knew that Mary Grace had lied to her about Brandi in their previous conversation and frowned, "Earlier today you said you had never seen her, but here she is, Mary Grace. Has she been here at the B & B the whole time?"

Mary Grace twisted her mouth and looked away as she considered what to say to Maggie. She decided to remain silent. She returned her eyes to Maggie, then Cagey, refocusing her gaze to the quiet water.

Maggie prodded her, "Do you know how she got in the water? Did she fall in, or did someone push her?"

Mary Grace cast her eyes toward the ground and continued with her silence.

Maggie frowned and picked up Cagey's camera and moved toward the two in the water. Brandi floated face down, inert in the water. She wore jeans and a gray t-shirt with her wet hair plastered to her head. Cagey shivered in the chilly water. and stretched his hand across her back trying to turn her over. "I don't think she fell in, Maggie," Cagey said. "She has a rope attached to her neck, and it's snagged up on the fountain. I can't turn her over without help. Where's the damn ambulance? I'm freezing!" Cagey had been in the chilly water cradling Brandi to keep her from being battered against the moat's bulkhead for the better part of an hour. With the noose entangled around her neck and shoulders, he couldn't steady himself well enough to set her free, and he was forced to wait for the coroner and ambulance to arrive.

"The EMTs are finishing another call and should be here in a few minutes. They'll help you take her out," Maggie assured him. "Hang tight." She continued to snap pictures of Cagey and Brandi, the moat, and the surrounding ground, which was a well-beaten path. She saw nothing of consequence.

"This water is so cold, and I want out," Cagey said. As he finished his statement, two vehicles— an ambulance, and an emergency service vehicle—arrived at the front of the castle. One of the EMT's ran toward the moat, dumped his shoes, and slid into the chilly water. The other two pulled a gurney and blankets from the ambulance and moved toward the moat. The coroner, WW Potter, followed the trio to the patio.

Maggie moved away from Cagey so that the EMT's could assist him and sat down beside Mary Grace who let out another loud wail with more tears flowing down her cheeks. She answered Maggie's question as if she didn't realize the conversation had been paused, "Well, yes, she's been staying here for a few days. I didn't want to tell you because she told me that someone was going to kill her, and here she is, dead, like she said." Mary Grace was sobbing now, and her breaths resulted in a coughing spell.

Maggie waited until Mary Grace quit sobbing and coughing before she asked more questions. "Did Brandi say who was going to kill her?"

"No, she didn't say anything, but she was obviously afraid. She locked herself in her room and told me not to let anyone know where she was. She stayed for two or three days, and I took her meals and once gave her a change of clothes. Reese and she are similar in size. That's Reese's t-shirt that she's wearing now. She said she was a vegetarian and didn't eat meat but ate eggs for protein. She asked for boiled eggs and a green salad. That's what she wanted to eat, boiled eggs twice a day, green salad, and water. I usually took her a half dozen at a time, I thought she needed the protein. Some hotels leave candy on the pillow, Brandi wanted boiled eggs. Go figure. Thinking it might calm her, I offered her a glass of wine, but she said no. She ate everything that I brought her and didn't ask for more."

The EMTs soon had Brandi covered with a blanket and moved her to the ambulance. Cagey dried himself with a towel, wrapped himself with a blanket, and headed barefoot to his SUV, "Let me get out of these wet clothes. I'll change and be right back, Maggie."

Mary Grace continued, "I first met Brandi when I was working at the CDR as Jay's bookkeeper, although I didn't know her well. She showed up one day, Jay liked her, paid her a lot of money, and she stayed. I liked her, too. She didn't strike me as the working girl type. She took care of herself and was gentle and kind to me and to the other women. I don't think she ever berated them or looked down on them. She saw them more as co-workers and accepted them as they were, not for what they were doing. She was more educated than most, and Jay adored her because she was pretty, smart, popular, and, of course, made him a lot of money. She was at the CDR for about four years, that's a long time in that business, and a lot of men were willing to pay big for her services," Mary Grace said.

"Did anyone ask for her while she was here, maybe her..." Maggie started to ask about her sister but cut off her sentence. She didn't want to reveal the Ace-Ginger-Brandi connection. She would keep that a secret.

Mary Grace didn't wait for the rest of Maggie's sentence, "No, no one but you, Maggie."

Chapter 44

Maggie and Mary Grace
Present Day

Maggie knew Mary Grace's comment wasn't exactly on point. Several others, besides the Barrier police, were looking for Brandi. Jay, Ginger, not to mention the Reno police. Mary Grace had lied to her, and now, she had closed off the conversation. Maggie said, "I want to check out Brandi's room and need a key, Mary Grace. Could you find it for me?"

The bed and breakfast had installed a two-key system for the rooms. As nearly every other hotel had done, they had switched to electronic locks, but Jay wanted to maintain a genuine medieval atmosphere and decided to add a system of large brass keys that looked and felt more authentic. They were trendy, and the guests enjoyed the return to the past. Most guests used both locking systems, which gave them a feeling of double security, but the brass keys often walked away when the guests left, leaving Mary Grace a two-sided problem, security and the cost of a new key.

"Brandi stayed on the second floor where both locking systems had been installed, although not every room has been completed. I have the electronic master key, but I need to pick up the brass key master, as well." Mary Grace went into the castle to retrieve the keys and returned in a jiffy with a ring full of shiny brass keys. "Room twenty-six is Brandi's room."

"Can we go in?" Maggie asked. "I really need to see the room."

"Yes, of course."

Maggie grabbed a roll of crime scene tape from her rig, and the two of them ascended the stairs. Mary Grace turned the key, then swiped the key card two or three times before the door swung open. Maggie attached the crime scene tape to the door jambs and entered the room.

Maggie entered first, "Are you sure this is Brandi's room? It doesn't look like anyone has been in it. Everything's perfect." She scanned the room but saw nothing out of place. It was a regular hotel room with the usual ice bucket, glasses, soap, shampoo, and a Gideon Bible. The bed was made, and the bathroom was pristine. Nothing was out of place, and they saw nothing personal in the room, closet, or bathroom.

Mary Grace looked dismayed, "Is something wrong? I had the cleaning staff scour it this morning, change the sheets and towels and wipe everything down. I can have them come in again if it isn't clean enough," Mary Grace offered.

Maggie inhaled a deep breath and held it, then said, "No, no, on the contrary, it's too clean. I wish they hadn't done anything. They should have left it exactly as it was when she was staying in it because some evidence could have been left behind."

It was mid-week, meaning the B & B was relatively empty, but Mary Grace said that only two rooms besides Brandi's had been occupied. Maggie recorded the names and addresses of the other guests in her notebook and visited those two rooms to interview the occupants. They were on the same floor, but not near Brandi's room. They claimed never to have seen Brandi and hadn't heard anything.

On his initial examination, the coroner confirmed to Maggie that Brandi had drowned, but he promised to perform an autopsy. Everyone was curious about the noose and its role in her death. Maggie phoned Reno Detectives Lawrence and Burns to notify them of Brandi's death/murder before returning to her office. They were the same detectives who had undertaken the Candice Dumont murder five years earlier.

Chapter 45

Maggie
Present Day

After Maggie returned to the sheriff's building, Brick and Cagey managed to slide the rusty gun safe out of Brick's car onto the handcart and wheeled it into Maggie's office. Splotched with plenty of matted debris, it left a trail across the sidewalk and office floor. They didn't know what it contained, guns or something else, but they didn't want to leave it on the sidewalk outside. Brick guessed it weighed a thousand or more pounds, but that didn't mean it was too heavy for gun owners who would be willing to risk injuring their backs for a safe full of weapons.

The wind had picked up, blowing the dirt and residue from the safe in gentle circles. Brick grabbed a broom and began to sweep the entryway when he noticed a small, skinny woman outside, peeking through the windows, obviously too shy to enter. She had a red mark on her cheek, and her hair drooped over her left eye. Brick gave her a wave, but she hung her head and did not return the wave. Brick had never met Ginger, despite living next door for a full year, but he recognized her from Maggie's description. When she finally looked at him, her eyes flared, and he knew she was angry, but he also realized she was frightened.

"You're Ginger, aren't you? Let me find Maggie for you," Brick said gently. "You'll want to talk to her." He guessed that she didn't know her sister was dead, but Maggie's gentle way would walk her through the situation without rancor. He hoped.

Ginger's voice was soft but firm. She knew what she wanted to say, "Yes, I'm Ginger, Ginger Wray. Ace's boss, Mary Grace, called me and said you put my husband in jail. My husband is Ace Wray, and I want to see him now."

Brick nodded, wondering if Mary Grace had also informed her about Brandi's death. It was likely that Mary Grace had not linked the lives of the two women and didn't realize they were sisters. Ginger had not mentioned Brandi, so Brick had to guess that she didn't know her sister was gone.

"Yes, Mrs. Wray, you need to talk to the sheriff, Sheriff Monroe. I'll locate her for you," Brick told her again.

Brick escorted Ginger into the sheriff's private office and offered her a cup of coffee while she waited for Maggie. Ginger accepted the coffee and began to question Brick about seeing her husband.

"Where is he? I want him to come home. The police blame him for everything, and whatever it is you think he did, he didn't do it. Where is he?" Her hands were shaking, and she sloshed the coffee on her lap. She stood up quickly and started brushing the wetness from her slacks. See what you made me do," she said angrily, glaring at Brick.

"Whoa, what's going on?" Maggie asked as she walked in the door. "Calm down, Ginger, let's talk." Brick closed the office door behind him as he left, knowing that Maggie would have her hands full, but would also calm Ginger down. It was one of her best traits.

Ginger once again demanded to see Ace, "I want to see him now. Why did you put him in jail, Sheriff?"

"We arrested him for the murder of your mother," Maggie told her. "The Reno police will be here soon, probably tomorrow. Detectives Lawrence and Burns are the officers on the case. They were assigned to solve your mother's murder originally."

Ginger rolled her eyes, "I know those cops. They are out for blood with Ace and me. Can't I see Ace now? He didn't kill my mother, and those policemen know it. They are trying to railroad him."

Maggie sighed. How would she tell Ginger of her sister's death when she was so focused on Ace? Not to mention the murder of Ace's father in Texas. One thing at a time. She said, "Ginger, I have another topic that I want to talk to you about. It's important, and it's going to be difficult for you."

"What's harder than having your husband falsely accused and in jail?" Ginger's mousy manner turned into a full-fledged tornado, screaming profanities and threats at Maggie. "This is all your fault. You arrested my husband. Why did you put my husband in jail? He didn't have anything to do with my mother's death. I know that for a fact. Let him out. I want Ace to come back home."

Maggie remained typically calm, allowing Ginger to vent, sure that her anger would pass, but the threats and profanity persisted. Cagey kept his eye focused on the pair through the glass windows of Maggie's office, doing nothing, but when Ginger stood and moved toward Maggie, he burst into the private office, saying, "Hold it, Ginger, you need to cool down."

Ginger immediately turned her anger toward Cagey and threw an unexpected sucker punch at Cagey's stomach, kicked him in the shin, followed by another quick kick to the kneecap. Cagey winced and doubled over, let out a shriek, and grabbed his knee. He tumbled to the floor in pain while Maggie, normally able to maintain her unruffled self, yanked her handcuffs from her belt. Moments later, Ginger was kneeling on the floor, trying to figure out what had happened. She glared at Maggie, and her tears turned to sobs.

Maggie assisted Cagey to his feet. He panted, "I'm okay. She caught me by surprise, that's all. She packs a huge wallop for such a little woman."

Maggie left Ginger on the floor while she found her a bottle of water and held it to her lips, allowing her to take a sip. Ginger quivered with fear and anger for several minutes but eventually calmed down, and Maggie helped her back into a chair. Maggie focused her eyes directly on Ginger, saying nothing, but carefully removed the handcuffs and began the interview. Ginger glared at Maggie, then dropped her eyes to the floor as the tears continued to flow down her cheeks.

Maggie lowered her voice, "When was the last time you saw Brandi?"

"Last week, she came by our house. She was angry because she had lost some jewelry and accused me of stealing it. We argued about it, and Ace ordered her out of the house. I told her that it couldn't have been me because I had never been to her room at the Chicken Dinner Ranch, but she didn't believe me. She said that no one, except me, knew about the jewelry."

"What kind of jewelry?" Maggie asked.

Ginger glared at Maggie but began to talk and didn't hold back. "She had all kinds of gems, rubies, diamonds, opals, emeralds. Brandi and my mother used to go to estate sales and buy old, broken jewelry. They would repair it and make it into new pieces and sell them on the internet. Mom invited me to help them, but I never did. They called themselves Q2. I didn't want to help them because I wasn't fond of my mother, and Brandi and I had never gotten along. I told Mom no because I wasn't interested in jewelry, but really, I just didn't really want to spend more time with them. Ace said I should have joined them because they made a lot of money. They'd pay a dollar for a broken earring and make it into a necklace with a return of five hundred bucks or more. Where's Ace? I want to see my husband," Ginger repeated.

"No, Ginger, you can't see him. I'm sorry, not today. Maybe later when the detectives from Reno arrive. What else can you tell me about Brandi? Why did she go to work at the CDR?" Maggie wanted to know.

Ginger teared up again and daubed her eyes, "I don't know. I don't know. She just did. She said she needed a job. That Jay guy offered her a lot of money, and she decided to take him up on it. She laughed and told me it was the first time she felt like she was paid what she was worth. Wait, where's Brandi? I want to see her, too. Don't I have any rights?"

"Brandi, I'm sorry to tell you, is dead, and her body is on its way to Reno," Maggie answered. "The coroner is going to perform an autopsy to try to figure out how she died, but we will find out who killed her. I'll call you when we find out anything."

Ginger let out a loud sob, "Her body? An autopsy? Oh, no. She's dead. My sister is dead? She can't be dead."

Although Ginger seemed to have a temper and had gone after Cagey, Maggie felt sorry for her. Having her husband in jail and losing her sister was a lot for anyone to take. "I'll take you home now but will call you tomorrow. Stay in town, though, if you want to see Ace. I'm sure I will want to talk with you again."

Chapter 46

Brick and Cagey
Present Day

Cagey's shin and knee were on their way to a nasty bruise. He was limping around the office when Maggie returned from taking Ginger home. While she was gone, Brick and Cagey had pushed the gun safe into her private office.

"This has been a hell of a week, and it's only Tuesday," Cagey said echoing Brick's comments to Maggie a few hours earlier. "Last week we were rattling around the office, looking for something to do, and now we have murder, a gun safe, and a possible tie-in to a murder that happened several years ago."

"And that's not all," Brick said, "because we haven't told you what we found in the bomb shelter." He looked over at Maggie and gave a little nod.

"The bomb shelter? What's up with the bomb shelter?" Cagey asked. "Isn't it empty?"

Maggie raised her eyebrows and answered, "Well, yes, we thought it was empty, and then it wasn't, and now it is again. We need to have another look. Why don't I keep an eye on Ace while you two check its current status?"

Brick and Cagey drove their separate vehicles to the sheriff's house while Maggie stayed behind. She called the Panorama and ordered breakfast for both. Burger, fries, and a milkshake for her, and a tuna sandwich on whole wheat for him. And two bottles of water. While she waited, she sat at her desk outlining the tasks that lay ahead. Added together, they all struck like a lightning storm. Undoubtedly, they were connected.

Brick unlocked the padlock to the bomb shelter hatch and swung both doors open wide. The doors groaned and instantly the stench from the bomb shelter erupted from the stairway to their nostrils. "Do we have a dead body? It smells like one," Cagey asked as he covered his mouth and nose. "Whew, it's a stinker."

Brick flipped on the flashlight so they could see better as they picked their way down the stairs. "We don't think there's a body in here, although the way things have been going, it's a possibility. But here's the story." Brick relayed the narrative of the treasures to Cagey, finding them, losing them, and the strange wall that opened when Maggie made her early morning trip alone and located a hidden light switch. "The light switch that Maggie found was double duty, turning on the overhead light and opening a wall. Let's see what that's about. She left the switch on and the wall open when she came back to the house because she wasn't prepared to chase crooks." He thought about Sarah, but didn't mention her. "She doesn't rattle easily but having a wall open clearly shook her up. She was out of breath and shaking when she woke me up." Brick found the switch she had told him about and turned it off. The overhead light flickered and went out as the wall began to close. He pressed the switch again and waited while it cracked open, and the dim overhead light crept on.

"Spooky. What are we looking for? The treasure or who moved it?" Cagey asked. The faint overhead light sputtered, and they could see that the wall next to the tiny bathroom had cracked ajar, barely a couple inches, but nevertheless open, as Maggie had recounted. Cagey and Brick stood inert, taking in the character of the bomb shelter. "Who built this?"

"We don't know who built it, but most likely it was built in the late forties or fifties. We can always check with the title company to figure that out. I read the abstract when we bought the house but didn't see anything about a bomb shelter. It was constructed before Barrier's gold mining boom and perhaps the title company didn't record everything they should have or would record now. Technology allows people to be a lot more thorough now with more detailed records." Brick flashed his light toward the collapsible table and said, "The money and gems were hidden under the table, but now they have disappeared. I don't know exactly what we are looking for, but let's go through the opening in the wall and see what we can find."

They unholstered their pistols and stood at the doorway. Brick kicked the door with his foot, and it creaked open a few more inches. "Is this a case of finders-keepers? I mean, if you find the treasure, will it belong to you?" Cagey whispered, "How much money do you think was in the box of money? Not to mention the value of all the gold and the jewels."

"I don't know. That'll be up to Maggie, but I know she'll follow the law. When you find something, you have to make a reasonable effort to find the owner, but in this case, figuring out who the owner is might be complicated. Of course, I wouldn't mind having a chunk of it, though, because sending three kids to college will cost a pretty penny," Brick admitted. "But we'll do what's right and legal."

Cagey pushed the door hard, and the door gave out another loud creak and opened wide into the next room. They flashed their lights around, hoping to find another light switch to help them see better but didn't see one. Both flashlights helped illuminate the room or tunnel, whatever it was, and they could see several yards ahead.

"This looks like another tunnel," Brick said, aiming his flashlight straight ahead. "A tunnel to where, I wonder. What direction are we going? I'm turned around. Are we headed in the general direction of Ace's house, the CDR, or toward Bob's?"

"My guess is that this tunnel goes toward Bob's house, but I could be wrong. We might be headed toward your house, for all I know," Cagey returned. "Between the dark and the twists and turns, I'm not sure."

"Let's see where it goes. It's gotta end up somewhere," Brick answered.

They crept along for five minutes and saw nothing except dirt walls, ceiling, and floor. "Brick, I don't think this goes anywhere. I'm a little claustrophobic down here, and it really stinks. Let's go back," Cagey said.

"I want to go a little farther," Brick said. "If this tunnel leads to either Ace's or Bob's house, we should be there in a minute or two, but if it goes to the CDR, it'll be another twenty or thirty minutes."

"Okay, but just for the record, I don't like this," Cagey grumbled. "I vote to turn back now."

They continued walking, and within a minute, they turned a sharp corner, and the tunnel took on a new appearance. "What's up with this? Astroturf on the floor, it's a good twelve feet. And the tile on the walls and ceiling, that must mean something." Brick said. "Maybe we are closer to finding something."

"Closer to what? We don't even know what we are looking for," Cagey answered. He wasn't sold that the tunnel would lead anywhere, but was definitely curious about the upgrades made to this part of it.

"Closer to whatever we're going to find, hopefully the lost boxes and bag."

"Why would they fix up this area?" Cagey carped, "To me, it would be a waste of money."

The tunnel lightened as they rounded another corner, and Brick stopped walking, "Uh, looks like we have run into some kind of gate," he said. "Let's hope it's unlocked, because I didn't think to bring any tools." He returned his pistol to his holster, and Cagey did the same. As they neared to the gate, the light of day grew brighter, and they didn't need their flashlights. Bars of a red metal gate stood before them, separating them from the open air and sunshine. Brick looked outside and said, "Well, what do you know? We're at the cemetery. The tunnel leads to the cemetery. Oh, great."

Chapter 47

Maggie and Ace
Present Day

Maggie finished her second breakfast and returned to Ace's cell to pick up his tray. "I'll be back in a few minutes because we need to have a talk."

He scowled at her and said, "That ain't happenin', not without a lawyer, Lady."

Maggie turned and looked at him, "That's Sheriff Lady to you, Ace, I'm the sheriff. We have one lawyer in town, and he's tied up a lot of the time, but I'll call him and make an appointment for you. What time would be good for you? Oh, yeah, anytime, because you aren't going anywhere anytime soon." Maggie's comments bordered on snarky because she didn't like wife-beaters, and she was sure Ace fell into that category.

"I hope this guy isn't a deadbeat lawyer because I want someone who will get me off," Ace groused.

She shrugged and replied with a smile, "I'll be sure to tell him that." She turned and left the jail area and returned to the office where she dialed Barrier's lone attorney.

Predictably, Barrier's attorney, Cy Rudd was busy and would see Ace sometime the next day, maybe at lunch time.

Maggie poked her head into the jail area, "Tomorrow, Ace, because your attorney Mr. Rudd, is tied up today, but he will come tomorrow around noon. Do you want to talk to me instead?"

Ace didn't say a word, and Maggie began to close the door to the jail area, but he changed his mind and sneered, "Okay, Sheriff Lady, I'll talk to you. You've got the keys, and when you hear what I have to say, you will let me out of here."

Maggie handcuffed Ace and moved him to the interview room where she attached the handcuffs to the middle bar on the metal table. She flipped the recorder on and read him his rights for the third time. She repeated the routine of asking his name and started the interview where Brick had left off.

"Can't you take these cuffs off me?" Ace asked. "I won't go anywhere. They rub my wrists raw. I promise I'll behave."

Maggie: Stop wiggling because removing them is not likely. You said that you wanted to talk to me. What do you want to talk about? I'd also like to talk about Candice, so how about her? What do you know about her murder?

Ace: I know that I didn't kill her and I'm fairly sure that Brandi did, but she has never admitted it to me or Ginger or anyone else that I know of. If she didn't do it, why did she run away and hide?

Maggie: That's a thought, but what motive did she have? From what I understand about the case, Candice and Brandi got along, and worked well together. On the other hand, Ginger hated both of them, which provides motive for you or Ginger.

Ace: As I have already told you, it was not me, and it certainly was not Ginger. The Reno detectives were all over us, but they didn't find anything either. I've told the Reno police plus that deputy, your husband, Brick or Rick or whatever the hell his name is, that I didn't kill her. Somebody killed Candice, but it wasn't me, and it sure as hell wasn't Ginger because she would never hurt a fly. Brandi did it. You should be arresting her, not me. Think about it, Sheriff Lady, she works in a brothel, not exactly the best job in the world. She went to college but ended up as a working girl. Does that make any sense? Can I see my wife? I'd like to see Ginger. She'll tell you that I didn't kill Candice. She knows.

Chapter 48

Brick and Cagey
Present Day

A rusted lock to the cemetery side gate hung free. Brick squeezed his hand through the bars and knocked it to the ground. The door grated open with a loud and long creak, enough to have awakened his wife. Brick glanced over at Cagey and said, "I think we've found the source of Maggie's creak; somebody used this gate to access the tunnel. I didn't realize that our house was so close to the cemetery. It doesn't seem that close when you drive by it, but it's a short shot using the tunnel, much closer than I thought. I've been thinking that Ace might have had access to the bomb shelter, but with this gate anybody and everybody has access to it, especially with that piece of nothing for a lock. I didn't know this gate was even here."

Cagey and Brick passed through the gate to the cemetery and wandered around, taking in deep breaths of the fresh air. "Getting out of that stench feels great," Cagey said. "I can breathe again."

Marking the existence and demise of Barrier's former residents, the trisected cemetery had more than passed its heyday. Although the city tried to maintain the dignity of its past residents, much of it had fallen into a state of neglect and dilapidation, partially because of lack of interest but also the expense of maintaining the grounds. Brick looked across the mostly dead lawn and said, "This cemetery is in shambles. The city needs to pay it some attention."

The cemetery was a mix of old and new graves, some over a century old and others fresh, dug recently. Barrier's first residents had laid out three labeled sections—Catholic, Protestant, and Jewish. Through the years, the graves had become mixed and now contained a mingling of old and new headstones of all types and faiths. The oldest section consisted of a few walk-in vaults with elaborate headstones with angels and flowers and even poems etched into the granite to commemorate lives and deaths of now-forgotten people.

A padlocked gate intended to protect the Catholic section from vandals and intruders had collapsed and provided no security, although a faded and pitted cement statue of the Our Lady of Guadalupe kept watch. Most graves in this section had headstones with waist-high wrought iron fences surrounding them. Weeds and wind-blown trash were trapped on the fences, and the entire section looked tired and in disarray.

The Jewish section, cordoned off by a large white chain, contained over thirty graves. The chain had rusted through in several places and sagged to the ground. Most gravestones in this section were tall and shaped like scrolls with a Star of David etched above the name of the deceased person. Three of the stones had writing in Hebrew, and two had been desecrated with swastikas. The gravestones were crammed together, and some of them had toppled to the ground either from age, weather, or vandals. "It's been a long time since I visited the cemetery. I wonder when these stones were vandalized. I'll talk to the city maintenance workers about removing those symbols," Cagey said. "It's not right."

The largest section was the protestant area, and it, too, had been divided into two areas. The largest section held hundreds of both large and small gravestones. Some were flat on the grass while others were above ground, but most were simple with a cross honoring the dead with the name, birth, and death etched on the stone.

Brick stopped and looked at one of the graves and commented, "You know, I've never understood why birth and death were the only important dates in a person's life, like this guy, Clarence Hightower, 1919–1999. He was born in 1919 and died in 1999, eighty years of life and work, and it's as if nothing else he did in life was important, being born and dying, that's all. His other life accomplishments, no matter how meaningful, were represented by the dash. It somehow seems unfair. What if he were a firefighter and saved ten people in a burning house or a doctor who delivered six thousand babies? Weren't those dates important, too?"

Cagey had moved to the smaller section where a small, yet respectful, sign reading, Lady's Lane, towered over quite a few graves. Wooden crosses and concrete plaques recorded the demise of the many ladies of the evening who had passed through the years. Many had a first name but no last name, no birth or death dates, and no dashes. "What about these ladies?" Cagey said, "They don't even rate a dash, it's like they are nobodies."

They wandered through the rest of the cemetery looking for signs that anyone had been in the cemetery recently and paused at a curious grave. It had a tall, nameless, and dateless headstone, and the grave was covered with an iron grate, which had been welded shut with multiple welds. It had seven bands of iron shoulder to shoulder and thirteen head to foot. Green grass peeked through the grate, in contrast to the brown grass of the rest of the cemetery. "What the heck?" Cagey said. "I've never seen this grave before. Is it keeping something in or something out? Ghosts? Vampires? Grave robbers? I'm done here, let's go, Brick."

They continued their walk looking for a path or sign that someone had been there but saw nothing. They returned to the house and locked up the hatch that led to the bomb shelter.

Chapter 49

Maggie and Brick
Present Day

Brick and Cagey returned to the sheriff's office just as she had finished prioritizing the list of responsibilities that had landed in her lap in the last two days. What had started off as a busy-body week had emerged into a list of critical duties, and now she was looking at three murders, only one of which belonged to her office. One was enough, but three? Related or unrelated, she didn't know yet. Three members of the same family were dead with no leads. Ace Wray, the dad in Texas, Candice, and now Brandi. Brandi's murder, along with Candice's cold case murder, obviously would head the list, but she didn't want wife-beating to turn into another murder, so she set it as a top priority, too. And what about the treasure disappearing in the bomb shelter? Maybe she would turn that over to Brick.

"What did you find?" Maggie asked, "Anything that will help?"

"No, we found nothing," Cagey responded with a shrug. "We toured the cemetery and found some graves desecrated, so I'll talk to Jay about cleaning those up. The whole cemetery can use a cleanup crew. Maybe we can ask the judge to assign it as a work detail."

"Cemetery? Why did you go to the cemetery?" Maggie asked, puzzled.

Brick paused before answering, "It's not exactly true that we found nothing. We found another tunnel that led to the cemetery, but we didn't find anything in the tunnel or in the cemetery, so we're no further ahead than we were a few hours ago, except for one thing—we figured out where your loud creak was coming from. It's an old metal gate that connects the tunnel and the cemetery. It's hidden behind some shrubs and away from the main part of the cemetery. The gate screeches when it is opened or closed. We could take fingerprints to see if whoever passed through the gate left anything of consequence. How about you? Did you make any progress with Ace?"

"No, I talked to him briefly, but didn't learn anything new. I called Cy Rudd, the lawyer, but he's busy today and will come around tomorrow. In the meantime, despite having three deaths, we're on hold. I made a list of whom we need to interview besides Ace. I added Ginger and Mary Grace, and I'll add Candice's husband because I think we need to take a closer look at him, but I'm stymied with who else. I think Ginger is more complicated than meets the eye, but it's a hunch, that's all. Every time we talk to her, she seems to leave gaps in the conversation, like she's leaving stuff out or hiding something. We'll talk to our coroner to see if his office can give us anything on Brandi's death. She could have drowned or been strangled by the noose." Maggie stood up and stretched. "I've been sitting too long and need to move a bit."

Brick nodded, "I'm hungry, so let's go home and eat something, and you and I can walk through the tunnel. Maybe you'll see something that we didn't. It's not like the other tunnels we've been through, and it surprised the heck out of me."

"I'll stay with Ace while you two have another look, but could you bring me back a hamburger or something? I'm hungry, too," Cagey said.

"We could, but why don't you call the Panorama and order it, something for Ace, too?" Maggie suggested. "His breakfast was skimpy this morning."

Terry and his crew were eating brown-bag lunches when Maggie and Brick arrived home. It didn't look like much had been accomplished that morning. "Did you find anything else that needs my attention?" Brick asked

Terry. "Graves or buckets of money? We can't wait to hear about more surprises." He was frustrated at the progress the pool diggers were making because every time he stopped by, they sat idly, doing nothing.

"No, nothing more, but we'll keep an eye out," Terry laughed. "Your yard is a whack-a-mole game. Cover up one thing up and another one jumps out at you."

Twenty minutes later, after tuna sandwiches and milk, Brick and Maggie reopened the lock and descended the steps to the bomb shelter. "It reeks like something is dead. Did you see anything dead as you walked through?" Maggie asked. "It has to be more than the mold. It could be a dead animal. Maybe a prairie dog that dug its way down here. Let's make this a quick trip, though, I don't think it's good for Sammy," Maggie said.

"Who's Sammy?" Brick asked, unsure if Sarah had been renamed Sammy, at least for the time being.

"I think the baby is a boy," Maggie continued, "and I like the name Sammy. Samuel. Sam. It has character."

"Sammy could be a boy or a girl, so maybe it's better than Sarah," Brick grinned. "I like the name Samantha or Samuel. Sammy's a good name."

They had just entered the tunnel when they heard a thud, as if somebody dropped something large. "What was that?" Maggie whispered, drawing her pistol and quickening her pace.

Before they had taken many more steps, they heard a loud creak similar to what she had heard previous nights. Brick fell into an easy lope and quickly outstepped her. Within seconds, Maggie heard him yelling, "You! Stop. Police." They both heard footsteps retreating and the gate creaked shut. In a heartbeat, Brick was outside the tunnel in the cemetery looking to see which direction the person had gone. He saw and heard nothing and called back to Maggie, "Damn, he's gone."

"Brick, the box! Our box is here. In the corner, look, somebody left it," Maggie called as she snapped a picture.

Chapter 50

Maggie and Brick
Present Day

With their pistols drawn, Maggie and Brick wound their way through the cemetery, twisting their heads to look behind graves and above-ground vaults for something, anything out of place. A soft wind blew through the trees and graves creating eerie sounds. Brick veered left, and Maggie went right, but they saw nothing or nobody.

As they started back into the tunnel, Maggie's phone chimed, and she saw Cagey's name on the screen. Cagey said, "I got ahold of the locksmith. He'll be here within the hour, unless I call him back to tell him different," he told her. "I assume you want to be here when he opens the gun safe, but I can call him and delay if you haven't left the tunnel and need more time."

"No, we're done here, so I'll be back in about half an hour. I definitely want to see what's inside, if anything. Hopefully, it's empty, because I'm done with surprises," Maggie answered, but didn't tell him about the person in the tunnel or the box that had mysteriously reappeared.

Brick put gloves on his hands and picked up the box, "Let's think this through, Maggie. Anybody could enter the bomb shelter through this tunnel. The gate is not locked, and the distance from the gate to the bomb shelter is an easy ten-minute walk even for a prego like you. We have a light switch on our side of the bomb shelter, and haven't seen a light switch on the cemetery side, and no lights either for that matter. Whoever came into the tunnel must have entered from the cemetery side. The wall was closed, so there must be another switch someplace."

They were standing near the metal gate in the section with AstroTurf, tile, and stone, and Brick trailed his light over the walls and ceiling slowly, revealing nothing. "I don't see anything, no wires, no switch, nothing that would carry or generate electricity, but somebody, somewhere has a remote switch."

Maggie looked around and took a deep breath, followed by coughing spell, "I suppose it could be a remote switch, but I doubt it, especially if it were built in the fifties. A remote control would mean it had been installed recently, but this whole tunnel, the bomb shelter, and the metal gate came from the dark ages, fifty or more years ago."

Brick commented, "I want to research the tunnel a little more, so let's put this box in the SUV. You and Sammy can go back and see the locksmith and figure out where we can store this box until we have time to look at it again. I don't trust that it will be secure in the bomb shelter or our house, and I hope that it's safer and sounder in your office. While you have a look at the gun safe, I'll stay here and do another search for a switch or remote. If I find something, I'll call you. Take the SUV, and one of you can come and retrieve me when I find a switch. I'm sure it's here."

"Okay, yeah, that sounds good. Sammy's restless and ready to leave. At some point, and sooner is better than later, I think we should have the tunnel and bomb shelter sealed. They are unsafe and reek and should be closed permanently. Besides, I don't like that anyone can be in a shelter under our yard. Can you believe all this came about simply because we wanted to build a swimming pool?"

Chapter 51

Maggie and Cagey
Present Day

Maggie returned to her office and waited for the locksmith to arrive, but she didn't have to wait long. His shirt tag read Jock, and he drove a fifteen-year-old pickup with a camper shell sporting the name, Jock's Locks. He was a talkative guy and began to chatter as soon as he saw the safe. "This is an old one! Maybe fifty years old or more. I'm sure I can open it, but it might take a little bit of work. It's fun to see what's in these old safes. If it is guns, who knows what condition they might be in. Or maybe there is some valuable treasure inside? Of course, it might just contain junk that someone else left for you to find. It's always a surprise." He had a husky voice and talked fast, spitting out his words.

"A few years ago, I opened a safe that this woman had bought on the internet for a hundred bucks. It was locked, and she thought it would be fun to see what was in it, so she called me to unlock it. She was hoping for money, but she was mighty happy when I unlocked it and found a few stock certificates. I would have liked them, too, as they were Apple stocks, from the early 1980s. That hundred dollars she spent on Craigslist ended up being a whole lot more." Jock gave out a chuckle, "I wish it had been mine. She didn't share either, even though I'm the one who got them out for her."

He continued with his stories, "And once I opened a safe and found firecrackers, a whole bunch of them. I was lucky they didn't explode. Thankfully, they were low grade and only gave out a little pfft when I opened it. It's a good thing they weren't better quality, or I might have lost my fingers." He waggled his fingers to show that he had them all.

Jock told a couple more stories that made Cagey and Maggie laugh, and fifteen minutes later the door to the gun safe swung open. "Whiskey, you got whiskey," he announced. "I'll be darned, a half case of Southern Comfort, that'll make someone happy, and it looks like two pistols and two rifles. This is for you, Deputy," Jock said, offering Cagey one of the rifles. "This beauty is a Springfield. It might even be a Civil War model, but I'm not sure," he added as he handed it over. It was a long rifle and in fine shape, no nicks or gashes, and the wood was smooth as fine silk.

"You might be right," Cagey replied, as he ran his hands over the weapon. "It's an old one, Civil War or about that time. I have read about them and seen photos. It's a muzzle-loaded rifle, but right on target when you shoot it. I'd like to try it out, Maggie, to see how it works."

"And this is for you, Sheriff, World War II for sure. A thirty-ought-six. It might be worth some money, too. It's a Smith-Corona."

"Smith-Corona? I thought they made typewriters," Maggie said, as she inspected the rifle. "I'm not sure they are still in business."

"Do you see any kind of name or address in the safe?" Maggie asked. "It must have belonged to someone, and I'm sure they'd like their guns and whiskey back."

Jock pulled everything out, "I don't see any names or address, but if you let the word out that you have it, I'm sure that you will have a flock of people come running. This is a rather good find, maybe not as good as the Apple stock certificates, but it's a good one."

Chapter 52

Maggie and Cagey
Present Day

The next morning Brick volunteered to stay with Ace while Maggie and Cagey visited with Ginger. Normally Maggie would have gone alone, but Cagey was still limping after Ginger's attack, which made them think Ginger was stronger than they thought, so they both went. Ginger might be able to take down one or the other, but not both.

When the sheriff and her deputy arrived at her house, the pickup was gone, and no one answered when they knocked. They walked to the back of the house but saw or heard no one. Maggie had removed the can of pepper spray from her pocket, but they heard nothing from Peaches either, and Maggie wondered if he was gone, too. Their list of suspects for killing Brandi was short, two people, Ace and Ginger, and they both had motives, but they didn't know about opportunity or means. Ginger hated Brandi, and Ace wanted money. Simple motives, emotional attachment and money, and either was enough motive to murder someone.

"I told her not to go anywhere. She's such a mousy character that I didn't figure she'd go anywhere. I wonder if anyone saw her leave?" Maggie commented.

"She might be mousy on the surface, but you should see the bruises on my leg. I went down fast and hard. She knows what she's doing," Cagey said, as he rubbed his knee. "It was like a karate chop or something."

Maggie cocked her head and stared down at Cagey's knee. "Something feels off here. We need to talk to her, so why don't you check with Bob and Joyce and find out if they know anything while I'll check with our swimming pool guys. Those guys probably won't know anything, but it'll give me a chance to see if they showed up to work. We are anxious to finish."

Cagey drove his SUV across the cul-de-sac to Bob and Joyce's house and soon Joyce gave him the scoop. "I was out for my walk and saw Ginger leaving. It was before the sun was up, not quite daybreak. She put that big dog, Peaches, in the back of the pickup and tied him to the gun rack. She's barely big enough to manage him, but she got him in the bed of the pickup and somehow subdued him. He barked once, and I saw her smack him with something, maybe a stick or a cane. He whimpered and lay down. She put some suitcases and a couple small boxes in the front of the pickup, and I wondered if she was leaving for good. Ace usually has the pickup, but I haven't seen him yesterday or today. It was dark so I couldn't exactly see what she was doing. I didn't know that she could drive because I've never seen her behind the wheel, in fact I've never seen her in the pickup."

"Do you have any idea where she went?" Cagey asked, knowing the answer before Joyce said anything. "Did she aim toward town? Or out to the highway?" he continued.

"I think she went toward town, headed that way, but she might have gone anywhere. It was early and dark, and I couldn't really see which way she went," Joyce said.

Cagey moved his SUV again, this time to Brick and Maggie's house, where Maggie was talking with Terry.

"How's it looking?" Cagey asked. "Are you making any progress?"

"Sure, the hole's dug, but now we have to shim off the excess dirt and level the sides, which will take a while because it has to be done by hand, not with a backhoe. Brick's going to bring in a group of kids from the high school to help with the floor of the pool, so we'll be mostly done tomorrow or the next day. Kids don't stay on task like adults, but we'll see. If Brick hangs out, they'll work harder."

Chapter 53

Brick and Ace
Present Day

Brick was anxious to interview Ace and called Cy Rudd again to confirm his appointment. He would be delayed a bit.

"I have a couple more questions for Ace, but I know the rules," Brick had told Maggie. "I want to know how they got to Barrier. Of all the towns in Nevada, how did they choose this one? Brandi lived here, but according to Ace, they weren't close. I'm gonna ask him a few questions, but if he refuses to answer, I'll back off."

Brick escorted Ace into the interview room and handed him a cup of coffee and one of the donuts that Cagey had brought from the Panorama that morning.

"I told you, I want a lawyer," Ace said. "I'm not saying anything without my lawyer. When's he coming again?"

"Yeah, yeah, I understand. He'll be here in a while," Brick told him, "but since he's not coming till then, I thought you might like a donut. We aren't barbarians you know, tossing you in the dungeon and letting you rot. I am curious about a couple things, though, and you don't have to answer anything until your lawyer shows up. I'm simply curious and want to pass the time of day."

"Hmm. I doubt that, but I won't turn down coffee and a donut." Ace drank a swig of coffee followed by a bite of the donut. "Not half bad. Thanks."

"Why'd you move to Barrier? It's an out-of-the-way place, not much to do here," Brick coaxed him.

"Ginger wanted to be near her sister, Brandi. We hadn't seen or heard from her in three or four years until we got a postcard. We didn't know she was a working girl, or we probably wouldn't have come. She must have been good at it because she made a lot of money, at least that's what she told Ginger," Ace said. "She was that guy Jay's favorite. She told us that, too. He protected her and made sure she had everything she wanted, but she got bored with him and tired of being a working girl. She had saved a lot of money and planned to leave and go somewhere, but he didn't want her to leave and offered her more money to stay. She had already made a lot of money, but you know the old saying, 'Money talks and...'"

Brick finished the saying, "Yeah, and 'bullshit walks.' That's what I heard."

"She convinced Jay to pay her more in exchange for staying with him for one more year, after which she planned to be leave. She had not spent the money from the jewelry business and hadn't done anything with the jewelry that she and her mother had purchased at yard sales and pawn shops a few years ago. She thought she might start up again and asked Ginger to help. And she also had all of the money she earned from her career, if that's what you call it. She told Ginger that she hadn't spent any money the whole time she was at the CDR. She didn't own a car and never went out to eat, except an occasional breakfast at the Panorama. She didn't buy anything for herself. Everything was provided by Jay, her meals and clothes or lack of clothes, no rent, no health insurance, a sweetheart deal, except for the possibility of diseases, like the clap. She had rented a storage unit in Reno for her stuff, including the car she had before she left, but never paid the rent on it and thinks the storage company auctioned it off. She didn't want anyone to know where she was, and if she had paid the rent, somebody could have figured it out.

"Ginger talked about us going with her, wherever that might be. She told us a lot about the business. Brandi had worked at the CDR for over four years, longer than most, because usually the girls leave after six months or a year, and Jay doesn't object. He says swapping his working girls out is good for business. New blood, so to speak. She said he tried them all out, but didn't want to become attached, except for her. She said he loved her, but she didn't love him."

Brick wanted a little more information but needed to be careful not to cross what might be a lawyer's red line in the sand. "Would you like another donut? We've got plenty. Out of curiosity, how much money does a woman make when she works at a brothel. Do you have any idea?"

"I'll take you up on the donut and a little more coffee, if you have it," Ace said. "I don't know how much she earned, she never told Ginger, but it was a lot. She said that Jay paid her well, and her clients, that's what Brandi called them, also tipped her in cash, casino chips, and occasionally gold nuggets. Jay and the IRS never saw that money. She bragged that she had a good stash of gold, but I don't know where it is or how much. It must be in her room or maybe she buried it in the desert. She never said."

Chapter 54

Brick and WW
Present Day

Brick heard the office phone ringing and hoped it was the coroner but was tied up with Ace and it went to voicemail. He gave Ace a third donut and locked him back in his cell. He listened to the message from the coroner, who said he would call back in ten minutes, but Brick didn't wait for the call and dialed. The coroner, William Walter Potter, who went by WW came on the line immediately. "WW here, thanks for calling. Is this Maggie?"

"No, it's Brick. Maggie's not here right now. I'm glad you answered, WW. Maggie's out catching crooks, as she likes to remind me. I'm not exactly sure what crooks she is catching or where she is catching them, but I'm keeping watch over our prisoner while she and Cagey are out. I know she's anxious to learn what you found."

"This is the darnedest thing; I've never heard of this before. You folks in Barrier sure know how to stump the coroner," WW said. He had a slight drawl, and he gave words like thing and stump two syllables. Thi-nnng and stu-ump.

"What do you mean?" Brick asked, "What did she die from? They found her in the Barrier B & B moat with a rope around her neck. Was she strangled, or did she drown? The rope had caught on something, and Cagey thought her death was one of the two."

WW inhaled a loud breath before answering, "No, neither. It was eggs. She died from a hard-boiled egg, actually a pair. She had two boiled eggs stuck in her throat, one was half-shelled and in a couple chunks and some smashed eggshell shards, but the other was whole, in the shell. We might find fingerprints on the shell if we're lucky. I sent it to the lab, but it's the darnedest thing," he repeated.

Brick was puzzled and wondered if he had misheard what WW had told him, "Do you mean that she died from eating eggs, maybe poisoned eggs or something? She was a working girl at the CDR and Jay, the owner, told Maggie that she loved hard-boiled eggs and barely ate anything else. Mary Grace said the same thing, but how did they get there? Did she shove them down her own throat, like suicide by eggs?"

"No, she didn't die from eating eggs, she choked on them. They were stuck in her throat, and she couldn't breathe. It looks like someone might have held her down because she had some bruises on her wrists and a big one on her pelvic area. It is possible that someone held her down and put a knee on her pelvis. Who is Mary Grace?" WW asked.

"Mary Grace is the manager of the Barrier B & B where Brandi was staying," Brick answered.

WW nodded, "I can tell you that she didn't drown, and she didn't die from the noose around her neck, although that's what we thought when we first saw her. She died from choking on eggs."

Chapter 55

Maggie, Brick, and Cagey
Present Day

Maggie looked at Brick as if he were crazy. "Eggs? How can you choke on eggs? Are you sure he said hard-boiled eggs?" She furrowed her forehead and twisted her mouth, "How does somebody choke on eggs? I've never heard of that before."

Brick gave Maggie and Cagey a full account of his conversation with WW, which seemed unreal to him as well. "They were hard-boiled, and she didn't eat them, rather she choked on them. One was whole, and the other was in a couple pieces with egg shell shards in her throat passage. WW thinks that someone rammed them down her throat. She had bruises on her wrists and one on her abdomen, and WW suggested that someone had placed a knee on her lower half to hold her down. She had two eggs in her throat."

Maggie agreed, "A whole, unshelled egg would definitely clog the throat. Mary Grace said that she only ate eggs and salad, nothing else, so when Brandi asked for them, she delivered both to her room with the eggs unshelled. I didn't see any sign of either eggs or salad when we walked through her room at the B & B, but Mary Grace had let the cleaning staff scrub the room, and nothing beyond the Bible and clean towels were in there."

Cagey said, "How'd someone force her to stay motionless? You don't sit quiet while someone packs your throat with eggs. Maybe she committed suicide by stuffing them down her own throat."

Brick reasoned, "She might have been able to stuff one egg down her throat, like the one without the shell. She could have gulped it down, but it's likely that she would have coughed it up. Stuffing in the second egg, which was still in the shell, wouldn't have been so easy, as she likely would be retching from the first. WW said that she also had some bruises on her hands and pelvic area, so perhaps two people were involved, one cramming the eggs and somebody else holding her down."

"Who knew that she liked hard-boiled eggs? Did the killer bring them with him or her, or were they the ones that Mary Grace had delivered?" Cagey asked.

"Good question, Cagey," Maggie said, giving out an awkward little laugh. "Premeditated murder by bringing hard-boiled eggs to the scene of the crime. Jay told me that she liked eggs when I first talked with him about Brandi's disappearance. And of course, her family, Ginger and Ace would know. Mary Grace knew, and some of Brandi's co-workers might have noticed. Co-working girls might be a better term. And maybe she shared this bit with a client or two. So, potentially a lot of people knew she loved hard-boiled eggs," Maggie said. "It wasn't exactly a secret."

"Where do we start, Sheriff?" Cagey asked, already knowing he would be trying to find Ginger to bring her back to the office while Maggie interviewed Jay at the CDR. Brick would head over to the Barrier B & B to talk with Mary Grace. At this point they had a lot of threads to unravel.

Chapter 56

Maggie and Jay
Present Day

"I always have time for you, Maggie," Jay said, when she unexpectedly showed up at the Chicken Dinner Ranch. He leaned over and kissed her on the cheek and clasped her hands in both of his. "It's a pleasure. We don't see enough of you. And the baby, is it a boy or girl?"

Maggie smiled and shook her head, "We don't know. It'll be a surprise. Sometimes it feels like a girl and other times, like a boy. I'm glad it isn't twins, though. Neither Brick nor I want to go through that again."

Maggie liked Jay. Despite his chosen profession, managing a brothel, he seemed to be a good person and went out of his way to help people. He had a good business sense and participated in community events. The CDR seldom had issues that required law enforcement, and he maintained high standards in cleanliness and demeanor for staff and guests. He owned Barrier's three largest businesses and had his fingers in a few more pies, including serving as the mayor, which he did well and would probably win a second term if he ran again.

"What brings you here?" Jay asked right off the bat. "Any news about Brandi?"

"Well, yes, we found her, but not how we wanted to find her. I'm sorry to tell you that she's dead, Jay, she died last night at the B & B. She was murdered," Maggie said. "Didn't Mary Grace call you? I thought she might."

Jay was upset but diverted attention by asking, "Would you like some coffee?" He called to his assistant, "Laura, bring some coffee and rolls for Maggie and me."

"Uh, coffee? No, thank you, I've had my quota for the day," Maggie said. "Did Mary Grace call?"

Jay's head was reeling, and he ignored her question for a second time. He concealed his emotions and once more called to his assistant. "Laura, Maggie doesn't want any coffee, but bring a cup for me, and a couple of those cinnamon rolls. They tasted better than usual this morning. I think Cookie added something extra, maybe more cinnamon or butter or something. I'll have to ask her what she did differently because they were sure good. You should have one, Maggie, they'll make your new baby happy." His phone buzzed, and he paused and looked at the screen. "It'll wait." He clicked off the sound button and laid his cell phone on his desk.

Jay's ability to separate himself from his emotions had proved valuable in his business dealings. "Now, what were you saying? Brandi died? How did she die?" Jay asked. "She was fine when I saw her last, a couple days ago. What happened?" He stretched to look toward the kitchen and yelled, "Laura, where's the damn coffee?"

Maggie's curiosity was surging. He was acting disinterested, as if he barely knew Brandi. What did Jay know that he hadn't told anyone? Her questioning would take a different route. "We're not sure yet," Maggie lied. "She's with the coroner, and we should have a report sometime soon."

"Hmm," Jay said. "Well, that's a shocker. I never expected for her to be dead, being so young and all. I just thought she needed a break from work. I don't think I will ever find another like Brandi, because Brandi was a good one, a real asset and filled my wallet with cash, as well as being easy on the eyes What do you need from me?"

"We need to know everything about her. You said you didn't know much, but surely you know something more than you've told us. She worked here for about four years, isn't that right? Have you told us everything?" Maggie pressed him, coaxing him to be more forthcoming.

"Nope. I can't think of a thing. She was a private person, never talked much," Jay added, as he picked up his cell phone again and rechecked the screen. "Maybe I should return this call. Can you hang on for a few minutes, Maggie?"

Maggie was becoming irritated. "Did she have any relationships besides her clients, like a boyfriend? Was she seeing anybody?"

"Nope, not that I know of. Like I said, she was a private person and kept to herself. She never mentioned seeing anyone, although I can't recall ever having asked her either," Jay said.

"We also want to search her room and need to close it off until Brick can do it thoroughly. He'll come by this afternoon, but I don't want anyone entering her room before he searches it," Maggie said firmly.

"Do you really need to search it again? Cagey and I already had a look a few days ago and found nothing. I doubt that Brick will either. Do you think someone killed her?" Jay asked. He obviously had tuned out the word murdered, that she had said a few seconds ago. "Who would have killed her? One of her clients? She was popular, but we also keep an eye out for trouble, and she never reported anyone."

"We need a list of her clients for the last year, her regulars, as well as those that she saw only once or twice. Have you seen her since you reported her missing, Jay?" Maggie asked.

"Seen her? No, I would have called you if I had, I told you that. What is this, Maggie? Why are you asking so many questions?" Jay raised his voice slightly, which caused Maggie alarm, but she pushed forward.

"Did you and she ever argue?"

"No, she was one of my favorite workers. We never argued, and she liked it here and intended to stay as far as I knew. Brandi was one of a kind, that's for sure." Jay looked at his phone again, "I'm sorry, Maggie, I have work to do."

"A few more questions, Jay. How did you manage to retain her for so many years? I thought most of the girls stayed only a few months, but you said she's been here four years." Maggie didn't like how this interview was going. Jay seemed disinterested in Brandi's death and helping Maggie find out who had killed her. She was curious as to how anyone could have worked here for four years without his knowing more about her. It seemed hardly possible.

Jay stood up and snapped, "Maggie, I said, I'm busy. I don't know anything, and I'm done answering questions. Brandi loved working here. And I loved having her here. She loved being a working girl. She's gone now and I don't know anything and I've got things to do. I'm sorry I couldn't be of more help," Jay said, as he cradled Maggie's arm to escort her from his office. "Maybe you are not talking to the right person."

"And who would that be, Jay?" she asked, as he slammed the door behind her.

She had considered Jay on the list of suspects, but he had ridden low on her list. Ginger and Ace were much higher, and of course the unknowns, like coworkers or Brandi's clients. Had Jay changed, or had she just not seen this side of him?

Maggie left the building, puzzled over Jay's comments about Brandi's murder. He seemed indifferent and aloof, and in reference to his last comment, who was the right person? Did Jay know anything or was he being sincere?

Chapter 57

Brick and Mary Grace
Present Day

After Maggie returned to her office, Brick drove to the Barrier B & B to talk with Mary Grace. She had been integral in the case regarding the priest, and he knew she would cooperate with him.

Mary Grace handed him a cup of coffee, "You drink it black, right?"

Brick took the cup and thanked her before saying, "Mary Grace, I want to talk with you about a couple things. Brandi, of course, but also about Ace. Let's start with Brandi though. I'd like to know everything she told you when she came to stay, which was when? Tuesday? Wednesday?"

A stout woman, Mary Grace panted a little as she spoke, adding an umph as she collapsed into her chair. She held a bottle of water, twisted off the cap, and drank a long swig. "Tuesday, but it was Tuesday night, late. The night clerk quit last week, so I was on duty. I hope to find a new person soon. I wanted Brandi to apply for the job because she said she was thinking about leaving the CDR, and she would have been ideal. I am not a night duty kind of person because those shifts wear me out, all day and all night. She said she was done with being a working girl. I thought she was a nice girl, rather woman, and she seemed happy to be giving up that line of work. When I talked to her, it sounded like she was ready to quit immediately and do something different, but she was so frightened that I decided to delay talking to her about working here."

"I see," Brick said. "Did she say why she was leaving the CDR?"

"No, but she was a bit shaken up. I thought that maybe someone had tried something with her, you know, like beating her up. Or worse, rape. Rape is rare among working girls, but it does happen. These women are still people, even though I don't much approve of their line of work."

Brick asked, "Did she have a car?"

"No, she didn't. She walked here, probably from the CDR. She paid cash for two nights with hundred-dollar bills and requested a room in the front of the castle. She said someone was after her and was going to kill her. I asked her who, but she shook her head." Mary Grace pursed her lips. "I've never seen anyone so terrified."

"After her? Did she say who?"

"No, she didn't say, but she was shaking, her face was blotchy, and her eyes were red. She had been crying. She pulled the blinds and moved away from the window," Mary Grace continued.

"Weren't you employed as...uh CDR...uh...person...when Brandi first arrived in Barrier? Isn't that how you knew her?" Brick asked.

Mary Grace's eyes bore through him and she snapped, "Yes, I worked at the CDR when she arrived, but I wasn't a working girl, if that's what you are insinuating. I wouldn't do that type of thing. I kept the books for Jay. Nevada requires a lot of paperwork for brothels, and that's what I did. Paperwork and nothing else. I worked at the CDR for a couple years before Jay hired me to manage the B & B, and I like this a lot better."

Brick gave her a half smile, "Mary Grace, I know that. I didn't mean to indicate you were a working girl. I know you better than that. I apologize if you interpreted my words differently. Did Brandi give any indication who was pursuing her? Male? Female? Maybe a name?"

"No, she didn't say anything else, just that someone was after her. Wait, Brick, that's not right, she said they were going to kill her. Kill her. But she didn't say who. But someone obviously did because now she's dead."

Mary Grace shook her head and wiped her eyes. "I asked if she was hungry because I would make her a sandwich or something, but she said no, but she asked if I had any hard-boiled eggs, she would eat a couple. We keep them on hand because you'd be surprised how many people eat hard-boiled eggs for a snack. She said she wanted three, so I brought her three, plus salt and pepper. Some people like salt and pepper on their eggs."

"Peeled or unpeeled?" Brick asked, faking a smile. He thought to himself, what a ridiculous question, how would they determine where she got the eggs that were the murder weapons?

Mary Grace twisted her face, "Does it matter? Unpeeled. I've found that most people like to peel their own eggs. It's a food safety thing."

"Did she act scared?"

Mary Grace paused before answering, "Yes. Like I said, she looked terrified. She kept looking around, out the windows, and when I showed her to the room, she peeked through the window once and yanked the blinds shut. I left after that, and I don't know how she got killed."

"Were other guests staying here, or was she the only one?" Brick asked.

"I told Maggie all this already, the day she got killed. Like I said, it was Tuesday, midweek, and we don't usually have many guests during the middle of the week. They mostly come in on Friday nights, and leave on Sunday night or Monday. Only two other rooms were occupied that night. I gave Maggie their information, and she questioned the occupants of both rooms."

"How about the eggs? Were they gone when you looked at her room after they found her?"

"I don't know, I was so upset that I didn't really pay attention. The room has been cleaned, and obviously nobody's stayed in the room since, so you can look if you want. What's so important about the eggs, anyway?" Mary Grace said.

"It probably won't do me any good since the room was cleaned, but I'll take a look anyway, after we talk about Ace, if you don't mind," Brick continued without answering her question.

"You probably know as much about Ace as I do, since he and Ginger live in your cul-de-sac," Mary Grace answered.

Brick frowned, "They keep to themselves a lot, and Maggie and I only recently met him. What's he like? Do you like him?"

"He's a proud Texan and reminds me of it every day. He's a talker and kinda boastful, likes to be the center of attention, and has his own mind. Kind of a jerk sometimes. I'm surprised he hasn't gotten to know you, because he's pretty outgoing and likes to talk about Texas. He's worked here a year and does okay, like I told Maggie, he shows up, is on time, and mostly does what he's told. I wish all my employees did that. But..." Mary Grace stopped talking.

"But what?" Brick encouraged.

"But. There is always a but, right?" Mary Grace asked, "This but is that I don't trust him. It's a hunch, a gut instinct, but something is off, even scary about him. I'm not sure what, though."

Chapter 58

Maggie and Ginger
Present Day

The second Maggie walked into the station after visiting Jay, Cagey knew something wasn't right. Maggie's face glowed irritation. He wondered what his brother had done this time.

Cagey had been with a handcuffed Ginger in the interview room when Maggie made her appearance. Maggie's eyes focused in on the bulging vein in his forehead. Cagey's face was red and angry.

"Sheriff, I'm glad you're here. How about I swap places with you, and you can interview Ginger? She's a little feisty today. When I went to her house to bring her in, she tried her judo moves on me again because she didn't want to come to the office. I had to slap on bracelets to get her to cooperate."

Tears ran down Ginger's cheeks, and she couldn't reach them with her cuffed hands, so she tried to lick off the tears, "I want to see Ace," she whined, although louder than necessary. "Where is he? I have my rights."

Maggie sat down across from Ginger and dabbed at her tears with a tissue. Cagey left, closing the door behind him. "Yes, Ginger, you have rights, but you don't have the right to see Ace. Let's talk, because at this moment, I want to ask you about Brandi."

"She was murdered, but I don't know anything about that." She started to cross her arms in front of her, but the handcuffs stopped her, and she looked at them as if she had forgotten they were binding her wrists together. "Take these off me. Please."

"Maybe in a while, but, first, I need answers." Maggie looked at the tape recorder, making certain it was switched on and said, "Let's start over. Please tell me your name."

Ginger: It's Ginger. You know my name. We've already spoken a bunch of times, and I live next door to you. Why are you asking me again?

Maggie: Protocol. What's your last name, Ginger?

Ginger: Wray. I'm Ginger Wray.

Maggie: Have you ever had another name?

Ginger: I was Dumont before I married Ace. Ginger Dumont. Dumont was my maiden-name.

Maggie: I see. And you have a sister, is that right?

Ginger: You know that, too, but you said Brandi's dead. And I have questions for you about that. Like, who killed her? And how did she die? I haven't seen her in three days. And now you say she's dead. Tell me right now what's going on.

Maggie: When did you last see her?

Ginger: She came by our house late Tuesday night. She had Tuesdays off, and this week she had Wednesday off, too.

Maggie: How long did she stay?

Ginger: Not long. She was angry when she came and said she had been robbed and accused me of theft. I was never in her room, and didn't know what she was talking about, although I figured it was her jewelry collection, but she started yelling. She blamed me for stealing her stuff, then for killing our mother. She was off her rocker. Ace didn't like it when we fought and told her to leave. She did, and that's the last I saw of her. I don't know anything else. Now can I see Ace?

Maggie: Why did she think you stole her stuff and why did she blame you for your mother's murder?

Ginger: She had been bringing small bags and shoeboxes of stuff over for a few weeks. She didn't say what they were, and everything was tied or taped shut like she was afraid someone would snoop. I would have had to use a knife to get into them and she told me not to open them. She was crazy about jewelry. I asked her what they were once and she blew up at me, so I didn't ask again. She blamed Ace for murdering Mom, but he didn't, and I guess she transferred that blame to me. She had a terrible temper, although most people didn't know about it. To other people she always seemed mild mannered. She said she was going to make some changes and needed a safe place to leave some stuff, whatever it was. I think she was hiding the jewelry that she and Mom had accumulated before Mom was murdered. Ace had told me about a tunnel he had discovered near the cemetery on one of his early morning walks. He said it was well hidden so I helped her stow the bags in the tunnel. I didn't tell Ace or anyone so nobody knew she was hiding stuff except her and me, unless she told somebody. I don't think she would tell anyone.

Maggie's heart quickened as she asked: Are the boxes and bags in the tunnel now?

Ginger: I don't know, I think so. Nobody knows about the tunnel, except Ace and me, but I don't think he ever went into it, although I never asked. He didn't say one way or another. I'm sure it is one of those mining tunnels that people talk about, but it's abandoned. It has a metal gate and I put a lock on it. The lock was rusted through, but I didn't have another, and it wasn't secure, I mean, someone could just lift it off. Brandi wanted me to buy a better one, but I kept forgetting. Plus, Ace didn't like me to leave the house. Maybe I should do that today after I see Ace.

Maggie: Brandi's dead, so we should have a look to see what she put in the tunnel. It might be valuable, like you said, jewelry or even old coins. And it might help us figure out who killed her. I'll grab Cagey and we can have a look. We'll help you move it somewhere safe.

Chapter 59

Maggie, Cagey, and Ginger
Present Day

Maggie wasn't convinced that Ginger would cooperate and left the handcuffs on despite Ginger's loud protest. The attack on Cagey had been enough to have arrested her, so Maggie was taking no chances. Brick had returned from his visit with Mary Grace and kept his eye on Ace while Cagey positioned and belted Ginger into the back seat of Maggie's rig.

The cemetery, located a couple hundred yards from Ginger and Ace's home, was hidden from view by trees and shrubs and a rather large pile of rocks. Ginger led them through the field and into the cemetery. They stepped over a small metal fence, dropped down a slight incline, and the red metal gate stood before them. The gate was closed, but the lock lay on the ground where Brick had dropped it.

"The padlock is off," Ginger cried out. "Somebody has been in here. This lock was there when I was here last, a couple days ago. I should have bought a new padlock. I wonder who has been in the tunnel. I wonder if Brandi's boxes and bags are still there!"

Cagey swung the gate open and entered. Maggie laid her hand on Ginger's shoulder and guided her through the gate. Ginger looked at Maggie, as if she wanted reassurance and stepped timidly into the tunnel.

Maggie and Cagey looked around, pretending they had no knowledge of this tunnel, even though they both had been in it recently.

Cagey rested his hand on his pistol but didn't remove it from his holster. Maggie remained back a few steps with Ginger while Cagey forged ahead, using his cell phone to light the way. He lit up one side of the tunnel, and Maggie's flashlight lit up the other.

"Where's the light switch, Ginger?" Maggie asked, hoping she had more knowledge of the tunnel than she admitted. "It's so dark in here."

"It's under the AstroTurf. If you uncuff me, I'll open it." Ginger said. She held her hands up showing Maggie her arms, as if Maggie didn't know the cuffs were on her. Cagey watched while Maggie frowned and slowly complied. Ginger leaned down and pulled up a corner of the AstroTurf and flipped a switch that had been embedded in the floor. A dim light from a small blue bulb emitted some light. It was so small that neither Maggie nor Brick had seen it.

"Thanks, that helps, but where did you put Brandi's bags, her treasures?" Maggie asked.

"They were here, but now I don't know where they are. Maybe they were stolen by whomever broke the lock off. Or maybe Brandi moved them without saying anything to me," Ginger said, looking around the tunnel. The tunnel was cool, and she folded her arms around herself.

"Let's go a little farther, maybe we'll see something," Cagey said, leading the way with his cell phone lighting the way.

They continued walking until they reached the door to the bomb shelter. "What is this?" Ginger said. "I never came this far into the tunnel. It's too dark and creepy, and I didn't like being here."

Cagey twisted the door that led to the bomb shelter and gave a fake pull, as he shined his light on the knob and around the sides of the door, "It's locked, Maggie. I wonder where it goes."

Maggie didn't say anything for a few seconds, but added, "Let's go back to Ginger's house, it's cold in here. We'll ask you a few more questions, Ginger, and then leave you alone for a while."

Cagey jumped in and said, "No, Maggie, let's go to the office. We'll have to deal with Peaches, and he's not a nice dog."

"Peaches is gone," Ginger said. "I didn't like him either, and when you put Ace in jail, I got rid of him."

"What did you do with him, Ginger," Cagey asked, thinking Peaches might become a stray that they would have to keep track of.

Ginger's eyes glistened with pleasure, "I used my rifle and shot him. I'm a good shot, and I buried him out in the desert. I didn't like him, but I didn't want the coyotes and buzzards to find him."

Maggie asked a trio of questions, "You killed your own dog? Won't Ace be mad? Where's your gun?"

Ginger answered with a smile, "Yes, I did. Yes, he will be. And, in my house."

Chapter 60

Maggie, Cagey, and Ginger
Present Day

Maggie, Cagey, and Ginger went to the Wray's house, the two officers hoping that Ginger would be more talkative and cooperative if they were in her house rather than sitting in an interview room at the sheriff's office. It was a ploy Maggie had tried before, sometimes it worked, other times not.

Maggie took the lead, "Ginger, this is the thing, if you want us to find Brandi's murderer, we need to know more about her. You were her sister and probably knew her better than anyone, so let's talk about Brandi, what she liked, didn't like, what she thought about being a working girl at the Chicken Dinner Ranch. She must have talked to you about her life at the CDR. You indicated you saw her often and it was a surprise when she didn't come by last week. Being a working girl is not a normal job, and she had a college degree and taught school, and apparently liked it, so let's start then, back in Reno, before your mom died. Tell us about Brandi and her life in Reno."

"I don't know, it was life, you know," Ginger began. "She taught school during the week, and she and Mom did their Q2 thing on the weekends. They didn't talk to me about it much, but they said they had fun. I couldn't see the fun in it because rummaging through other people's throwaways and old stuff, felt like a foolish waste of time. I thought the jewelry was junk, mismatched, broken, and grimy, and they had to work hard to restore it. Mom would spend hours polishing a little piece of a ruby or chipped emerald. So tedious and boring. I couldn't see the use in it. It certainly gave me no joy," Ginger said. "I tried it once, but my fingers got sore."

"But they earned quite a lot of money, didn't they?" Cagey asked.

"I'm not sure because you couldn't believe Brandi. She said that they turned pennies into dollars, but she didn't buy any better clothes and her car was old and beat up. She didn't travel or go to plays or do anything that people do if they have extra money, so my thought was that if she earned so much money, wouldn't she have bought some things to make her life more pleasurable?" Ginger avoided Cagey's eyes as her eyes darted from floor to ceiling and back again.

"Did she ever talk about the money?" Cagey asked, urging her to continue.

"Before Mom died, I asked Brandi about the money once, and she got mad and told me it wasn't any of my business. But later she admitted that she didn't really know how much they earned because Mom tended their earnings and put them in a bank in Reno. Neither of them trusted banks nor opened bank accounts, but rather used safe deposit boxes. The police in Reno have already asked me these same questions, so why are you asking them again?" Ginger asked.

"Because you talked to the Reno police and not us, and I haven't seen their files, so continue, please," Maggie said bluntly.

Cagey was convinced that the root of the mysterious two deaths had to do with money, so he pressed on. "Did Brandi ever tell you how much money they had? Hundreds? Thousands? It might make a difference in what she did with it, like investments, savings, donations," Cagey repeated. "If she didn't spend it, what did she do with it?"

Ginger frowned and set her lips in a straight line and laughed. "They didn't trust banks, as I said, so I don't think they invested their money either.

And as far as donations, Brandi would never have donated to anybody except herself, so I don't know about that. I don't know how much money they had or what they did with it. Maybe they had a lot, but Brandi never said. She was secretive. She did tell me she closed the safe deposit boxes a few days before she left Reno though. She must have kept that money."

"How much money was in the safe deposit boxes? Did she say?" Maggie asked.

"No, she didn't say, but maybe a lot because Brandi discovered that our mom had two safe deposit boxes, not just one. I reasoned she had one for the jewelry they bought and repaired and one for money," Ginger said, "but that wasn't how it was. Mom had two boxes because she was hiding part of their income."

Maggie's eyes darted from Ginger to Cagey, "Your mother was hiding money from Brandi? What did she do?" This was new information. Perhaps not the smoking gun, but something that was not included in the reports she had read.

Ginger paused, wondering if she was saying too much. Brandi had kept that information a secret from the police and her. No one except Brandi had known the existence of a second safe deposit box until she accidentally divulged it in a fit of rage. This shouting match had gotten Brandi tossed from their house. But now, as Ginger sat silently with Maggie and Cagey, she realized that she could tell all because Brandi was dead, and she was likely the sole heir to whatever Brandi had stored away and that would be terrific. Ace would like it, too.

Ginger began to tell her story, "No one knew about the second safe deposit box, especially the police, but when Brandi looked for the key to the box that she knew about, she discovered the second key. It turned out that Mom was cheating her, not splitting the money as they had agreed because Mom did a one-for-you and two-for-me type of deal. They had repaired and sold jewelry for two or three years and accumulated a tidy sum, but Mom avoided talking about how much money was coming in, and Brandi never pressed her. Who would think that her own mother was stealing from her? You want the motive for Brandi killing Mom, you found your motive. Her own mother was stealing from her."

Ginger's face tightened, and she looked at the two officers. "Mom had retired early and couldn't live on her pension and social security. She liked to do things with her friends, golf and lunches and day trips, like everyone else her age did. Brandi was the brains behind their business with a designer's eye, and she had a much better business sense than Mom. She was first in everything, and she wanted to be the expert on their business as well. She designed the jewelry and bargained with the people running the estate sales, and had the internet expertise to sell online. The biggest mistake was when she turned over the actual transaction part of their business to Mom, who thought that cleaning and polishing the gems was worth more than half of their earnings, because it was hard work. And she needed the money. Brandi kept so busy with school during the week and estate sales on the weekends, she didn't have time for anything else. I don't even think she dated."

Maggie asked, "Did Brandi ever tell you what was in the safe deposit boxes?"

"She never said, but I assume it was cash and maybe some jewelry," Ginger answered.

"How about gold?" Maggie asked, thinking of the cigar box they had found in the bomb shelter.

"She didn't mention that she had been paid in gold, except one time she showed me a gold nugget that somebody had given to her as a tip at the CDR. She said it wasn't the first. She didn't know how much it was worth, but it was about the size of a large marble, and she laughed about it. She told me that she had worn a blond wig, and he called her 'Goldilocks,'" Ginger said. She smiled, thinking of their conversation.

"Did she open a bank account or have a safe deposit box at the bank here in Barrier or someplace else?" Cagey asked.

Ginger answered, "As I have already said, she doesn't like or trust banks. So, if she did, I would be surprised. I guess you could check, but I don't know. She didn't have a car, so she would have used the local bank if she changed her mind. Maybe we'll find a statement or a key in her room. I'd actually really like to see her room. I've never been in it."

"How about friends? Did she have many friends?" Maggie asked. "It seems everyone liked her, so I would think she would have had a lot of friends, you know, people she liked to hang out with."

Ginger shrugged, "I don't think so, just her coworkers. She never mentioned anyone except Jay by name, and nobody came with her when she came to our house. I've never seen her out with anyone because I mostly stay home. She told me a lot of the working girls went to church, but she didn't. She stopped for coffee many mornings at the Panorama Hotel after her walk. She liked hearing the stories of the young women who were new to the United States. She walked four miles every day to keep herself fit and used the gym equipment that Jay provided. She was in shape with taut skin. Ace called her buff."

Maggie continued, "How about boyfriends? Did she have a boyfriend? She was a working girl, but even so, she was young and attractive. Surely, she had somebody special. Did she talk about anybody in particular?"

Ginger offered an explanation, "She had a lot of regulars, she called them, men who came back a few times, but she didn't call them boyfriends. I don't think she dated anyone if that's what you mean. During high school, boys were wild about her because she flirted. She had a date every weekend, sometimes two, and she'd stand one or both of them up and go hang out with a different group and flirt with those boys. Then, she would laugh about it, but they came back. I remember once being in the cafeteria, and I noticed a big crowd of boys, maybe a dozen, and she was right in the center of the group. She had incredible charisma.

"But Brandi had a dark side, too. She liked to lie and trick people with her lies. When we were kids, she lied to and about me all the time, which got me in trouble with our parents. She would conjure up a scam, pull off the prank, and I'd be the one blamed for it. Some were tame, like switching out various food items, one for another, like seasoning cookies with chili powder instead of cinnamon. Those were mean, but we learned to live with them. And watch for them. Mom bought a new set of golf clubs once, and Brandi was so mad about something that she hid the driver under the car. When Mom drove to work, she ran over it and smashed it. I was no angel, but I wasn't like her."

Cagey sighed, "But didn't she have anybody regular? Barrier doesn't have a lot of available young men, most are married, but it seems that someone might have given her a look during the four years. She was a good-looking woman, a knockout even."

Maggie glanced at Cagey wondering why he hadn't given her a look and raised her eyebrows, but she would hold those questions for later. She had never known Cagey to date anyone, but he had noticed Brandi and called her a knockout.

Ginger didn't answer for a minute, then said, "She made me promise not to tell, but she's dead now, so I guess it doesn't make any difference. She did love somebody for a long time, but he ended it, although she didn't tell me why. She was in love with Jay."

Cagey's head snapped up at the mention of his brother. "Are you saying she had a thing for Jay? That can't be right. He's my brother, and I don't believe you because he once told me that he would never date one of the working girls. They weren't his cup of tea."

"I never saw them together, but that's what she said. Something happened though. I don't know what it was, but when he broke it off, she wanted to leave Barrier and quit the CDR. I think that's why she was putting stuff in the tunnel. She was sneaking everything out, maybe planning to disappear one day. She and Jay kept their affair quiet, but when he broke it off permanently, she went crazy and wanted to walk away, to leave and escape him. She wanted me to leave Ace and go with her. She said she had enough money for us to go to a deserted island and lie on the beach all day where no one would bother us."

"Like I said, Jay told me he would never date a working girl, too much mileage," Cagey repeated.

Ginger smiled and said, "I'll bet that was before he met the bewitching Brandi."

Chapter 61

Maggie and Brick
Present Day

Maggie and Cagey removed the handcuffs from Ginger and left her at home. They returned to the sheriff's office, but instead of going inside, Cagey went a different direction. He hadn't said a word in the car, but his face had reddened, and his lower lip trembled. He switched cars and yelled out the window to Maggie, "I'll be back after I talk to Jay. I want to know what the H this is about. I don't think he was involved with Brandi. He viewed the working girls as that, working girls, and would never have gotten involved. No, he wouldn't have."

Maggie started to say that he should wait, but Cagey roared out of the sheriff's office parking lot, leaving a cloud of dust.

Maggie took a deep breath and went into the office where Brick was waiting. "Hey, Maggie. I need to go back to the house to see how Terry is coming along on the swimming pool. He said they would probably finish digging today, but I'd like to check their progress. I interviewed Mary Grace and wrote out the notes from our conversation so you can see what she said. Brandi was scared and thought someone was going to kill her, but who? Ace or Ginger? Who else?"

Maggie said, "I have another name for our list that might answer your question about who else. Jay. Cagey and I just came from a conversation with

Ginger. She led us to the tunnel, but I don't think she had walked beyond that first ten feet that is bricked in, but she knew where the light switch was. She said that Brandi had put small bags of something in the tunnel, but they disappeared, vanished, at least not in plain sight. She didn't know what Brandi had stored in the bags, so that's another puzzle. It could be money or gems or gold or something else. We walked all the way to our door of the bomb shelter, and it seemed like she had never seen it before. I don't think she was acting, but if she was, she should be winning academy awards.

"Cagey and I decided to interview her at home, and she finally relaxed, and we got her to talk about Brandi. At first, she was wishy-washy, didn't know or admit to anything, but later she threw us a wrinkle. She said that Jay and Brandi had been having an affair and had recently broken up. After they broke up, Brandi decided to quit the CDR and Jay had objected, of course, because she made a lot of money for him. I wonder why he broke it off. If he were in love with her, that would add some spice to the stew."

"Jay? Holy cow! As far as I knew, Jay never messed with any of his girls. He saw them as money makers and cared for them, but never got involved with any of them. I've never seen him with any of them outside the CDR," Brick said.

Maggie nodded, "Cagey went to the CDR where he's going to confront Jay about their relationship, and maybe we'll add Jay to the list of people who might have motive to kill Brandi."

"I'm having difficulty thinking that Jay would kill anyone, let alone Brandi. She was his number one moneymaker. Besides that, he's the mayor, and although people don't necessarily approve of the CDR, they like him," Brick answered. "I'll tell you what, you and Sammy can stay here and rest while I join Cagey at the CDR. Cagey has a good sense of direction, but he and Jay are brothers, and we don't want this to go sideways. I'll check on Terry after I return."

Chapter 62

Maggie and Joyce
Present Day

Maggie poured herself a cup of coffee and sat down and raised her feet, placing them on a chair. They had been swelling at night, and she thought elevating them might help. It had been a trying morning, and she welcomed a little respite. Sammy seemed to be hyper-active this week, maybe reacting to her stress. The easy week she had anticipated shot out the window, with one thing after another, and her mind was cluttered with problems waiting to be solved. She was in the process of sorting out the issues, prioritizing, and piecing things together when the phone rang.

"Maggie, it's Joyce Givens. Do you have a minute?"

Maggie answered quickly, "Sure, Joyce. Is everything okay? Did you lay eyes on our potential prowler yet?"

"No, that's not what I am calling about," Joyce snapped. "I'm calling about our neighbor, Ace. I understand he's in jail, and I'm curious to know why. I heard he murdered somebody, one of the working girls at the CDR. Is that true? We can't have a murderer living in our rental property. We just can't. I thought the Wrays were a little odd, but never considered that he was a murderer. And what about Ginger, is she a murderer, too?" Joyce was talking fast, and her voice was cracking.

"Slow down, Joyce. Where did you hear this?" Maggie asked.

"Bob heard it at the pizza shop. He said it's all over town, and I'm nervous. How could we have an ax murderer living in our house? How could we? Aren't you and Brick worried, too, with your little boys outside?"

"Slow down, Joyce," Maggie repeated. "There's no ax murderer."

Maggie spoke slowly and definitely, "I'm really not at liberty to tell you anything right now, Joyce, and won't until we manage all the details we know so far. You and Bob are safe enough and shouldn't worry. Cagey and I will sort all this out, and I'm sure you'll hear all the details soon enough."

"And another thing, Maggie, just so you know, earlier in the week, I was looking out the window. I might have already told Cagey this, I don't remember, but I've been watching for the prowler, like Cagey said we should, when I saw a young woman run out of their house and down the incline toward town. Actually, I didn't tell Cagey this because I'm just remembering now. It was fifteen or twenty minutes later and had gotten darker, when I saw another person run out the front door, but that person jumped in a vehicle. I think it was a pickup or van. I don't know if it was a man or woman, could have been Ace or Ginger, but I don't think so. The person was a little hunched over and moved more slowly, so I'm thinking it was someone older. I'm not sure as it was barely light. Was Ginger's sister the one who was killed? Bob said she was a call girl at the CDR. Did Ace kill her? And one more thing, Maggie, what about that dog? He's gone. Maybe Ace killed him, too. I didn't like him much, but I don't think he's at their house anymore."

"That's one thing I can tell you about. Their dog, Peaches, is gone, and you don't have to worry about him anymore."

Chapter 63

Brick and Jay
Present Day

When Brick arrived at the CDR, two tour buses sat outside, both with red and blue labels emblazoned across the length of the buses, reading See Nevada First! He smiled to himself at the thought of senior citizens filling out their bucket list by telling their friends they had once been in a brothel. They would eat a meal, but elaborate that they had done other things, too. Jay offered free pie for bus drivers, and with the already inexpensive food, everyone was happy.

"Where's Jay?" Brick asked the hostess. "I need to see him."

"I think he's in his office with his brother. You know where it is, don't you?"

Brick nodded and picked up his pace toward the rear of the building, noting the crowd of white-headed men and women enjoying the traditional chicken dinner and trimmings, including home-made apple pie. Even if they didn't tell their friends about the brothel, they would tell them about the fried chicken and apple pie.

Brick rapped on the office door, "Jay, it's Brick, could we talk?" A few seconds later, he swung the door open and saw Cagey and Jay sitting across from each other but neither smiled when they saw him.

"I suppose you want to know about Brandi, too. She was murdered, and now you two think I had something to do with it," Jay growled.

"I didn't say you had anything to do with her murder," Cagey scowled back, "I want to know why you never told me about her. You always said the brothel girls were off limits."

Jay answered, "It's really none of your business, Cagey. I don't have to tell you who I date or don't date. High school was a long time ago."

"It is my business when somebody is killed and she was, so you need to be..." Cagey snapped as his forehead vein grew bigger.

Brick interrupted the bantering, "Stop it." He glared at both and they knew he meant business. "What kind of relationship did you and Brandi have, Jay? Romantic? Sexual? Friends? We're trying to figure out who killed her, and it seems odd that no one knows anything about her."

Jay responded without hesitation, "I don't know much about her. She showed up here with a truck driver four years ago and clammed up about the rest of her life. She told me she had a sister, Ginger, and one day Ginger and Ace appeared in the bar for a meal. I met Ace one time, and by the way, he was an ass. I kicked him out of the CDR, and as far as I know, he's never set foot in my establishment since."

"You don't kick many people out of the CDR, so what did he do to annoy you?" Brick asked.

"He and his wife, Brandi's sister, were eating dinner. Brandi walked by and he grabbed her. You know I don't let anybody manhandle my girls, so I threw him out. Her sister finished her meal, but she's never returned either, at least not that I'm aware of."

"Why don't we start at the beginning, the day you hired her?" Brick asked.

Jay sat back and crossed his arms. "That's easy, a one-liner. She showed up, I offered her a job, she said no, then changed her mind and said yes, and went to work. That's it, nothing more. She said she was from California, but all my girls claim to be from California. It must be the place to be from."

"Did you know her last name was Dumont?" Brick asked, "Dumont, as in the Candice Dumont murder in Reno about five years ago? Do you recall that murder? It was high profile, all over the news."

"I didn't connect when I hired her, but I do now. I had heard of the murder, but I didn't realize that she was Candice Dumont's daughter. I'm not a cop, so I don't think the same way you two do," Jay answered.

Brick looked at Cagey before asking the next question, "Did you ever date Brandi, I mean, take her out to dinner or spend extra time with her? Did you sleep with her?"

"Hell no! She was like all the others, making a buck at what she did best, and she was good at it, too. She had a knack for convincing customers to return and it's the repeat customers who keep money coming in. She had a bunch of regulars," Jay said. "Between her looks, her physique, and her other talents, she was a busy girl and made me a lot of money."

"Do you sleep with your girls?" Brick was watching Jay closely, trying to figure out if he was lying or telling the truth. He knew Jay had been honest with him in the past, and he hoped he was now, but his story and Ginger's were at odds.

Jay paused before he answered this question, "It would be dishonest of me to say that I haven't, I mean, that's the business I'm in, and it's in my best interest to know their style. Whether they have aggressive or passive sexual inclinations, what they like to do, that type of thing, but I don't bedroom hop, if that's what you mean. I didn't treat Brandi different from the other girls. She had a way about her that made her clients feel special. Incredibly special. She had a gift."

Chapter 64

Maggie and Reno Police
Present Day

Maggie sat alone in her office, outlining their case on her white board—who was telling what, the contradictions, and unanswered questions. Her sketch looked like a bad road map. Maggie saw three possible suspects for Brandi's murder: Ginger, Ace, and the newest person of interest, Jay. Inconsistencies drilled holes in their stories, and the three suspects contradicted each other in nearly every aspect of the case. It would take at least one more round of questions, possibly more. She decided to switch out interviewers and she would interview Jay, Brick would visit with Ginger, and Cagey would discuss the case with Ace and his attorney. Something was out of place, but she didn't know what was missing, had been omitted, or moved.

A Reno police SUV pulled into her parking lot as she was completing her map and timeline of what they did and didn't know. She looked up as two men entered the office and introduced themselves, Detective Burns and Detective Lawrence, both members of the Reno police. She didn't know them, but they both looked like cops. No doubt about it. She had been half-expecting them to show up, but they hadn't called.

Detective Burns pulled out a handkerchief and mopped his brow. "Can I have some water, please? Our air conditioning quit working on the way here.

No one in Nevada should be without air. It feels good in here." His eyes noted her badge but quickly fell to Maggie's swollen abdomen. He offered Maggie a toothy grin and said, "I guess that's a baby, Sheriff. Congratulations."

Maggie opened her mini fridge and pulled out two bottles of water. "Thanks, and it is true, June does get mighty warm some days. Today is brutal. I don't think I want to know what we have in store for July and August."

They apologized for not having called, and she invited them to sit down and ask their questions.

Burns said, "You and I haven't met, but we have talked on the phone. I'm sure you remember that we investigated the Candice Dumont murder of five years ago. We've never stopped looking, but it's now a cold case since we've had no luck making progress about who killed her. Ace Wray has been on our mind, but something always seems to get in the way of charging him. And now Candice's daughter, Brandi, is dead. Is Wray a suspect in her murder, too? We thought that Brandi Dumont knew more than she let on, but she disappeared, and we couldn't find her, never considering that she would go to work in a brothel. Apparently, a brothel is a good place to hide, not to mention the fact that Barrier is so small that it's hardly on anyone's radar."

Maggie remained silent, letting the two officers tell their story.

Lawrence continued, "The sisters, Brandi and Ginger, were suspects. Brandi was caustic and didn't want to talk with us, which prioritized her as a suspect. She withdrew from life, hiding, first in Reno and then falling off the grid when she came to Barrier. The other daughter, Ginger, dragged her feet about talking to us but was such a mouse that we couldn't believe that she would have killed her mother. She looked like she wouldn't harm a fly. Those two girls were sure different."

Maggie sat listening without responding, but thought, *maybe not that different. Ginger attacked Cagey and killed her dog. That was something. Maybe she has more depth than you think.*

Burns' dull expression became duller, "We want to talk to Ace, Ginger, and the owner of the brothel. We think our Candice case and your Brandi case are tied together and maybe we can help each other, Sheriff."

Maggie said, "Sure, we can help you, but I'd like one of us to be a part of the interviews. I have only two deputies, but the three of us cover a lot of ground. I'm guessing that when we divulge everything we know about both cases, we will find several commonalities between the two. I think we should dive in and see what we can figure out. Who wants to go first?"

"I think we should start with Ace. If he's locked up, let's talk to him first," Burns said.

"Yes, he's locked up, but he's also lawyered up, so we will need to locate his lawyer. His lawyer is excellent at what he does and can be a pretty smooth operator, but mostly he cooperates. He's continuously busy, though, so it might be tough. He is the only lawyer in Barrier, which makes him the part-time public defender. He also has a private practice, mostly mining and real estate law. I'll call him and see if he is available right now."

Cy Rudd, the public defender, knew everything worth knowing. He hadn't been in Barrier long but was an extrovert and knew nearly everybody and everything that happened in Barrier. Maggie speed dialed him, and he answered immediately. He had a secretary, but unless he was with someone else, he answered his own phone. "Personal service, that's what people want," was his motto.

Cy had desert allergies and had a habit of snorting when he started to speak. "Hrrgggg. I was coming later, but I can break free in about an hour, and I'd love to see you, Maggie. Will an hour work for you?" Cy was a country lawyer, a good-old-boy type guy, and not much got by him.

"An hour, Detectives. Cy will be here in an hour, so why don't you go across the street for a slice of pepperoni or cup of coffee. Just don't be late getting back here because Cy won't wait," Maggie said with a smile. Country lawyer or not, he was slick and would put the two detectives through the wringer.

Chapter 65

Maggie and Cy
Present Day

Cy arrived at the sheriff's office ahead of schedule. "Hrrgggg, I know I'm early," he said, "I don't like these city slicker detectives and want a head start on them. They think we are hayseeds and don't know nothin.'"

Cy and his wife Ruth had retired to Barrier two years before and found a nice acreage ten miles from town. They aimed to raise llamas and alpacas during the day and drink good whiskey at night. That plan kept him occupied for the better part of a year, but he found he missed the challenges of a law practice. When the public defender position came open, he jumped at the chance to reopen his practice. Ruth was glad to have him out of the house and agreed to care for the animals when he went back to work. He was happy as a hyena because, unlike the big city, in Barrier, he didn't have to wear a suit and tie and could work as many or few hours as he wanted. He found that he didn't care much for tending the animals, so left them to Ruth. When he had extra time, he fished for bass and crappie.

Originally from Pahrump, Nevada, Cy had attended a premier law school on the east coast but returned to Carson City where he built the largest and most successful firm in the city. He purposefully developed an unmistakable twang, which made other lawyers think he was a country bumpkin, which was far from the truth. In fact, he was a brilliant attorney and could out-think and out-pace his legal opponents, leaving them trying to figure out what happened.

And now, he would represent Ace.

Maggie offered Cy a bottle of water and started talking, "I'm glad you came by early because I wanted to mention another issue with your client, too, Cy. You might have heard a rumor about the murder of one of Jay's working girls, and Ace is a suspect in that killing, too. Her name is Brandi Dumont, and she's the daughter of Candice Dumont—the woman murdered in Reno five years ago and she is also Ace's sister-in-law. His wife's sister. Depending on the time of death, he could have killed her, but he might have already been in jail. WW hasn't determined the time of death yet, as she was in the moat and the water distorted her body temp. Ace has not been charged with that killing, in fact, we haven't mentioned her death to him. I'll be watching his reaction when we do."

Cy inhaled quickly, "Hrrgggg. I'm glad you told me. What about his wife? I've forgotten her name. Has she been charged?"

"Ginger, her name is Ginger. No, she has not been charged yet, and we've got another suspect, as well, but I will fill you in on him later," Maggie said. "What I will say is that right now, we've got a lot of ends on this ball of twine, and it keeps growing bigger."

Chapter 66

Maggie, Ace, and Cy
Present Day

Detectives Burns and Lawrence entered the office three minutes before their appointment and were surprised to see Maggie and Cy Rudd deep in conversation.

Maggie introduced the men and Cy said, "Hrrgggg. I'm glad to meet you. I haven't seen my client yet so I'd like to spend a few minutes with him. You can join us in about fifteen minutes, then you can ask your questions," Cy told them as he headed toward the interview room. "Sheriff, can you bring him into the interview room for me? Hrrgggg."

Two minutes later, Maggie escorted Ace to the interview room, attached him to the table's center bar, and left the room to rejoin the two Reno detectives. Burns said, "Fifteen minutes? That is all the time he wants to talk with his client that he's never seen before? That's hardly enough time to say hello."

Maggie laughed, "Don't worry. He'll have everything he needs in less than fifteen minutes."

Exactly fourteen minutes later, Cy called to Maggie, "Hrrgggg. Time's wasting, so let's get a move on, Sheriff. You had something you wanted to tell Ace, so you can go first. Detectives, you'll have to wait a little longer."

Maggie told Ace of Brandi's death, omitting the cause of death and that he was a suspect. Ace shook his head, "Dead? Brandi? Was it one of her johns, I mean her clients? I don't understand. Was she shot at the CDR?"

Maggie watched him carefully, watching for any inconsistencies in what he said and how he reacted, but didn't see any. If he was lying, he was doing a good job at it.

"No, she wasn't at the CDR. She was at the bed and breakfast, where you work. Do you know anything about her murder? Did you see her at the B & B?"

"Does Ginger know? I never saw her at the B & B. She came to our house occasionally, but I don't think she was ever at the B & B. In fact, last year when I told her I worked there, she asked where it was because she had never heard of it."

Maggie returned to her office, gathered five bottles of water, and invited Detectives Burns and Lawrence to join them. She clicked on the recorder while Lawrence pulled out his notebook and began taking notes. Burns unfolded his list of questions and began the conversation, "Hello again, Ace, long time, no see."

Ace: Too soon for me.

Burns: How about we start where we left off a year ago? Tell us about the night your mother-in-law was murdered. Where were you?

Ace: You know the story, Burns, I was at work. I was a janitor at the casino, working graveyard shift.

Lawrence: That's what you said, but didn't you take a break in the middle of your shift and were late when you came back on duty? You've never really answered that question, so why were you late?

Ace: I already told you, I had to take a dump and it took longer than the ten-minute break.

Lawrence: That's what you said, but did you talk to anybody?

Ace: Do you talk to people when you take a dump?

Cy: Hrrgggg. Enough of the dump talk. This is inane. You don't have to answer any more questions, Ace."

Ace: I have one more thing to say. I'm sick of this harassment and I suppose it will start again about Brandi's death. But I'm in jail, so how could I have killed her?

Maggie: Nobody said you did, Ace but somebody did, so if not you, who? Ginger?

Ace: No, not Ginger. She loved her sister. Well, maybe not loved her, but they were still sisters. It was more resentment because Brandi and Candice did hurtful things to Ginger.

Maggie: Like what?

Ace: For example, neither Brandi nor Candice bothered to come to our wedding and that really got in Ginger's craw. They finally sent a present, a cutting board, shaped like the state of Nevada. I'm sure they thought it was great, but we thought it odd. And Ginger never got over the bike thing.

Maggie: What bike thing?

Ace: It was total jealousy. Sister rivalry, but it stayed with Ginger all these years. For her eighth birthday, Candice gave Brandi a fancy, brand-new banana-seat bike, Ginger thought her parents would buy her one when she turned eight, too, but on her eighth birthday, they didn't even make her a cake, let alone a bike. She cried and cried, and a few days later, Candice found a used bike at a garage sale and bought it, but it wasn't like Brandi's bike, all shiny and pretty with a pink banana seat. The seat was duct-taped together, one of the grips was missing, the brakes didn't work, and it had a flat tire.

Maggie: That's pretty awful, but it was twenty-odd years ago, a long time to hold a grudge.

Ace: I suppose, but Ginger never forgave Brandi.

Maggie: It wasn't Brandi's fault, Candice did it. Why would she hold a grudge against Brandi?

Murder in the Brothel

Ace: It wasn't the only time, but this one was the one that she remembered, and it comes up on her birthday every year. I've even thought about buying her a brand-new bike. Eight-year-old girls can be irrational.

Burns: I wish I had known how distorted their relationship was earlier, maybe we could have saved some heartburn. Do you have any other information that we might want to know about?

Ace: No, their relationship was rocky, but why don't you ask Jacque? He might be able give you more details than I can.

Lawrence: Jacque? Candice's husband? He's never been in the picture. You and Ginger said you didn't know where he was, and he's never come back to Reno. At least, we've never seen his name come up in our research. He had already blown town when Candice died and both Brandi and Ginger said they never saw him after that. We thought he was dead. Is he alive?

Ace: That's not true. There were lies about that. Neither Brandi nor Ginger wanted any involvement with their dad. He lived in Carson City when Candice was killed.

Burns: Is he alive?

Ace: Yes, he is, I saw him yesterday and he might know more than you think.

Maggie: How could you have seen him yesterday? You were in jail.

Ace: Oh, that's true, but I have a window and he was here, right here in the sheriff's office. For about an hour. He drove a pickup with a camper shell on it. His name is Jacque, but he must have Americanized his name. It's been six years since I last saw him, but he looked the same, a little grayer and a few more pounds, but it was him. The logo on the truck said Jock's Locks.

Cy: Hrrgggg. No more. This conversation is over.

Chapter 67

Burns and Lawrence
Present Day

It was late in the afternoon and still over ninety degrees outside when the Reno police left the sheriff's office. They had spent much of the afternoon speculating about Jacque or Jock, whichever name he preferred. No one had seen his pickup since he had opened the gun safe and left the office. Maybe he had departed Barrier.

Earlier in the day, Burns and Lawrence had deposited their car at the repair shop to address the air conditioning, but the owner said he'd need at least 24 hours. That meant the Reno officers were not only stuck in Barrier, but also were on foot. They debated which of the three locales they should stay in. All were owned by Jay Guzman with a variety of offerings.

Detective Burns wanted to stay at the Panorama, located within a two-minute walk from the sheriff's office. It was ancient, a part of Barrier history, and had great food and reasonable rates, well within the Reno Police Department's budget. Burns was tired and thought that a good meal and glass of whiskey would put him to sleep.

Detective Lawrence thought otherwise. His wife had been lobbying for a weekend excursion to the Barrier B & B, and he thought this would be a good opportunity to check it out, with the police department paying the tab. No doubt that it would cost a bit over their budget, but if they supplemented the cost with a few dollars, the department wouldn't object. It would be a memorable experience and he could report its possibilities to his wife. But, with the murder investigation, was it a good idea?

Lawrence and Burns laughed about the third choice, the CDR and its great food, they didn't think the accounting department folks in Reno would understand.

They crossed the street to the Pizza Shoppe to drink a beer while they debated the pros and cons of each venue and found Cagey, a half beer ahead of them. He had ordered a pizza and invited them to join him. Cagey signaled Bob to bring them beers, and two Oly's appeared in record time.

"How did he know that I would want an Oly?" Burns asked. "It's the only beer that's really beer, but I can't buy it at home, except at the grocery store. All the restaurants and watering holes only carry craft beers these days."

"Bartender Bob is magic," Cagey chuckled, "besides, all he carries is Oly. It's a Barrier thing, beer minimalism. Where are you two hanging your hats tonight?"

Lawrence replied, "We aren't sure yet, but we should spend the time looking for Jacque. Do you think Ace was lying?"

Cagey answered, "My opinion? Ace would say anything to get himself off, but the pickup he described is accurate, so maybe he's coming clean."

Lawrence took another swig of his beer, "Tomorrow. We'll deal with Jacque tomorrow. In the meantime, let's finish this beer and decide where we are going to stay tonight. Burns wants to go to the Panorama. It is cheap and close, and they have food, since he is always hungry. But I want to go to the B & B. It's a destination place that my wife is crazy to visit, so I hoped to check it out. It's a little farther though, and Burns doesn't want to walk in the heat, so we're debating."

"I'll give you a lift, but you should go to the B & B. That's where Brandi died, and we haven't been able to gather much information from the manager, Mary Grace Brownly. No one will recognize you as police, and maybe you will see or hear something from one of the staff or guests that would be useful. Besides, that's where Ace worked. Lots of info is probably floating around someplace, but we haven't been able to gather much. I might be able to convince Maggie to pay the extra cost, too."

Chapter 68

Maggie and Ginger
Present Day

Maggie sent Cagey home for the rest of the day. His visit with Jay had worn him down and his usual positive disposition had turned sour. He hadn't had time off in three days and she thought a night away from the office would help. She left Brick with Ace and headed once again to see Ginger. She took the long way around town, watching for the pickup with the Jock's Locks logo on it, but she didn't see it. She felt sure that he was somewhere in town but had no idea where he would be. Although Barrier was a small town, it had many back streets and alleys where people and vehicles could be concealed or lost. Maybe he was with Ginger, which would make sense, but she hadn't spied his pickup from her own house next door. When she arrived, Ginger answered on the first knock.

"I'm looking for your dad, Ginger. Do you have any idea where he might be?" Maggie asked.

Ginger turned her head away from Maggie and said, "My dad? I don't know where he is. I haven't seen him in a long time, maybe since before Mom died." This was a half-truth because in fact, she hadn't seen him, but she knew of his comings and goings.

"Ginger, how am I going to find Brandi's killer if you keep lying to me? I believe you have seen him more often than you have told me, in fact, I think you have seen him recently, maybe even today. Ace told us that he, you, and Brandi lied to the Reno police about his whereabouts after he left your mom. I'm done with your lies and want you to come clean about your father."

Ginger sighed but invited Maggie into the house. "I don't like talking about my dad. He's a horrible person, and I don't want to have anything to do with him. He's one of the reasons that Brandi and I didn't get along. Maybe the main reason."

"I thought it was your mother that you disliked so strongly, not your dad. You've blamed your mom and Brandi for everything and have barely mentioned your father in any of our talks," Maggie said, clearly puzzled. Ace had also indicated the rift between Ginger and her mother, blaming it on the bike. Maggie knew that sibling rivalries could be brutal.

Ginger teared up and grabbed a handful of tissues as her cheeks grew wet. "None of this matters now that Brandi's dead. We did lie about him because we didn't want to have anything to do with him. He had been gone from our lives for a long time. He and Mom divorced years ago, I don't exactly remember when, but it was before Brandi went to college. I was just a teenager, maybe fourteen or fifteen, not much older.

"He was awful to us when we were kids, but I thought he was awful only to me, not Brandi, because he paid no attention to me. I was jealous because he and Brandi went places together and he bought her presents, like a birthday bike, and bragged about her, but he was much worse to her. I didn't know it until recently though."

Maggie prodded, "Yes, Ace told me about the bike. Long ago, but the hurt doesn't go away fast."

"Until we arrived in Barrier, I didn't know that he had sexually abused her all those years, starting when she was about five or six and continuing until she went to college. All those times when he bought her presents or took her for ice cream, he forced sex on her, abused her. Brandi said that Mom knew about it but didn't do anything and covered it up by paying extra attention to her, too. He had a sexual addiction and should have been locked up long ago." Ginger's jaw tightened, and her eyes showed fear and sadness.

"This was horrible, horrible for Brandi, but also you and your mother. Can you tell me more about what happened? Do you think he had anything to do with Brandi's death?" Maggie asked.

"He might have. I wondered if he killed Mom, but I had no proof, nothing but my dislike for him and how he treated us. Neither of us wanted to have any contact with him, obviously for different reasons. He had left Reno, moved somewhere else, but we hadn't seen or heard from him in maybe five or six years. The police never asked about him either, and as far as I know, they didn't follow through on our stories about his whereabouts.

"This is my theory, as stupid as it sounds, he killed her over golf. She loved to play golf, but he hated it and thought it was a waste of time. She had played at a local golf course all these years with a mismatched set of old garage sale clubs and mostly walked the course because she had no money to rent a golf cart, like her friends did," Ginger answered solemnly. She had not answered the sheriff's question, but Maggie let her go on. Maybe they were finally moving ahead.

"Sometime after Brandi went to college, Dad found Carlotta, a former call girl at one of the brothels near Carson City and married her, or at least lived with her. He said they got married, but I didn't believe him.

"Anyway, financially, when Mom and Dad were together, they were okay for retirement, but when he left her, he took whatever money he had with him, and she had nothing but a tiny school pension and her social security. I am guessing that she wanted more, like most of her friends had, but most of all she wanted to play golf more. I know she called him for some reason and was surprised when Carlotta answered and informed Mom that she was his new wife. Mom hadn't known about Carlotta, but when she investigated, she discovered her past. Evidently Dad had been seeing her for many years. Mom wanted revenge and tried to put a squeeze on him for more money by threatening him to expose his wife as a hooker, but he wouldn't budge, and two days later, she was murdered. End of story. Maybe he did murder her, but as far as we knew, he had mostly vanished from the picture."

Maggie said, "Hmm, that's more of a theory or hunch, not real proof of anything, but I understand why you might think that. What's mostly vanished mean?"

Ginger continued, "It means, he reappeared in the worse way after we got to Barrier. As long as Dad and Carlotta were together, as long as she was alive, they controlled his sex addiction, but Carlotta died a few months ago, and he was back on the prowl again."

"How did Carlotta die?" Maggie asked.

"I don't know, maybe she was murdered or maybe she died of some dreaded disease," Ginger gave a mini-shrug. "Since she had retired as a working girl, Dad thought she had grown old before her time, and the police didn't make much of it. He told me the police crammed her death into the pile labeled, Unknown, Who Cares, and he said that he sure as hell didn't care. He said those words, not me. I never met her, but she died, and no one, as far as I know, was arrested.

"Somehow, he ended up here in Barrier at the CDR. Brandi had seen him a couple times, hanging out with some girls in the bar, but he hadn't seen her, and she kept as far away from him as she could. He didn't know that Brandi was a working girl. A couple weeks ago, though, he had been a little drunk and paid his money and picked a name from those listed on the working girl menu and chose Brandi, never dreaming it was his own daughter. He laughed about it and told the hostess that he loved the name Brandi, the name of his firstborn. When he arrived in her room, they were both horrified. After years of abusing her, her own father had paid money to have sex with her. It was more than she could handle."

Maggie's eyes grew big. She had not expected this. "What did they do?"

"Brandi told me that Dad went nuts, threatened her, and insisted that she quit the CDR. He told her about Carlotta's death, and he blamed it on old age because her body and soul were worn out. Carlotta was about forty but had the body and looks of someone much older.

"After he yelled at her, he started ripping up the room, looking for money, and Brandi ran out of the CDR. She stopped to see Jay long enough to tell him she wouldn't be back, and ran to our house to hide from Dad. She said Jay was furious, of course, but didn't stop her. She didn't tell him anything about Dad, only that she was leaving. When she got to our house, she was sobbing and told me that it was time for us all to leave Barrier. Dad didn't know that I lived in Barrier, but he must have figured it out and followed Brandi. Or maybe Jay told him because all of a sudden, the three of us had an unplanned family reunion."

Ginger gave out a noise that sounded like something between a laugh and a sob. She continued, "As soon as she heard him on the porch, she ran out the back door, running as if her life depended on it. Dad yelled at me and looked for Brandi in every room. When he couldn't find her, and I wouldn't tell him where she had gone, he smacked me and held me in a choke hold until I told him where she was going, to the B & B.

"He screamed out, 'I'll kill her,' and then called me some names before he jumped back in his camper and left. I don't know where he went, maybe he followed her to the B & B. It was late, but Ace hadn't gotten home yet because he was working. Dad went after her and said he would kill her. That's all I know."

Chapter 69

Maggie
Present Day

Maggie had learned a lot from her conversation with Ginger. She now had set her eyes on Jacque, but where was he? After the talk, she stopped at their home for a bathroom break, and checked on Terry and the pool. The plumber had installed the pipes, and the electrician had wired for the pump. Both had left, and Terry was wrapping up for the day. Two more days and they would be ready for the basketball team to smooth out the floor, and next week they would insert the liner. It was beginning to look like a Fourth of July pool party could be a possibility after all.

Maggie drove her rig through town, slowly meandering through the streets, hoping to see Jock's vehicle, but saw nothing and pulled into a parking space in the front of her office. Cagey's rig remained parked on the side of the sheriff's office, and she wondered if he were back at work, despite her insistence that he take the night off.

Brick sat at the front desk of the office with his feet propped up and a crossword puzzle book and pen in his hand. "What did Ginger have to say? Has she seen her dad?"

Maggie retrieved a bottle of water, "Yes, she did. And what a story she told. She said they had been lying about her dad the whole time, like Ace told us. She informed me that Jacque was a sex addict who sexually abused

Brandi through the years. The corker of the story was that he visited the CDR to partake of their services, and the woman he selected turned out to be Brandi, his own daughter."

"Good God Almighty. I can't imagine," Brick exclaimed. "How awful for Brandi."

"After talking with Ginger, I don't think Ace and Ginger had anything to do with either murder. After learning what I just did, Jacque has moved to the top of my list. We also can't eliminate the possibility that Jacque had something to do with the death of his second wife, Carlotta. Her death continues to be unsolved. If Ginger's being truthful, which at this point she has no reason not to be, Jacque is now my number one suspect, and we need to find him. I've taken a couple detours through town and didn't see his pickup, but I have a feeling that he hasn't left Barrier."

"Cagey had located him to open the gun safe, so he probably has a phone number. We could call him and say, 'Did you kill Candice and Brandi?' He seems like such a nice fellow that I'm sure he would tell you the truth," Brick said with a smile.

Maggie twisted her mouth into a sarcastic smile, "Where's Cagey?" Maggie asked. "His rig is outside, but I told him to go home."

"He's not here, and the two Reno detectives left for the night, too, although I don't know where they went," Brick said. "Maybe the three went for a beer together someplace."

Maggie said, "I want to ask Mary Grace a few more questions, to find out if she knows anything about Jacque. Maybe he was the one who was updating and rekeying some of the rooms at the B & B. Maybe she saw him. I want to believe her, but she sometimes omits things. I won't be long, but somebody has to spend the night here in the office, watching over Ace. You need to check out the swimming pool to find out when they will be ready for your team, so I'll keep watch over my one-guest flock tonight."

"You should hire another person when we have guests in the jail," Brick said. "Can't you find some money in your budget?"

"I don't even pay you, so I doubt the county will find money for a night watchman, but maybe it's time. I'll bring it up with the county commissioners at our next meeting."

Maggie hugged Brick, left the office, and immediately saw the three policemen exiting the Pizza Shoppe. She called out to them, and they waved and moved toward her. They had each imbibed a couple beers and were cheerful and happy to see her.

Cagey mock saluted her and said, "Hello, Sheriff Maggie, I'm taking these fine detectives to the B & B. I called Mary Grace and she has rooms available. We might eat dinner, too, although we just finished off a pizza. Do you want to join us?"

Maggie frowned at the three. They had obviously been drinking and would be of no help finding Jacque. They were also in no condition to drive to the B & B. "I was headed that direction myself because I want to talk to Mary Grace. I've developed a sudden interest in our friendly locksmith, Jock, because Jock, J-O-C-K and Jacque spelled J-A-C-Q-U-E- are one and the same—Brandi and Ginger's father. Do you happen to have his phone number, Cagey? How did you contact him to open the gun safe?"

"That was purely coincidence. I saw his pickup with the Jock's Locks logo on it when I was out at the castle and asked Mary Grace about it. I figured he might be a locksmith. She introduced us. He was staying at the B & B in his camper, changing out the locks, you know making those brass keys and the electronic locks work together. He'd already been in Barrier a few days, but Mary Grace thought he would be at least another week," Cagey said.

"So, he's staying at the B & B?" Maggie asked for clarification.

Cagey answered, "Sort of. He has a cot in the back of his camper, which is hooked it up to electricity, so he has power and lights. He has a portable latrine. It's actually a pretty slick system. When I found him, he was parked in the parking lot behind the B & B, where the employees park. Jay built a storage shed out back a few years ago to keep the lawnmowers and tools in. It has water and electricity so is an easy hook up."

"You guys have been drinking so there's no way I am going to let you drive. I'll drive these fine detectives to the B & B, but I need help, Cagey. I need you to watch over Ace while Brick and I find our friendly locksmith. Drink some coffee or water, and I'll explain everything when I return."

Chapter 70

Maggie, Brick, and Jacque
Present Day

Maggie parked in front of the B & B and she and the detectives entered through the front door, but no one was at the desk. She called out to Mary Grace and opened the door behind the desk, but that room was empty. Maggie and the detectives waited for a few minutes before she went upstairs to see if she could find Mary Grace or someone else who could help them.

Brick drove his SUV to the rear of the building, and sure enough, the white camper was parked where Cagey had said, but he didn't see Jacque. He walked around the shed and opened its door but it, too, was empty. He not-so-gently rapped his knuckles on the camper's door but heard nothing. He rattled the handle and the flimsy door gave way and opened wide.

"Brick! What are you doing? Get out," Mary Grace demanded. She was half dressed and sitting atop a man, who must have been Jacque. Her hair was sticking out and her face was red.

"Who are you?" the man said. "You can't burst into my camper like that."

"I'll be happy to wait outside," Brick offered, closing the door. *Seek and ye shall find,* he thought to himself.

Mary Grace, now fully clothed, burst through the door. She was smoothing her hair and tugged on her shirt to bring it below her flabby belly,

"I can't believe you opened the door, Brick, like it was nothing. It's where he lives, his house, his residence. How humiliating."

Brick said, "I'm looking for Jacque and I knocked, but nobody answered. I'm sorry, Mary Grace, I had no idea anyone was in the camper. I didn't mean to open the door, but when no one answered my knock, I rattled the door handle thinking he might hear it and it fell open. Is that Jacque with you?"

"Yes, that's him, not that it's any of your business. What do you want him for? Are you going to arrest him, too?" she snapped as she stormed toward the back entrance to the B & B. Her shoes were on, but she had not tied the laces and they flapped in the dirt.

The door to the camper slowly opened and Jacque stepped out. Brick introduced himself. "The sheriff has some questions for you. She's in the B & B, so let's go in and let her decide where she wants to interview you." He had a good idea that they would be returning to the sheriff's office, and perhaps Jacque would be another guest.

"Am I under arrest?" Jacque asked. "What does she want to talk to me about? I have questions, too, for example, why did you open my door? It's where I live, not a public building."

"The door opened by itself, I rattled the handle and it popped open, and I apologize to you and Mary Grace. You should fix the handle because it will do it again," Brick said, as he clasped Jacque's elbow and began walking toward the B & B. "I think one of your screws is loose or missing." Brick smiled to himself, wondering if Jacque recognized his pun.

Chapter 71

Maggie and Jacque
Present Day

Maggie placed Jacque in the backseat of her SUV, while Brick offered the two detectives a ride with him. "We thought he was dead," Burns said. "We stopped looking for him three or four years ago. Whoever would have thought he'd show up here? We were interested in Brandi, but now we would enjoy talking to her father."

"Am I under arrest?" Jacque Dumont asked Maggie as she shut the door of her vehicle. "What did I do? It's your deputy who should be under arrest because he entered my domicile without being asked. And he embarrassed Mary Grace. She's a nice woman, I could love her." He was a talker and complained and jabbered until they arrived at sheriff's office ending with, "Who are those other men, anyway, the suits?"

"Haven't you met them before? These detectives come from Reno and have been investigating your wife's murder. Their names are Detective Burns and Detective Lawrence. They have questions about Candice's death, and I have questions regarding your daughter Brandi."

"I don't know anything about those murders, but if you ask me, I'll tell you they both deserved to die. Candice was a money-hungry bitch who tried to wrestle money from me for her golf habit, which was like an addiction, playing every day, no matter what. She wasn't any good but wanted the best of everything. She said she would improve her game with better clubs and a fancy golf cart. She enrolled in some lessons once, but they didn't help. I bought her one of those pull carts for her birthday one year, so I don't know why she complained. I told her that walking was better for her health, and a golf cart would make her lazy and fat, but she never listened." Maggie found herself wondering if Jacque had rehearsed this speech.

"And Brandi, well, she ended up working in a brothel as a working girl, and after all I did for her, she never returned the favors. She was a waste of good sperm." He chortled at his attempt at humor. "Do you know that the only thing she would eat when she was a kid was hard-boiled eggs? I'd take her out to some fancy restaurant, and she'd order eggs. She was crazy for eggs." Maggie considered what he said and how he said it. Jacque should not have known that Brandi was dead, yet he didn't question her about it and didn't act surprised. Instead, he criticized her.

Maggie accompanied Jacque to her office and closed her office door. She read him his rights, but he blew her off, "I didn't do anything, so why are you reading me my rights? Candice's murder was years ago, and I know about statues of limitations. It's been beyond the five years."

Maggie smiled and looked Jacque directly in the eye and didn't blink, "Not really. First of all, they are statutes of limitation, not statues. A statute is a law, and a statue is a tribute to someone, totally different. And secondly, murder has no statute of limitations. I don't know where you heard that, but that's wrong, so we've got a lot to talk about. I'm not going to talk to you about Candice. Those two men from Reno will discuss Candice with you. I want to ask about Brandi. This might be a long night for you, Mr. Dumont."

"I don't know diddly squat about Brandi, Sheriff. I haven't seen her in about six years. Maybe longer. Like I said, she was a waste of energy on my part."

"Did you know she was dead? Murdered?" Maggie asked. Information about Brandi was available through the grapevine, but he had not seemed the least bit curious, asking how, when, or where she died. It almost matched Jay's demeanor when she told him that Brandi was murdered.

Jacque sat silent as an unused drum and Maggie had to prompt him. She repeated, "Jacque, can you answer my question? Did you know that Brandi was dead, murdered?"

He paused, but finally answered. "Yeah, I heard about it. I heard about it from Mary Grace."

"When did she tell you that?"

Jacque paused before answering, "She told me last night."

"How long have you known Mary Grace?"

Jacque was indignant, "What difference does that make? We have been friends for a long time, and she called me some time ago, wanting the locks on the guest room doors changed so that the electronic locks would work with either a key or an electronic card. It's tricky and I had a hard time figuring the system out, but I finally got them to work together. I've been fixing them for her. I do a few every day, but I'm not done yet," Jacque gave out a long yawn, as if he were bored with the whole conversation. He stretched his legs trying to become comfortable in the old wooden chair.

Maggie said, "I hope I'm not boring you. Brandi had lived at the CDR for a few years. Did you know that she was here?"

"I heard about it. My wife told me that she was here. Carlotta. She worked in a brothel, too, for a while, not this one, but she knew a lot of the other women. It's a fairly tight network."

"Did you see her after you came to Barrier?" Maggie asked.

"Who? Carlotta? No, she's dead. She died a few months ago," Jacque said.

Maggie shook her head and said, "No, not Carlotta. We are talking about Brandi. Did you see Brandi after you arrived in Barrier?" Maggie paused. She wanted to know about Carlotta, too, but decided to wait. One death at a time.

Jacque snapped, "No, I told you, I have not seen her for several years."

Maggie came back, "Did you ever go to the CDR?"

Jacque had to think about this one for a minute, "Sure, of course, I had to eat, and they have excellent chicken dinners. Cheap, too. You should try them out."

"So, Jacque, if I talk to the hostess, would she say that she has never seen you before, or would she recognize you right away?"

Jacque wanted to avoid answering her questions, but said, "I need to use the head. Where is it?" Maggie signaled Cagey to accompany Jacque to the bathroom.

Maggie stood and moved around a little to work the kinks from her legs, and Brick joined her. She shook her head, "I think he murdered Brandi, but he's not admitting to anything, which is not a surprise. Let's bring Ginger here, and maybe he'll change his mind. We might as well have a little family reunion, as Ginger mentioned, bring everybody together. Ask Cagey to find out which hostess was on duty the night he paid for his own daughter. Let's bring her here, too."

Chapter 72

Ginger
Present Day

Brick knocked on Ginger's door, and she opened it with, "Now what?"

"Your dad is talking to the sheriff in her office, and she wants you to come, too, so she can talk to both of you. She sees some inconsistencies with what you told her and what your dad is telling her, and she wants to straighten it out."

"I really don't want to see him. And I'm fairly sure he won't want to see me. Does he know what I told Maggie?" Ginger's eyes blazed with contempt, and she gave Brick the once-over.

Brick didn't know if the contempt was for him or for her father, but Ginger said, "He was a horrible father, and the more I think about him and that night, the more I hate him. I'm sure he killed Brandi, and I feel sure that he killed Mom as well. And maybe Carlotta, too. He's slippery, and it's not a surprise that the police couldn't find him."

"I don't know what your dad said because the sheriff talked to him alone, and she didn't tell me. She asked me to bring you to the office, so let's go," Brick demanded. "Get your jacket, it's a little chilly right now."

"Okay," Ginger said, moving toward the back of the house while Brick waited by the front door. "I'll be back in a second." She returned with her windbreaker and purse. "I can't imagine that Dad's story and mine disagree," she said sarcastically, "he's never told the truth about anything in his life. He's a lying SOB." Her voice was low and harsh, filled with anger.

Within five minutes, Brick and Ginger entered the sheriff's office. Jacque saw her and leaped to his feet. He started to take a step toward her but drew back, "Shit."

Maggie pulled out her handcuffs and slapped them on Jacque's wrists before he even knew they were a possibility. She responded, "Sit down, Jacque. You aren't going anywhere."

The door to the sheriff's office remained closed. The people in the two areas could not hear each other, but Ginger said bitterly, "Dad, what a pleasure. I'm so glad to see you. You killed Mom and you killed Brandi and...what about Carlotta. Did you kill her, too?"

Ginger snatched her pistol from her purse, and she pointed it at her father. A bullet flew out of the barrel before Brick could stop her. "Damn you, Dad. It's bad enough that you loved them more than me, but did you have to kill them, too? Should I expect the same?" She spat the words out like bullets from a machine gun.

Brick pushed toward her as she fired, but he was a half-second too late. The glass wall exploded, and her father fell to the floor, bleeding profusely. It could have been the shoulder, or the chest, maybe the heart, but blood was everywhere. He tried to focus his glassy eyes on Ginger and said, "You have to know...I'm sorry...your mother...Brandi...eggs," and he said no more.

Brick grabbed Ginger's pistol and snapped the handcuffs on her wrists and set her down in a chair with his hand on her shoulder.

Cagey was already on the phone to the EMTs, and a few seconds later they heard the sounds of an ambulance, but it would be too late.

Chapter 73

Ginger
Present Day

Four weeks later, Maggie sat at her desk wading through the mountain of paperwork that had accumulated as she prepared for Ginger's trial for killing her father. She had organized everything, timeline, affidavits, warrants, interview documentation, as well as her sometimes sketchy and incomprehensible notes. Brick and Cagey had done the same. Her due date for their baby was a quick two weeks away, and she felt uncomfortable, ready to pop. The baby couldn't arrive too soon. Even though the Fourth of July party was still on the books, Maggie and Brick doubted that Sammy would wait that long.

When Maggie's team, with the help of the Reno police, searched Jacque's camper, they found a single golf club, a driver, and determined that it had been used to bludgeon Candice to death. They were finally able to confidently label that case as Solved.

The sheriff from Post County, Texas applied and received extradition permission to return Ace to Post County for the murder of his father. The sheriff noted that although his arrest was primarily by the process of elimination, they had acquired some evidence that would lock him up for a few years. Perhaps not for murder, but for abuse, certainly.

Ginger sat in the Barrier jail, awaiting trial, and Cy was banking on the defense that "Jacques was a guy who needed killing," which had been a defense in a Florida murder case some years before. In that case, the jury agreed that the murdered drug dealer was a menace to society and needed to be killed, and the perpetrator had gotten off scot free. While Jacque hadn't been a drug dealer, he was perhaps a serial killer, having brutally murdered his first wife and daughter, and most likely his second wife. Cy said, "Hrrgggg. I've always wanted to use that defense, and Barrier seems like a town that just might buy it. Ginger shot him in cold blood with witnesses, but maybe the jury will sentence her to fewer years, anyway. I love rural juries. Hrrgggg."

Near the bottom of her pile of paperwork, Maggie ran across the list she had created of the issues she had on her plate that Tuesday morning a month before. She picked up a pen, checked them off, and wrote a comment for each:

- ✓ Pool: Complete. Filled with water. Swimming lessons start next week.
- ✓ Boxes of money, jewels, and gold in bomb shelter: Locked inside the sheriff's vault.
- ✓ Screeches: The gate opening and closing as Jacque moved boxes in and out of the bomb shelter. Continuing to figure out the finders-keepers law.
- ✓ Brandi's disappearance and death: Jacque
- ✓ Candice's death in Reno: Jacque
- ✓ Ginger's abuse: Ace. She wouldn't incriminate him, but he was under arrest in Texas. Problem solved, at least temporarily.
- ✓ Gun safe: Don't know why or how the gun safe entered into the issue, but it led to finding Jacque. Calling it a happy coincidence.
- ✓ Jay. He really didn't know anything after all. He was Jay being Jay.

She added to her list:

- ✓ Carlotta: probably murdered, turned over to Reno's police.
- ✓ Jacque: dead, Ginger on trial.

Everything bounced back to Jacque, someone she didn't know existed when she had scratched out her list. She had been correct in thinking that everything was tied together because when he died, the noises had stopped, and everyone was safe and sound.

- ✓ Sarah: She crossed out Sarah and wrote Sammy. When?

Maggie sat back in her chair and smiled. Everything is tied up, now I can rest. She sighed and suddenly felt warm water oozing between her legs. "Brick, my water broke. We've gotta go now!"

Read on for a sneak peek at the next book in the
Maggie Monroe series: **Murder in the Diocese**

Chapter 1

Angel, Saturday

Praising God and cursing Him at the same time, Angel fell to her knees. Wasn't she one of the faithful, one who prayed without ceasing? Hadn't she always attended Mass? Hadn't she always thought of Him first? Hadn't she sacrificed enough? Thank God, the babies looked healthy. Thank God, the pain was over. But why two? And one darker than the other. A black baby and a white baby? Wasn't one baby punishment enough? Why had they picked today to be born? Couldn't they have waited until next week?

Angel, as her stepfather called her, knew little of childbirth, babies, or caring for them. She did not believe in abortion. Babies were God's creation. She would not, could not destroy them. As a youth, she aspired to greatness and disciplined herself to achieve her goals, but these past years had worn her down. Now in her late 30s, she struggled with saying no to people, and her obsessive work habits had begun to exhaust her. She compensated for her passivity with gruffness, which others considered aggressive behavior. And these babies, they were unwelcome. She would never say unwanted, but they were unwelcome.

Hail Mary. She looked at the babies. Two. She didn't know there would be two. And the race thing. How could that be? Shouldn't twins look alike? According to her calculations they were due in four weeks, but they chose today to be born. Wearily, she recalled that violent night. At first, he had been gentle, teasing and smiling, then suddenly he changed and had become angry, brutal, even vicious. With his anger she became more passive, hoping he would leave. But her docility only made him more violent. He forced himself on her, then threatened her. She knew that revealing the secret would destroy all that she had worked for.

She had not seen a doctor during her pregnancy and relied on WebMD to learn about prenatal care. Later, she went back to the Internet to see how to deliver a baby, and had even purchased new, sterile scissors to cut the cord. No one had to know. She could ignore seeing a doctor; what did they know anyway? Tell you to push the baby out, pat you on the back, and send you home. This way, it was between her and God. Throughout her pregnancy, she had not drunk alcohol. Of course, wine didn't count. Nor did the daily Blood of Christ. And she didn't smoke. When the babies finally made their appearance, she severed the cords with her new scissors and tied them tightly. She then wiped the babies' mouths and noses free of mucus. From what she could tell, they appeared healthy. So, at least there was that. Praise God.

But the two babies. One white, one black. Had God played a joke on her? An unfunny, thoughtless joke? God was kind. This wasn't in His nature. I am white, she thought to herself. How could I have a black baby? Was he African American? No, that's impossible, she thought. He had dark hair, but his skin was so light. Could he have been black? She didn't know anything about him. God had played jokes on her before, but why now? All the fingers and toes were intact. She counted them twice. It made no sense. She would look in the Scriptures and perhaps she would discover the answer. Judas was black. At least she thought he was black. She was confused on so many levels. People said that God only gives you what you can handle. Had God forgotten that rule this time around? She thought so.

Chapter 2

Angel, Saturday

Mass would begin in a little over an hour. If she left now, she could deposit them under a pew. Some kind soul would take them to the hospital, and she would be free of them. "No one has to know whose they are," she repeated to herself. "No one has to know." She was exhausted and needed to rest, but she forced herself to get dressed. She wanted to get to Mass on time.

Angel started to clean herself and the babies. She ran water until it was hot, then cooled it. It needed to be warm, not hot, she remembered as she carefully washed them, and gently patted them dry. They finally were free of the mucous that surrounded them for eight long months. The towel she used was rust stained but clean. I should have bought a new towel, too, she thought. Her mind was in overdrive. The only thing she knew how to do was to make them look better, more appealing. Please let someone want them. I want them to be wanted. She thought of Mary. Jesus had been born of a virgin. True, she wasn't a virgin, but maybe she was a chosen one, like Mary? A holy one. She frowned.

She rambled to herself in her mind. Shit, I only have one blanket. I didn't know that I would need two. What am I supposed to do now? She saw her new scissors and decided to cut the blanket in two, clipping the dangling threads. After, she had two jagged halves. The blanket had been too large for a single baby anyway. I should have bought a new blanket as this one will scratch them. I should have thought of diapers, too. I was not prepared. Praises that I have an extra rosary. She knew nothing about babies, bottles, or diapers, but she did know about rosaries. She knew the rosaries would protect the twins and bring them luck.

She kissed the two rosaries and placed one with each baby as she bundled them up and placed them in a cardboard box. They whimpered a bit. "Shut up," she snapped. "Shut up. Please don't cry." She shuffled out the door to her pickup and placed the box on the floor of the front seat. "No one can know. No one can ever know."

Angel somehow bolstered the strength to attend Mass that day but was too weak to do her normal routine. She entered the sanctuary and placed the babies in the rear of the church, knowing that someone would sit near the door, anxious for an early exit. Someone always sat there. She positioned them under the kneeling rails sure that eventually they would make a fuss. She thought this was a good plan as the babies needed to be found, and soon. She had two chances: one at the 5 p.m. mass and another at the 7 p.m. service. They were silent now and breathing easily, but as soon as someone discovered them, the questions would come. People would wonder who they belonged to and worse, they would ask why one baby was black and one white. They would wonder who could have left them there. They would feel sorry for the babies and take them to the hospital. No one would know they were hers, and she couldn't let them find out.

St. Gertrude's was one of the super-churches, semi-circular interior with room for over 400 parishioners who flooded each of the five weekend Masses. The stained-glass windows and muted bulbs darkened the room, but the candles illuminated it enough to allow people to read. Angel loved candles and the aura that they created at St. Gert's. Burning candles symbolized prayers ascending to heaven and lots of candles meant lots of prayers. She looked around. No one was there yet. She dropped two quarters into the prayer box and lit two candles, one for each baby.

As planned, once she placed the babies beneath the kneelers, she made her way to another section of the sanctuary. She thought over the events of the past few hours. Away from the babies, she knelt on a kneeler and prayed that they would be found by somebody young, someone with other children, someone who would love them. Of course, with her luck, some ancient, do-gooder would find them and kick up a fuss during Mass.

Before she left the sanctuary, she remembered that she failed to leave their names in the blankets. I should have remembered, but now it's too late. Marie and Louis would be good names. Marie and Louis, her mother and her father. I'll get the names to them somehow.

Maybe my luck will change. Angel prayed, "Glory be to God. Glory be to God."

Chapter 3

Gwen, Saturday

Hail Mary, full of grace, the Lord is with thee. The few parishioners who gathered recited the age-old phrase. Rosary beads jangled against the backs of the wooden benches and prayers ascended. Some would be answered. Some wouldn't.

Gwendolyn Harte settled into the pew waiting for Mass to begin. A born Lutheran who had converted to Catholicism as an adult, she struggled with the concept of Mary and how Mary could be without sin. She had read and reread the literature that the priests offered her but couldn't manage to pray the Hail Mary. She sat quietly and listened to the drone of other parishioners who semi-articulated the prayers as they thumbed the beads of the age-old Catholic prayer. Her mind drifted as she sat waiting for the priest to enter. Who would recite Mass today? Would it be the French priest who avoided looking at the parishioners as he talked? Would it be the professional Irishman who feasted on Rolaids? Or would it be her boss, the Iron Man, who doubled as principal of St. Thomas More, the local Catholic high school? They were all different, and each had his own agenda and responded to the Holy Gospel in dissimilar ways. One could argue that the word of the priest was the Word of God, but if that were true, why were they constantly contradicting each other? She fought these thoughts as she readied herself for whomever might show up.

Gwen and her husband, Clancy, and their three children had relocated to Basin two years before. Basin was a small city of about 250,000, a suburb of Reno, Nevada, and it was a far cry from the 700 people in Hawley, their previous home. It seemed colossal with its paved streets, sidewalks, mall, and traffic lights. Hawley had no stoplights, but in Basin, one flashed on nearly every corner, tempting motorists to run red lights in order to get where they were going faster. The ever-present inversion contrasted to the clear, starry nights of the mountains. Their lives in the city varied from their existence in Hawley, but Gwen's jobs were the same: wife, mother, and teacher. She enjoyed going to work, teaching school, returning home, playing games with her kids, and holding hands with her husband. Simple things made her happy.

She attended Mass alone today. Clancy had traveled toward Lake Tahoe to fly fish in one of the state's many fast-running streams. Their children were spending the night with Granny, and she was looking forward to a little R&R that Mass afforded before the gang returned home. She sat near the back of the church so she could make a quick getaway. She was already thinking about her comfy spot at home where she would stretch out in quiet to eat popcorn and watch a new Netflix movie. Attending Saturday night Mass would allow her to sleep in on Sunday, one of the benefits of the Catholic Church. She rose as the fat French priest entered. The gossip mill rumored that he was 37 years old, but he looked ready for AARP. He was stooped, wizened, and shaped like an hourglass with large hips and paunchy chest. He wore his tightly cinched belt high on his waist, which drew attention to his bulging stomach that sagged beneath. His body looked distorted, even comical. Eczema patched his red-faced nose and cheeks. His complexion was spotty, making Gwen wonder if he had been tested for skin cancer. His pale, shiny hair was streaked with gray and covered his shoulders. It might have been clean, or it might have been greasy. One couldn't tell. A good haircut would do wonders for his appearance. She thought he looked especially off today. Perhaps he was a little under the weather. His robe masked his physical being. He looked clerical, except for the Birkenstocks that peeked out of his robe. He wore no socks.

As Father Rene Leclerq strode in, he stared straight ahead, as if in a fog. Gwen automatically reached for the kneeler and started to pull it down. It snagged on something and wouldn't budge. She tugged again and looked down but didn't see anything. She ducked her head down to look closer and noticed a navy-blue piece of cloth that blended in with the carpet. And it moved. Oh. My. God. Oh, my God. She leaned down for a closer look and picked it up. It was a baby. A dark-skinned baby who couldn't have been more than a few hours old. She glanced behind her and to the sides. No one was within five rows of her. She had arrived 20 minutes earlier and had seen nobody except the few early bird parishioners who were reciting their Hail Mary's. She leaned down to check for a bag or note—anything that might explain the presence of a newborn under her kneeler. She laid the baby on the pew and scrunched under the kneeler. She didn't see a note or bag, but she spied another blanket. And another baby. This baby was fair skinned with blue eyes staring up at her. It was also but a few hours old. Twins? One black and one white? That can't be. Oh, my God. She gazed around again in all directions but saw nothing that would explain the presence of two babies. In fact, the whole rear section of the church was empty, and she sat alone in the pew. "This is impossible," she thought to herself. She touched their faces and thankfully they were warm, and alive, both shifting slightly at her touch.

After she had placed both babies on the pew, she tiptoed to the rear of the church to see if there was anyone who might explain the presence of two babies. She checked the women's bathroom, the entryway, and the cry room. She looked outside the doors of the church. No one. Confused, she returned to her seat. The babies were not moving, eyes shut, rasping restlessly. To whom did they belong?

The priest was mid-way through the Mass and about to begin serving the Eucharist. His squeaky voice grated on her ears, but she was not listening anyway. Before Gwen proceeded to the altar to receive the Holy Communion, she placed them back on the floor. Perhaps her proximity frightened their mother away and she would reappear while she was at the altar. She glanced around as she walked down the aisle, searching for someone who might have recently given birth. This was the 5 p.m. Mass, known for its elderly patrons. Two wheelchairs, a half a dozen walkers and canes in every pew. No mother was to be seen. Perhaps the mother was ill or in her car. When she returned, the babies hadn't gone anywhere. Their sticky eyes tried to open, but they made no noise.

Nothing in Gwen's historical toolbox told her how to manage what was mysteriously set before her. What do you do when you find two babies? Did anyone know? One thing was sure. Hail Mary, full of grace, was not going to solve this problem. Gwen placed them carefully back on the pew, one on each side and bided her time until Mass ended. Hopefully, someone devout would come over and claim them. Her eyes moved from side to side, from baby to baby, from black baby to white baby and back again. Could it have been a coincidence that two mothers left two babies? Her eyes alit on the statue of the Virgin Mary toward the front of the church. A miracle birth, two? God help her. Gwen was a convert. Miracle births? Two miracle births? These babies should have been in the incubator at the hospital.

When Mass finally ended, the priest and his entourage departed. No one looked her way. No one stopped.

Gwen sat still, remaining in the pew, uncertain of what to do. Nearly everyone had vanished, even those with walkers and canes. The usher was gathering the wayward bulletins and tidying up before the next Mass, which would begin in less than one hour. Gwen beckoned to him as he approached, "Excuse me." No answer. She cleared her throat and repeated a little more loudly, "Sir, excuse me."

"Did you need something?" he asked. That was an understatement. Of course, she needed something. A mother would be good.

"Uh, I have a little problem here. I sat here in this pew, but when I went to put the kneeler down, I found, uh, I found two babies. Both are only a few hours old," Gwen noted. "They might be twins. I don't know." His nametag read, "Frank Bilbaostrigo, Senior Usher."

"Babies? Whose babies?" Frank Bilbaostrigo exclaimed as he sidled between the pews to have a look. "Well, I'll be. They are babies, all right. And one is black, and one is white. I'll be," he exclaimed again. "Who do they belong to? They're not yours, Mrs. Harte, are they?" Gwen was surprised that he knew her name. He grinned, as though he had caught her in a secret. Gwen didn't know many people at St. Gertrude's, but Frank apparently knew everybody.

"Of course, they're not mine, and I don't have any notion who their mother is. I don't know how they got here or to whom they belong. Could you find Father Leclerq and ask him to come here, please?" Gwen was becoming concerned that she was going to be responsible for these babies. She continued, "I peeked into the blankets and didn't find any identification. No note or anything. This one is a girl, pointing to the darker of the two, and that one is a boy. The only thing in the blankets is a rosary. One with each baby. But I want to get them out of these blankets. Not only are they filthy and damp, but I am guessing they are scratchy wool, the kind you get in the military or when you are going camping. They're not the kind you should wrap newborn babies in. Plus, they aren't wearing diapers or anything else. Could you help me carry them into the cry room? It is brighter in there, and maybe if we unwrap them, we can find identification inside the blankets."

They each picked up a baby and headed toward the cry room and placed both in the crib. Gwen stripped off the wrappings while Frank set out to retrieve Father Leclerq. The well-formed twins might not have been full term but were well developed and had all their fingers and toes, but no identification. Some toddler-sized paper diapers and a couple of scruffy, but sort-of-clean blankets lay on a folding chair. She folded the babies into the too-big diapers and wrapped them up in the softer, cleaner blankets. They had been silent during Mass, but now were becoming a little fidgety. They gurgled rasping noises that babies make and stretched their arms and legs to work out the kinks of their nearly nine-month cramped fetal positions. She guessed they were about three or four pounds each but maybe born a few weeks early. They did not wear hospital bracelets and did not appear to be medicated. Their cords were cut and tied off with string.

Frank returned sans Father Leclerq. "He's disappeared," Frank stated. "In fact, everyone has disappeared. It's you, me, these little bambinos, and a few people moseying in for the next Mass. Did you find any identification?"

"No, only these dirty blue blankets and the rosaries. I guess they were not born in a hospital. They were born somewhere else, and the mother abandoned them here. Isn't the church one of the Safe Havens under the law that allows mothers to abandon their babies if they don't want them? The law was designed to keep babies out of trash bins. I remember reading about it some years ago. Are you aware of any pregnant girls in the parish who were about to give birth?"

"I don't know who the mother might be, but what I do know is that the 7 o'clock Mass will begin in about 20 minutes. The 5 o'clock Mass mainly has older folks, but families attend the 7 o'clock Mass. This room will fill up with a whole bunch of kids, and there will be a lot of questions and a lot of germs. Why don't we put them in your car? Can you transport them to the hospital? We could call 911 and get an ambulance, but that would cause a lot of questions. I know I shouldn't speak for Father Leclerq, but I don't think he'd want this type of publicity. It is also a health issue. The hospital will know what to do. Perhaps they can locate the mother. I'd go with you, but I need to get home to my wife. She's got the flu. I'll call you later to find out what the hospital suggested." She agreed and gave Frank her cell phone number.

Frank and Gwen bundled the two up and carried them out to Gwen's car. Gwen squinted in the sunlight and held the blanket over the eyes of the girl baby. Frank instinctively did the same with the boy baby. The sun shined brightly. It was a typical evening in June, about 75 degrees with a hint of a breeze. The lack of clouds made it perfect. They placed the children on the floor of the back seat of her SUV. As an afterthought, Frank ran back into the church and picked up the two blue blankets and took them out to Gwen's car. They used them to wedge the babies in place.

The parking lot was filling again, but Frank didn't see anyone who looked like a new mother minus her new children. Gwen's children were older, and she had no infant-safety system. She knew it was against the law not to strap children in their seats. She thought to herself, Drive slowly. The last thing I need is to get pulled over by the police. Of course, now that I think of it, maybe that would be good luck.

Chapter 4

Gwen, Saturday

Gwen Harte maneuvered her SUV up to the emergency room entrance and honked the horn. No one came. The semi-circle in front of the automatic doors was vacant with a couple of signs that read, "No parking." A valet-less valet stand held a sign reading: "Closed Saturday and Sunday nights." I'll risk it, she thought. What's the worst that can happen? She set the brake and exited her car. She somehow picked up the two babies and toted them inside. They were asleep, but their eyelids jumped as she moved them. She stepped up to the admissions window while balancing the babies on her waist and opened her mouth to tell her story. The clerk replied, "Take a number." She did not look up.

"But...," Gwen stammered.

"Are you bleeding? If not, take a number. Triage will see you when your number comes up." She sounded as if she had been there all week. Her ashen hair stuck out from her attempted ponytail, and her hands were stained from a leaky pen.

"But..."

"Look, Ma'am, we'll see them as soon as we can. Take a number and get out your insurance cards." More loudly she said, "Number 422, please."

Gwen took number 428 from the number dispenser and obediently carried the babies to the waiting area and manipulated them into a chair. The hospital was a paradox. The chrome arms on the black vinyl chairs gleamed in the bright sun-lit room, but the tattered magazines were askew on the floor, table, and chairs. An overflowing toy box contained a variety of toys reminiscent of a second-hand store's toy department. The security guard absentmindedly fiddled with a hand-held computer game and critically eyed the visitors on the lookout for anyone scheming to hijack the emergency room. A sign on the wall boasted, "Your Emergency Is Our Emergency." Definitely not feeling that now, Gwen thought.

The babies had been cleaned some, but sallow, splotchy mucous and afterbirth stuck to their bodies. They looked the same, yet different. One woman, waiting to be seen, vacillated her gaze from Gwen to the babies and back to Gwen who returned the stare. Having one black baby and one white baby was sure to raise some eyebrows in or out of the emergency room.

In about 15 minutes, the clerk called number 428. Gwen carried the little bundles up to the counter to hand them over dutifully. The triage nurse asked her a couple of questions and eventually figured out that they weren't hers as Gwen had answered every question with "I don't know; I found them." The triage nurse's nametag identified her as "Luella."

"May I see your identification, please? Who is the mother?" Luella demanded curtly.

Gwen handed over her driver's license. "I don't know who the mother is. I found them at St. Gertrude's Catholic Church at Mass." Luella glared at Gwen.

"I see," Luella responded. "And who is the father?"

"I don't know. I found them at St. Gertrude's Catholic Church at Mass." Gwen answered while Luella tapped her pen and raised her eyebrows.

Luella needed more information for her forms and continued her quest. "I see. When were they born? Where are their mothers? Why are they different races? What's that about?"

"I already told you. I don't know. I found them at St. Gertrude's Catholic Church at Mass," Gwen could feel her rage building.

Luella was not happy with Gwen's answers and continued. "You realize that we can't help you, don't you? Newborn babies who are not born in the hospital are not allowed to be admitted as newborns. You are aware of that, aren't you?" Luella added more eye moves and mouth twists.

Gwen's patience was wearing thin. "No, I am not aware of that. I found these babies. I cannot care for them and can't leave them on the street."

Luella sighed and said, "I'll check with the charge nurse. Do you have insurance? Could I see your cards, please?"

It was Gwen's turn to sigh. "I have insurance, but these babies are not on my insurance plan, because I found them. They are not mine. How many times do I have to tell you?"

Luella persisted, "You must be a guardian. Are you the legal guardian?"

"I am not. I found these babies at Mass 45 minutes ago," Gwen reminded her again. "Look, Luella, I don't mean to be rude, but I found these babies. They are not mine. I don't know what to do with them. I need some help here. I don't blame you for not believing me. I'm not sure that I would believe me, but I need some assistance."

Luella smiled and wrote something on the form. "This is very rare. The Safe Haven law says we must take abandoned babies, but as far as I know, we have never had any abandoned children and haven't established a protocol." She told Gwen to move her car before heading back into the emergency waiting room. "The staff will look them over and decide how to deal with them. We will consider you as their next-of-kin until someone tells us differently." She finished filling in the form noting Gwen as next of kin.

How could Gwen be next of kin? She was merely a Good Samaritan doing a Christian deed. Luella wrote out the triage report and noted in large red letters that there was no insurance. She called for an ER nurse.

Gwen continued to balance the two babies on the counter as Luella pushed the door-opening button. Within minutes of returning from moving her car, another nurse appeared and helped her carry them behind the stainless-steel doors of the emergency room. Her name was Linda. She repeated the same questions as Luella, and they discussed whether the babies were twins since they appeared to be of different races. Linda was certain they could not be twins. Gwen didn't know if twins could be of different races or not. Other nursing staff threw in bits of experience and knowledge. The consensus was that no one knew whether twins could be of two races or not. Linda took their vitals and began to clean the babies. Their healthy color and their persistent whimpers conned Linda into some formula. Someone gave Gwen the emergency number for Health and Welfare. She called it and got a recording. I am glad that I wasn't being beaten, she thought as she pushed buttons through the menu to emergency children's services. She left a message with her cell phone number requesting Health and Welfare to call her back. She provided Linda's name and the emergency room number.

The emergency room was sterile with shining stainless steel at every turn. The nurses smiled, but they too reflected steel sterility. Every medical gizmo lay at their disposal, but would any of their fancy machines produce a mother for these babies?

Gwen pondered their introduction to life. Tiny, innocent, and unwanted. How could someone discard them? How could someone not want these babies? Babies were a gift from God, magic in most people's books. One minute you have a fetus, and the next minute you have a baby. Joyful. Truly a miracle.

She remained with the babies for an hour and watched the nursing staff come and go. They used thermometers, took blood, gave sponge baths, put on diapers that fit, and attached wires that extended from the babies to monitors. They were efficient and polite, and Gwen knew they were in good hands. The preemie bottles were measured in CCs, and the babies struggled to get a few drops of the formula down. The nurses finally wrapped them in blankets: one pink and one blue with matching caps. Gwen decided to go home to change her clothes. She would return tomorrow to see how they were doing. She gave Linda her phone number on the way out.

Chapter 5

Gwen, Saturday Evening

When she arrived home, she couldn't think of anything except those two babies. Her mind wandered all over the place: from Mass to Father Leclerq to Hawley to her own children. The phone rang, and her first thought was, Thank heaven! Health and Welfare. The Caller ID read, "Restricted."

"Hello. Thank you for calling me back," Gwen started, not waiting for the caller to identify herself.

"Are they okay?" the hoarse voice rasped. "I want them to be okay. Take good care of them, please. When you get them back from the hospital, safeguard them as your own children. Tell them that I love them. I named them Marie and Louis. Raise them with God, Mrs. Harte." Click. The caller hung up. Gwen checked the caller ID again. Restricted.

Stunned, Gwen sat down. Who was this person? Why is she giving her children to me? I have a life. I have a husband, three children, a job, and enough to do without twin babies. Her head spun as she thought about what had transpired.

The phone rang again. She checked the caller ID. Restricted, again. "Who are you? Why are you giving me your children?" she almost shouted into the phone.

"This is Violet at Health and Welfare responding to your call."

Gwen's conversation with Violet was as calamitous as the one with Luella. Violet asked questions for which Gwen had no answers. Violet couldn't answer the questions that Gwen had. Gwen described the phone call that she had received. It was disturbing that the caller knew that Gwen had found the babies and had turned the babies over to the hospital. She indicated that she wanted Gwen to keep the babies. How did she know who had taken them?

"The babies are safe for the time being, however, I have no available foster homes in Basin right now. It is Saturday night, and the hospital will take care of the babies until Monday. In addition, it will be difficult to secure a foster home for two newborns. We don't know about their family. For the moment, Mrs. Harte, you are their next of kin. Did you call the police?"

"No, I did not call the police, and I am not the next of kin. I drove them to the hospital and called you." Gwen was becoming irritated.

Clancy and Gwen had undertaken the responsibility of being foster parents once before. A 14-year-old boy tried to commit suicide with a pistol but missed his brain and severed the optic nerve blinding himself instead. They cared for him while the child welfare workers investigated the family and the child. The department needed to learn the whys and wherefores of the attempted suicide before returning him to his home. Clancy and Gwen dealt with the delays, broken promises, and tangled red tape. They knew the system. The department had rules, but there were many ways to circumvent them. A resourceful social worker could accelerate the process. A genuine, dyed-in-the-wool bureaucrat could cause a foster family to jump through hoops forever. Social workers could make the foster family's life as easy or difficult as they desired.

Violet persisted, "The mother evidently knows you. She might have chosen you on purpose or was glad you found them. She called you, didn't she? They'll stay in the hospital for the weekend. Monday, I'll expedite your case to certify you as foster parents, if you will assume that responsibility."

Gwen stammered a bit, "Well, uh, I don't know. I must talk to Clancy. We served as foster parents once before, but that was a few years ago. That boy was a teenager, and it was for only a few days. When do you need to know? What will happen to them if we don't take them?"

"You've already been foster parents? Oh, good. That makes it easier. The mother contacted you once and may call again. If she does, please assure her that the babies are safe. You should call the police and request that they keep an eye on your house in case she comes by. You could request a tap on your phone to allow them to trace the call should she call again. I'll have the department designate you as a foster home first thing Monday."

Gwen thought it was inconceivable that Health and Welfare and Violet would assume that the Harte family would just take these babies in. Her thoughts were running rampant, Health and Welfare has decided that we're going to be responsible for these babies. First, the hospital decided I was next-of kin. Now Health and Welfare announces that we're playing finders-keepers. What will be next, the hokey pokey?

Gwen didn't express those thoughts, but suggested to Violet, "Don't you want to see them, and wouldn't you want to meet us before you just sign them over to us?"

"Patience, Mrs. Harte. I'll see them on Monday. They're in good hands now, and I can't do anything more this weekend. The system works slowly. You must be a fine woman, because you found them at church, didn't you? If you were a bad person, you wouldn't go to church," Violet responded brightly.

Gwen's head was churning. She could not believe what was happening. It wasn't that she didn't want to help. It was just that this wasn't what she had in mind for the week. But these newly born children, Marie and Louis, had never been held in the arms of someone who loved them. She wondered what Clancy and their three children would say. And what about them being of a different race? *How could I explain that when I didn't even know it was possible?*

"Okay, Violet, call me Monday. I don't know about being a foster home, but if we get certified as a foster home, we'll keep them for a few days starting then. Meanwhile, I'll call the police and file a report, but what do I file? A missing person's report. A found person's report. I have never done this before. And, before I forget, may I have your cell number please? Your number did not come up on my caller I.D."

"Just call the police and tell them you found the babies. You wouldn't want to be charged with kidnapping," she chortled at her private joke. "I'll talk to you Monday." Click. Violet hung up without leaving her phone number.

Chapter 6

Detective Maggie Monroe, Saturday Night

Sheriff Maggie Monroe was exhausted. She had been looking for a job in law enforcement for two weeks with no success. It was a Saturday night and she had exhausted her pool of law enforcement agencies. She and her husband Brick were enjoying a glass of wine, both frustrated with the whole hiring process, wondering what would come next. She had recently retired from her position in Barrier, a one-horse town that no longer had any horses. It had a good hotel, a casino, and of course a brothel. It backed up to the Sierra Nevada Mountains with plenty of both character and characters. Brick, prior to their marriage, had moved to Barrier as an escape from Los Angeles and the big city ways in order to teach school but ended up as the high school principal. They were the community's "power couple" with a lot of influence.

A Marine, Brick had always been a picture of health, but suddenly he wasn't. The VA's thorough evaluation had diagnosed a brain tumor, which had destroyed glandular function in his pituitary from exposure to burn pits during his first tour in the Middle East. They said his multiple injuries were inoperable, yet they had hope that he could continue his normal life, but he needed to be closer to a VA facility. The five-hour, twice weekly drive to Reno had exhausted them both. Reno's VA was excellent, and it specialized in burn pit syndrome. It was a perfect move, except Maggie had been unable to find an acceptable position in law enforcement.

After Brick's diagnosis, with his apparently failing health, they pulled up stakes and moved to Reno, finding Basin, a small suburb close to the VA for his weekly visits. Maggie had no prospects for work when they arrived but applied for positions with the Washoe County Sheriff's Office, the Nevada Highway Patrol, Reno Police, and finally with the much smaller Basin Police Department. She was told "No," repeatedly. As a former sheriff, she was overqualified for most open positions, which were at officer-level, and she wondered if the upper management unit considered her experience and qualifications a threat to their male-dominated hierarchy. None of the law enforcement agencies were hiring, they said, and disinterested because they were looking for someone younger, who was trainable in their methods of law enforcement, which she saw as a way of keeping the "good ol' boy" network alive and well. As sheriff, she answered only to voters, and she was the boss, albeit for a tiny department in a tiny county. Brick teased her by calling her the "High, by God, Sheriff," and he meant it.

Maggie wanted to stay with law enforcement and in the state retirement system for health and retirement benefits, especially with Brick's illness. But things didn't seem to be going her way. As a last resort she and Brick talked about private detective work, which didn't appeal to her. They were about to go to bed when Johnny Tucker, the Basin chief of police called her. "You still interested?" he started, sounding tired and frustrated. She hesitated. Yesterday he had not been interested, but tonight he was. It was nearly eleven o'clock. What was going on?

"Well, yes, I am. What's the position?" she asked.

"It's a detective position. Not high paying and I'll assign a patrolman to you, you know, so you won't be in any danger," the chief said. "It'll mostly be minor cases, misdemeanors, or family issues. No murders or anything complicated, those go to our experienced officers."

"You do know that I'm experienced, don't you? I was a sheriff for twenty years, and we handled everything. We didn't have a big office and staff like here, so my deputy and a half and I handled everything, even murder."

"Yeah, yeah," the chief said, brushing her off. "We'll give you a shot and see how it goes. You'll be the only woman on our staff and don't have any uniforms, so you can wear civies. Just make it professional, Detective Monroe. Can you start tomorrow?"

The truth was that Chief Tucker had been served with a discrimination citation for not having females on the staff, except for clerical help, and he hoped that hiring Maggie would get the county attorney off his back. "Tomorrow," he repeated. "Can you make it tomorrow, even though it's a Sunday?"

Maggie didn't like the sound of this job, but knew she had to get her foot in the door somehow, so agreed. "Does that mean I can't wear my bikini?" she answered, flippantly.

Chief Tucker responded, "Bikini, no, but something that makes you look like you know something about kids. Be here first thing so we can get all the paperwork done; I've got something right up your alley."

"Sounds good, I'll be there."

About the Author—Helene Mitchell/Gail Cushman

Born and bred a small-town Idaho girl in the beautiful intermountain west, my life has been a myriad of adventures. I am a Marine Corps officer, a former high school principal and superintendent, and I love to write. My readers may recognize that I write my blogs, my *Wrinkly Bits* series and newspaper columns as Gail Cushman, my birth name. I love writing these humorous stories and enjoy receiving the fond feedback. My heart is full when I read your comments. Thank you!

Before I penned my *Wrinkly Bits* series, I had written a serious mystery and crime series revolving around a female sheriff named Maggie Monroe in rural Nevada. Now I find that I need to switch hats, from the silly, flowery bonnet of Gail Cushman to a new hat, a detective's fedora, for my nom de plume or pen name, Helene Mitchell. One cannot wear two hats at the same time, so when I put on the humorous hat of Gail, I write funny nonsensical stories that occur in everyday life, and when I put on my detective Helene hat I write about murder and mayhem. Every day, I choose which hat I will wear as I say good morning to my computer.

I hope you enjoy this third book in my *Maggie Monroe* series. And watch out, I have several more in the pipeline. Enjoy life, my friends because as Scarlet O'Hara said, "After all, tomorrow is another day!"

Gail Cushman's books

- *Cruise Time*
- *Out of Time*
- *Wasting Time*
- *Flash Time*
- *Bits of Time*
- *Loving Again: A Guide to Online Dating for Widows and Widowers* (co-author Robert Mitchell)

Helene Mitchell's Books

- *Murder in the Parsonage*
- *Murder Almost*
- *Murder in the Brothel*
- *Murder in the Diocese* **Coming Soon!**
- *Murder on the Rez* **Coming Soon!**

gailcushman.com

Made in the USA
Monee, IL
04 September 2024